D0456340

IDENTITY THEFT

ANNA DAVIES

POINT HORROR

Copyright © 2013 by Anna Davies

All rights reserved. Published by Point, an imprint of Scholastic Inc., *Publishers since 1920*. SCHOLASTIC, POINT, and associated logos are trademarks and/or registered trademarks of Scholastic Inc.

No part of this publication may be reproduced, stored in a retrieval system, or transmitted in any form or by any means, electronic, mechanical, photocopying, recording, or otherwise, without written permission of the publisher. For information regarding permission, write to Scholastic Inc., Attention: Permissions Department, 557 Broadway, New York, NY 10012.

ISBN 978-0-545-47712-3

Library of Congress Cataloging-in-Publication Data Available

10 9 8 7 6 5 4 3 2 1   13 14 15 16 17

Printed in the U.S.A.   40

First edition, May 2013
Book design by Natalie C. Sousa

To the NYC crew:
For always keeping me on the right side of sanity

CHAPTER 1

I paused for a moment outside the royal-blue doors of Bainbridge Secondary School. Around me, groups of kids were buzzing about lakeside bonfires, evenings spent driving around town, and thankless summer jobs whose only benefit came in the form of cute coworkers. Even though I'd gone to school with these kids my whole life, I hadn't seen any of them since I'd left for the summer debate intensive at the University of New Hampshire.

But I wasn't looking for a catch-up session. Instead, I pressed my back against the ridges of the oak tree outside the door, pretending to be supremely interested in examining my senior year schedule as Keely Young, Ingrid Abramson, and Emily Hines walked across the parking lot toward the entrance. Once my best friends, they'd pretty much ditched me midway through freshman year, when I quit the field hockey team to concentrate on my grades. Ever since, they'd made it clear through sideways glances and snide comments that I'd made the wrong decision.

Among the kids streaming into the entrance, the three of them stood out. Keely's highlighted blond hair and glowing skin made it seem like she'd breezed in straight from a Nantucket beach. Ingrid was now sporting a tiny silver stud in her nostril, most likely obtained during her two-month-long backpacking trip through Europe. I'd read all her Tweets about it, but seeing her in person — the way the stud glimmered in the light, the way her scarf was perfectly draped around her neck, the way her shoulders were held back in stark contrast to Keely's signature slouch — I felt a wave of betrayal.

It should have been me. In eighth grade, she and I would spend hours clipping articles from travel magazines and dreaming of trips we'd take when we were older. We'd even made a list of everything we'd do: getting as many piercings as possible, being driven through Paris on a Vespa, meeting a hot boy on a train (her), and being mistaken for a native Parisian and being kissed by any boy at all (me).

Jealousy knifed through my stomach. I couldn't help but wonder what else she'd crossed off the list.

"So I think this year I'm only going to date guys from the U," Emily said in a vapid voice that made it clear her main extracurricular of the summer was watching way too many episodes of *Keeping Up with the Kardashians*. She was wobbling on five-inch heels as if she were a baby deer nursing a shin splint. "I think that dating high school guys when you're a senior is kinda pathetic, you know?"

"Eh, it depends on the guy. You know what I think is even more pathetic?" Keely asked in an actress-y voice that forced me to look up despite myself. We locked eyes and I immediately glanced away, but not quickly enough. Keely was about to go on the attack, and I was going to be the victim. "Girls who don't date at all in high school. Like, they think a guy will wreck their GPA."

Emily snorted. "Or they make up a boyfriend and put him all over Facebook. I think *that's* even worse."

"Seriously, I'm done with Facebook anyway." Ingrid sniffed. "It's so . . . insular. Everyone who's anyone uses Instagram."

"And then uploads the pictures on Facebook. Besides, I saw you just posted your new Europe album, so don't even talk to me about quitting," Keely said. "Although even the losers are joining," Keely hissed as she walked by me. I lowered my head until I heard the fading echo of Emily's heels clicking on the ground, surprised that another insult hadn't been lobbed in my direction. Keely's assertion wasn't entirely correct. Because while they certainly thought I was a loser, I definitely wasn't on Facebook. They'd made sure of that back in ninth grade.

Once they were a safe distance away, I walked through the double doors of Bainbridge Secondary School. The lobby smelled the same as it always did: a combination of Lysol, floor wax, and Axe body spray, courtesy of the freshman boys. To me the scent was as welcoming as apple pie or the perfume-filled air of a department store. It was the scent of home. The nostalgia caused my shoulders to drop and my gaze to lift. Here, I didn't have to worry about snarky comments and former best friends.

To my left was the Bainbridge trophy case, where no fewer than ten different plaques chronicled my achievements: HAYLEY WESTIN: OUTSTANDING ACHIEVEMENT IN PHYSICS. HAYLEY WESTIN, SCHOLAR-ATHLETE OF THE YEAR. HAYLEY WESTIN, NATIONAL MERIT SCHOLAR. I smiled to myself as I looked at my name etched in metal. I tried not to think about the fact that I had more awards than friends. After all, these awards had led me to my Ainsworth scholarship nomination, which all I'd wanted since freshman year. The Ainsworth was a big deal, a scholarship for ten students nationwide that paid full college tuition and room and board, as well as a $5,000-a-year travel stipend. I had to win it. It was the only way my mom wouldn't have to worry, where I wouldn't have to choose the major that promised the most money upon graduation. The Ainsworth didn't ask that their nominees be oboe-playing phenoms or Olympians. All the Ainsworth asked for was excellence. The plaques all proclaimed that was what I had. I just hoped that the nominating committee would agree.

"So, then, we ended up having this *epic* party at this house share in Nantucket? It was, like, all these college guys?"

As I turned the corner, my reverie was ruined by the uptalky conversation between Hilary Beck and Rachel Martin. Both juniors, Rachel and Hilary always hung out at the Ugly Mug coffee shop after school. Because I'd worked there, and because their voices were so loud, I was intimately familiar with Rachel's boy drama and Hilary's acne problems. I shuddered. Even though I'd miss the paycheck, quitting the Ugly Mug to focus on winning the Ainsworth was worth it.

As long as I won.

"Ugh, really? I'm so jealy! I wish I'd done that instead of going to stupid Greece with my stupid parents. We went on a stupid cruise. Hello, did they never see *Titanic*? Plus, the rooms were, like, the size of my closet," Rachel huffed, drinking the dregs of what I instantly recognized as the Espresso Yourself Icy Frozen Blend. I knew it well, having made approximately one billion over the past three years, about half of which were ordered and drunk by Rachel.

I whirled around and caught Rachel's eye, but she gazed through me, as though she'd never seen me before. As if that was even possible in the Ugly Mug–mandated orange-and-purple apron and hat.

"Everything will be worth it," I whispered under my breath as I hurried up toward the math and science wing. It was my mantra whenever things got tough.

Quickly, I slid into one of the side desks in the AP Calc classroom. It wasn't until I'd already settled and had pulled out my notebook and pen that I realized I'd plopped down right next to Adam Scott.

"Hayley." He nodded curtly in my direction as though we were two opposing lawyers sitting in front of a judge instead of two classmates who'd known each other for twelve years.

"My favorite seatmate." I smiled tightly. Adam and I had been frenemies since kindergarten, when he came in after winter break announcing he could read chapter books. I'd immediately gone home and demanded to my mother that she help me sound my way through *Jane Eyre*. And ever since then, the rivalry for number one had been intense.

"How was your summer?" Adam asked, pulling out his iPad and setting it on his desk.

"It was all right. Lots of work, not so much play. The usual." I couldn't help but notice that he looked good. His shoulders filled out his blue button-down more than I remembered last year, and his curly brown hair had grown out so it was a teeny bit shaggy, a nice change from the buzz cut he'd sported for at least the past decade.

"How was debate camp?" he pressed. I glared at him. Yes, we were in AP Calc, aka the varsity squad of nerds, but did he have to say *debate camp* quite so loudly? Besides, it wasn't like he cared. The question was clearly his not-so-subtle attempt to suss out whether or not I had an upper hand when it came to the Ainsworth application. So I decided to mess with him a little.

"Why? Worried your foreign field trip wasn't academically rigorous enough?" I teased. Ingrid wasn't the only Bainbridger to have passed the majority of her summer in Europe. Adam had spent six weeks in a language immersion program in Aix-en-Provence in France while I'd labored away in the cinder-block dorms of UNH. He'd been able to enjoy evenings in cafés drinking espresso while I'd listened to monotone professors discuss policy. He'd had the opportunity to explore the world. And I'd spent another summer being a type-A overachiever.

"France was cool. I had fun. But I worked hard, too. In any case, I'm sure the experience will give me plenty to talk about with the Ainsworth committee," Adam said with a smirk.

"Great." I shifted in my chair. Sure, Adam wanted it. But he didn't *need* it the way I did. His dad was a Harvard legacy and corporate lawyer and his mom was the provost at the U. He lived in one of the fancy houses up on the Ridge, and his family would have no problem getting into — and paying for — any school he wanted. Realizing that brought our rivalry up a few notches beyond good-natured competition, and I couldn't help but feel that, for the time being, I shouldn't be as friendly as I'd been in the past.

At that moment, Dr. Osborn strode in, wearing a chalk-covered corduroy blazer over a T-shirt that read WHY DID THE CHICKEN CROSS THE MOBIUS STRIP? Behind me, Jake Cross, a thirteen-year-old who took high school classes, chuckled so hard he snorted.

"First rule of Calculus, and it's an important one. Never drink and derive," Dr. Osborn boomed. He looked hopefully around the room, but his only response was another high-pitched snort from Jake.

"Well, of course, since you're all underage, you wouldn't be drinking anyway, but I'm saying this only because it's a play on words, and it is true that derivatives must take your complete and total attention," Dr. Osborn sputtered as he wrote an equation on the board. I hastily began copying it into my notebook. Beyond his dorky sense of humor and chalk-stained clothing, Osborn was a serious teacher who could make or break my straight-A average. Next to me, Adam was scribbling away, too.

It was good to be back.

AP Calculus, AP English, AP European History, gym, and it was finally my lunch period. Most seniors left the building at lunch. They'd either head home to hang out with their significant other while their parents were at work, or they'd drive to the strip of sandwich places on Main Street. I rarely left campus. I preferred to eat a PB and J and get stuff done that I didn't have time to do during the day. Even though it was the first day of school, I still had plenty on my to-do list, starting with selecting the editors for class sections for the *Spectrum*, the award-winning Bainbridge yearbook. I'd been procrastinating on that project all summer, pulling out the folder, then pushing it back into the depths of my desk drawer to deal with later. No matter who I ended up picking, someone was going to get mad, and that would lead to another round of whispers and talking behind my back. It wasn't something I'd wanted to think about in the summer. But now, I didn't have a choice. Besides, it wasn't like people were begging me to head out to the sandwich shop with them.

I grabbed a seat in the corner of the cafeteria, pulled my sandwich from my bag, and began to look through the applications.

Around me, scared freshmen were swarming into the cafeteria like spooked wildebeests, unsure of where to sit or whom to avoid. A small, skinny girl with owl-like eyes behind round glasses and tangled, wiry hair paused by my empty table.

I glanced up and gave her an encouraging smile. I knew how she felt. But instead of sitting down, she scampered away. I wanted to tell her that it got easier, that eventually, she'd find a place for herself, even if it was just sitting solo and doing work. That despite what you saw on the CW network, friends weren't necessarily the most important part of high school. That, in a way, not fitting in meant you had the opportunity to stand out, in the best possible way, to teachers, college admissions officers, and scholarship officials — who were really the only people who mattered.

But I didn't have time to give advice. I spread the junior-class applications in front of me, wishing I had a red pen or a pair of glasses to feel more editorial-official.

The first was from Kayla McDonough. A field hockey player with a surgically altered nose and a modeling agent in Concord, she clearly wanted the position to ensure that pictures of her friends were prominently featured in the yearbook. The second applicant was Jessica Adamson, an honors student who'd also applied for the editor in chief position last spring, even though she'd been a rising junior. Traditionally, the spot went to a senior, but that wasn't a hard-and-fast rule. Luckily, Mrs. Ross, our advisor, had kept to tradition and chosen me. I was grateful, because I knew that Jess would have won by a landslide if students had voted on the position. She hosted bonfire parties at her lakeside house and invited Hacky Sack kids and honors students. She played lacrosse in the spring and hung out at football games in the fall. She made sure to wear blue and white on School Spirit Day. In short, she lived the type of laid-back, fun, high school dream life we created in each page of the yearbook layouts. Or, rather, *I* created in each page of layouts as everyone else was actually out having fun. I did everything from ensuring that people actually showed up for *all* group activity photos that they were part of (people tried to skip Marching Band and Select Chorus photo calls for the dork factor, but not under my watch) to policing senior quotes for anything un-PC (which pretty much meant rejecting any lyric by anyone except Taylor Swift). I knew that all of my own proofreading and double-checking and editing was the reason why the yearbook always looked awesome. But this year, the recognition would be mine — something I was confident admissions officers and Ainsworth application readers would appreciate.

And as much as I hated to admit it to myself, I was a teeny bit jealous of Jess. Mostly, it was her confidence — how she could assume she even had a shot at the position when I was the one putting in hours and hours of actual work, hunching over in the yearbook edit room while she was putting blue and red ribbons in her ponytail or baking cookies to sell during halftime. She even went so far as to throw a fit when Mrs. Ross gave the position to me, citing a conflict of interest because I was also the editor of the school paper, the *Bainbridge Beacon*. It was a stupid argument, but she wouldn't let it go, even going so far as setting up an anonymous survey online asking for my removal. And, for once, the apathetic student body worked in my favor. No one bothered to vote. Still, that didn't mean Jess wouldn't make things extra hard for me this year.

I glanced back and forth at their applications as I took another bite of my sandwich. I paused at Jess's application. She was good. Kayla was not. But in the end, it came down to Slacker versus Backstabber.

Slacker, I decided, ripping up Jessica's application. Yeah, I'd pretty much have to do Kayla's job to ensure the junior section didn't suck, but I wasn't afraid of hard work.

Whoever said it was lonely at the top was right, I mused as I pushed my chair back and headed out of the cafeteria to make an appointment with my college advisor. I saw a few seniors walk in carrying Zoomie's milkshakes. They were laughing and hanging off one another, as if they were extras in some face wash commercial about how awesome it is to be a teenager. Meanwhile, I felt like I was an overworked, underappreciated corporate attorney. *It would be worth it.*

I pushed open the heavy oak door to the guidance suite, relaxing as the door clicked behind me. Set in the center of school, the brightly lit guidance office was large, airy, and a million times more inviting than the dark and claustrophobic cafeteria. At one end of the room was a glass-topped conference table, where ten or so freshman — including Keely's sister, Laurel — were in the mandatory Intro to the Guidance Office meeting every new student had to attend. Laurel widened her eyes at me. I looked away and hurried toward the secretary desk at the opposite end of the room.

"Hi, Miss Marsted," I said politely to the sixty-year-old secretary who co-owned the pie shop downtown with her sister. A lot of kids only came to the guidance office because they hoped for a snack. Today, a strawberry-rhubarb pie and an apple tart were sitting on the counter alongside a stack of paper plates.

At the sight of me, Miss Marsted's doughy, wrinkled face broke into a smile.

"Miss Westin, how lovely to see you," she said warmly, as though I were an unexpected houseguest. "Now, I know you're probably falling down busy on your first day back, but you *must* have a piece of pie and you *must* tell me all about your summer. It's your favorite kind." She bustled to the front of the desk to cut a thick slice of the strawberry-rhubarb.

I shook my head, ignoring the vague rumbling of my stomach. I was well aware that Laurel and a few of her friends were watching me curiously, and I didn't want the next generation of Bainbridge students to think I was the weird girl who was BFF with the guidance office secretary.

"Are you sure?" Miss Marsted asked, the knife still poised above the lattice crust.

"Yes, thank you. I just need an appointment with Mr. Klish. As soon as possible. It's in regard to my Ainsworth application."

"Oh, of course." Miss Marsted bustled behind the desk. "I can schedule an appointment tomorrow morning before first period. Will that be all right?"

I nodded, feeling strangely grown-up. I could so clearly imagine myself in ten years as an attorney at a law firm, trying to set up a time to meet with a partner. I'd wear a charcoal suit, just like the one I always wore to debate tournaments. My dark brown hair would be pulled back into a low chignon, and my lips would be a sexy, subtle coral color that I was never able to master with my current makeup bag of drugstore cosmetics. It would be great. No, it would be better than great. It would be perfect.

"Seven forty-five all right?" Miss Marsted asked.

"Of course." I pulled out my pink Filofax and wrote down the appointment, noting the tiny blank squares that were all about to be filled with obligations, deadlines, and interviews.

"You still write on paper. Just like me!" Miss Marsted enthused loudly. I heard a few giggles emanate from the corner. Awesome.

"I don't believe in computers," I said tightly. She beamed back at me, oblivious to my abrupt response, which only made me feel worse. I spent so much time telling myself I didn't care what other people thought of me. I just wished it could be a little more true.

"All right, see you tomorrow, Miss Westin. And if you want any pie, well, you know where to find it."

"Right," I mumbled. I knew that a full schedule would fulfill me way more than a full stomach would.

CHAPTER 2

"All right, so let me announce the new *Spectrum* executive board." My voice cracked, and I quickly took a large sip of my coffee. I noticed my hand was shaking, but I couldn't tell if it was nerves or caffeine jitters.

It was seven a.m. the next morning, and I'd already drank a sixteen-ounce coffee at home and was halfway through my second oversized thermos. Two years ago, Principal O'Neill had come up with the genius idea to have most clubs, including Yearbook, meet during zero period. And since most people preferred sleep to saturating their college resumes, membership had declined sharply. Even our faculty administrator, Mrs. Ross, was nodding off in the corner of the room, occasionally emitting a snore that sounded like a high-pitched teakettle.

"Shouldn't you wait a few minutes? Make sure that everyone is here?" Jess asked from her seat directly opposite me. Her blue eyes were wide and innocent, but I understood the subtext: Attendance was sparse and the majority of people in the room were freshmen.

I took a deep breath. The past *Spectrum* editors in chief had made running a meeting seem way easier than designing a layout or editing a story. After all, they just had to stand up, talk, and assign. I was used to making speeches in front of strangers through debate. But this was different — and I was reminded of that every time I looked over at Jess. Her unblinking stare made me feel like I was on a tightrope. One wrong sentence could cause everything I had worked so hard for to topple.

"No, I think we're fine. We have a lot of ground to cover today," I said firmly, arching one eyebrow in her direction. One of the techniques taught at debate camp was that raising an eyebrow is one of the key gestures that will make your opponent realize that you're in charge.

I looked down at the list, willing myself to stop letting Jess undermine me. I might not have been as charismatic as Jon Keselica, our editor in chief last year, or as pretty as Meg Smith, the editor in chief from two years ago, but I'd gotten the job. I deserved it. No matter what Jess thought.

I smiled at Libby Dorn in the front row. Also a senior, she'd been on Yearbook since freshman year. She smiled back. She was nice enough, but I barely knew anything about her, beyond the fact that she had four sisters and hoped to be a poet when she grew up. She hung out with the slam poetry kids and the other artsy hipster types who tended to spend lunch in the atrium by the auditorium. I wasn't one of the creative kids, and it wasn't as if Libby had ever invited me to eat with them, anyway.

"All right, so our freshman editor is Dominick Jenson. Congratulations, Dominick." I nodded in the direction of a skinny ninth-grader with bleached-blond hair and thick glasses. He turned beet red and beamed, then threw his hand in the air and waved it.

"Yes?" I asked nervously. Jess's previous question had thrown me off balance.

"Can I call my mom and tell her?" he asked excitedly.

Laughter erupted from the back corner of the room. I was so relieved to no longer be the center of attention that I didn't bother to stifle a smile as I nodded. Truth was, I was thankful for his enthusiasm, even if he had been the only one to apply. All he had to do was interview other frosh, about how they were adjusting to pep rallies, what they thought of high school, and what they kept in their lockers, and with a little help, he'd do all right. I added *Figure out freshman section* to my mental to-do list.

"Sophomore-class editor is Christina Jenner," I said, locking eyes with a beaming, glasses-clad girl whose cello case was propped against her desk. That had been an easy decision. She'd done a decent job as freshman-class editor last year.

Just then, the door opened and Matt Hartnett sauntered in. A hush fell over the room as everyone, including me, turned to stare. Even though he was wearing jeans and a button-down — the unofficial boy uniform of Bainbridge — he stood out. He was taller and more built than most guys, but it was beyond that. He seemed wholly comfortable in his own skin. He never gave the impression that he tried to be anyone else. Even though Keely, Ingrid, Emily, and half the female population of Bainbridge seemed to follow him around, Matt had never had a serious girlfriend. I sometimes wondered if he, too, realized there was more to life than high school.

"Yo, Hayley. Mad sorry I'm late," he said sheepishly.

"That's fine, just have a seat."

"Cool." He waved his way between desks, oblivious to the stares that followed him. He'd been the sports editor since freshman year, and even though I often had to rewrite his stories so his sentences contained more than four words, he was pretty diligent. He'd once told me that he wanted to be a sports reporter after college. I liked that about him. Platonically, of course. But it was nice to see that he had aspirations beyond prom king or winning soccer sectional finals.

Finally, he perched on the radiator in the back of the room. I hoped the relief wasn't evident in my voice. But seeing him was the feel-good equivalent of an A-plus on a test, a sign that everything was *fine*.

I smiled broadly and squared my shoulders back, allowing my gaze to fall straight on Jess. "And junior-class editor is . . . Kayla McDonough," I said, realizing before her last name left my mouth that she wasn't even there.

Silence hung in the air. I wasn't sure what I had been expecting. Maybe Jess to yell, or immediately complain to Mrs. Ross. But instead, she stared silently down at her desk. I noticed her knuckles were white from clutching her travel mug. It was a gesture I knew all too well myself, something to focus on to stop any tears from forming. I looked away.

"And senior-class editor is Libby Dorn," I said, smiling at Libby. "So we'll have a special class editor meeting next Tuesday morning to brainstorm stories. But for now, since the cover is due to the printer by next month, we need to come up with a theme and title for the book." I glanced over at Jess, but her head was still bowed low, making it impossible to tell whether or not she was upset.

"What are you thinking, Miss Westin?" Mrs. Ross prompted.

"Of course. Well, I was thinking, um . . . *Ever Upward*, I guess. I mean, *Ever Upward*," I corrected. *Um* and *I guess* weren't confident.

"I hope everyone here will agree that it's fun, it's inspirational, and I think it exemplifies the high school experience on a few levels. Plus it's classic. If we do something from a song or a movie, it dates the book too much. What do you guys think?" I asked. I'd already worked on a few preliminary sketches to go along with the theme. I liked it. It was simple, yet direct, and wasn't one of those cringe-worthy ones like *Teenage Dream* or *Dancing Queen* that people are guaranteed to make fun of at all future reunions.

Immediately, Jessica's hand shot up. Her eyes flashed at me, and if she'd been close to crying a minute ago, she certainly wasn't now.

"I don't like it. What does it mean? It sounds so cheesy. Like, seriously, if I had to show a yearbook called *Ever Upward* to my college roommate, I'd be really embarassed," she said, not even waiting for me to call on her.

Of course Jess doesn't like it. You knew she wouldn't, I reminded myself as I felt my heart lurch from a canter to a gallop. Ten minutes into my first meeting and Jess had messed with my mind. I needed to put a stop to it. I couldn't let it seem like she could bully me. And I couldn't seem threatened. I took a deep breath, exhaled through my nose, and focused on the spot right between her eyebrows. "What's your idea?"

"Well, I think it should be more like *That's What Friends Are For*. Or maybe *Lean on Me*. You know, something that has a message about friendship. What people want is a title that exemplifies the high school experience. And isn't that what it's all about, Hayley?" she asked pointedly. "Won't the biggest thing you'll miss after graduation be your friendships?"

I froze. All eyes were on me, and I felt blood rushing to my face. I turned toward the board so people couldn't see me blushing.

That's What Friends Are For. I wrote with a shaking hand. And then *Lean on Me*.

Unbidden, my mind drifted back to when Keely, Ingrid, Emily, and I were a foursome. We called ourselves HIKE after our initials. In middle school, we'd even gotten permission to leave gym class for HIKE club meetings. We'd managed to convince Coach Ervin it was an official group led by our Earth Science teacher, and had managed to spend half a semester gossiping during gym before he'd caught on. That was around the time that we realized HIKE could also be a contraction for Hot Guys We Like. We'd write pros-and-cons lists on each of them, contemplating their kissing potential and whether or not we should date them now or wait until the end of high school, when the romance was likely to last longer than a month. Of course, I'd known even then that none of the guys on the list would have actually dated me. Not in ninth grade. And definitely not now.

They were drawn to Keely's confidence; Emily's short skirts and long, mermaid-like hair; and Ingrid's sense of adventure and ability to flirt. None of the boys cared about my math skills or ability to quote Shakespearean monologues from memory. No matter how hard I tried, I couldn't compete with Emily, Ingrid, or Keely. And the worst part was that I could never figure out what I was doing wrong or how I could change.

That was when I began really focusing on schoolwork. I'd always been smart, but in ninth grade, I wanted to become exceptional. Because academics made sense in a way popularity didn't. It was an equation: You worked hard, you got a good grade. Not so with guys. I could say the same thing as Ingrid and they'd ignore me, but when Ingrid said it, they'd smile. I tried flipping my hair the way Emily did, but my hair never grew much beyond shoulder length, and too much flipping would cause it to tangle. I'd begun to resent HIKE. I wanted out. And I'd gotten it. Keely had made sure of that.

I squeezed my eyes shut to block out the memories floating into my head. I needed to focus on now.

"So, you're saying you feel our high school experience is best exemplified by the title of a cheesy song from the seventies?" I gripped the chalk so tightly it split in two with a loud crack.

"I think it would be exemplified by what *normal students* want," Jessica said with a condescending smile. "Besides, I was thinking off the top of my head. *Some* people didn't spend their whole summer thinking about Yearbook," she said smugly.

I turned away from the chalkboard and stared around the room. The tension was electric, and I knew that the way I handled Jess in the next two minutes was key in keeping control over the rest of the staff. If everyone saw her get to me, she'd have won, and it wouldn't matter that I was the official EIC. They'd listen to her.

"Fine, we'll have a vote. Anyone who has a theme idea that's as brilliant as Jessica's, please e-mail me and I'll have Mrs. Ross send a survey to the student body."

"What?" Mrs. Ross jerked her head up and glanced wildly around the room. Matt gave me a small smile, and my stomach slightly unknotted.

"Not important." I shook my head brusquely. I silently thanked debate camp's endless practice rounds for allowing me to fake my steely resolve. "I just need you to send an e-mail survey blast to the student body. I'll draft the text after class."

"All right. Sounds like you have everything under control," Mrs. Ross said.

"I do." An awkward silence fell over the room.

Matt raised his hand. "Yo, I like *Ever Upward*. It's cool, you know?"

"Thank you. Hopefully everyone else will agree." I stared straight at Jess even though part of me wanted to hug Matt.

"What?" Jess said defensively. "You don't need my approval. You're the editor. And you don't need to worry about setting up the survey. I can do it myself. And I already know the ropes about section pitches. That *is* what you're about to discuss, right?" She smiled.

"You don't need to do that," I said uncertainly. I knew she wasn't trying to help me. But I couldn't figure out what she was trying to do.

"I want to." Jess flashed me a smile before packing her bag, slinging it over her shoulder, and sauntering out of the room.

The door slammed shut.

"Guys!" I clapped my hands, cringing when I realized that was exactly what Madame Wenstrom, the senile French teacher, did to call the class to order. "Guys!" I said again. "This week, I want you to think about interesting stories, and pitch them to your editor by Friday. You just need a few sentences in the pitch, and make sure to include any details that are relevant, such as event dates or photo concepts," I said. The more I talked, the more confident I felt. I was *fine*.

When the bell finally rang, I felt like I'd run a marathon. I'd been coasting on adrenaline, and now that the room was empty, I felt wobbly and off balance and I sensed a tension headache rolling in from the sides of my brain. School was *definitely* back in session.

As I turned the corner, I paused by the water fountain. I pulled out my economy bottle of Advil, popped two in my mouth, and took a large sip of the chlorine-y liquid. Then, I rested my forehead against the cool green tile above the fountain. I was exhausted and I hadn't even gone to first period yet.

"So, Westin, cured cancer yet?"

I immediately whirled around and found myself gazing into Matt's green eyes. His dark hair flopped over his forehead and his lips looked slightly chapped, like someone who spent too much time kissing. I was glad he'd been sitting in the back. Looking at those lips in the first row would have been seriously distracting.

"Huh?" My heart resumed hammering in my chest.

"I want to hear what you did this summer. So if you didn't cure cancer, what did you do? Write the Great American Novel? Invent the new Facebook?"

"No, was just . . . doing stuff. . . ." I studied a spot on the gleaming linoleum floor and waited for my insane blushing to subside. How was it that I could win a gold medal in debate, onstage in a packed auditorium, but I couldn't come up with one remotely flirtatious one-liner?

"What about you? How's soccer going? Make any goals?" *Make any goals?* This was getting worse and worse. Soon, I'd be asking him if he'd *felt up any future opportunities*, which was the ridiculously embarrassing phrase Mr. Klish always used when he meant to ask whether or not we'd researched colleges.

"Doing stuff with *who*?" Matt grinned.

"No one! I mean, like, studying and watching movies!" I said quickly. I mashed my lips together, ensuring I'd shut up and not share the fact that instead of hanging out at the lake, status updating, or doing anything remotely normal, I spent the rare free time I had watching cheesy movies like *Notting Hill*, *Love Actually*, and *Sixteen Candles*. No one knew that, and I wanted to keep it that way. But one more question from Matt and I'd most likely be blabbing all about it.

He shot me a look, but before he could say anything I spotted Jess scurrying out of the guidance office. I narrowed my eyes. Had she been talking about me? It was likely, and I was going to find out.

"I have to go. Bye!" I practically sprinted toward the guidance office, eager to pump Miss Marsted for Jess details before my Mr. Klish meeting. I was also kind of relieved to excuse myself from the awkward Matt conversation.

"Mr. Klish will just be a moment. He said to wait for him in his office," Miss Marsted said, waving me past the desk without looking up from the mountain of course schedule switch requests on her desk. The one day I actually wanted to linger at the desk and talk to Miss Marsted, and she was busy. Great. What could Jess have been *doing* in here?

I headed into Mr. Klish's corner office and sat down at a pockmarked oval table in the corner, piled high with precarious stacks of college pamphlets. The yellow paint-chipped walls were covered with posters from various elite institutions and summer programs. As always, I examined the UPenn one that was posted directly above Mr. Klish's desk. The largest poster in the room, the main photograph featured a group of students walking across a leaf-strewn campus at twilight. UNIVERSITY OF

PENNSYLVANIA: ACCESS THE WORLD, the text screamed in forty-eight-point Calibri font. As always, my eyes zeroed in on one specific photo subject: the guy wearing rectangular glasses, his curly dark hair floppy on his forehead. A checkered blue scarf was tied at his neck and he was holding a copy of Plato's *Republic* in one hand. He looked like he could be an Ian or a Morris. And while I wouldn't say Ian-or-Morris-or-whoever was the *whole* reason I wanted to go to the University of Pennsylvania, I would have been lying if I said he wasn't a contributing factor. Mostly, it was because he represented the type of person I wanted to meet in college: intense, committed, focused. Ian-or-Morris would have toiled away thanklessly in high school. Ian-or-Morris would understand where I was coming from. He wouldn't be like the guys at Bainbridge, who only wanted to copy my Calc homework, or the guys at debate camp, who'd see me as competition as soon as I defeated them in a practice round. He'd understand me, even if I didn't do the Emily hair flip or laugh in that *heh heh* way at lame comments, the way Ingrid always seemed to whenever a guy tried to crack a joke. In college, I wouldn't have to pretend to be anyone I wasn't.

"Miss Westin?" Mr. Klish entered the room and settled heavily in the leather club chair behind his desk. He was wearing a corduroy jacket with leather patches on the elbows in that non-ironic way that only college professors and grandfathers — both of which he was — could get away with. He emitted a large sigh before clasping his hands over his expansive belly. I tore my eyes away from Morris.

"Sir?" I asked. I didn't like the sound of his sigh.

"I just spoke with Mrs. Ross." He squinted down at a thick file folder that I realized was a three-inch-thick record of all my accomplishments from the past year. "I realize you're editor in chief of the yearbook as well as working on the newspaper. Are you sure you'll be able to do both and keep up your academic record? Because the committee for the Ainsworth will be picking through your activities and résumé with a fine-tooth comb, and it would be far better to drop one of the positions now than resign later. I know Jessica Adamson had expressed interest in the yearbook position, so if you wanted to step down, you could help her in an advisory capacity."

Fear sliced through my stomach. So *that* was why Jessica had run out of the meeting — to reignite last spring's controversy. Since when had overachieving been a crime? "Have I ever quit anything, Mr. Klish?" I asked in a low, measured voice.

"No, Miss Westin. Your record is impeccable. And that's why I want to make sure it stays that way. I wouldn't want your extracurricular activities bogging you down from your academics, or from debate, or from your college search. I'm suggesting you think over your schedule, come up with a list of priorities, and then work together to shift anything around. You don't need to feel like you're taking on too much. Jessica could do a fine job as the editor, and it sounds like she's quite keen for the position. You could still be on the committee, but I don't want you to feel like you're shouldering so many leadership positions. After all, even a seriously impressive young lady such as yourself can't be in two places at once."

"I appreciate your concern." I smoothed a wrinkle in my red skirt. Mostly everyone wore jeans to school, but I preferred to dress more formally, drawing inspiration from style blogs geared toward professional twentysomethings. I believed in dressing for the job you wanted. And the job I wanted was Ainsworth scholar. I looked back up at Mr. Klish.

"I've got everything under control. I want this, and I always get what I want." I locked eyes with Mr. Klish, pleased to see a flicker of agreement in his eyes.

"I am concerned." Mr. Klish continued to press the issue. "When will you sleep?"

"I'll sleep when I'm dead," I said tightly, realizing after the words escaped my lips how clichéd the phrase was, especially for the yearbook editor in chief to admit. But the entire conversation had put me on edge. I hated being questioned, especially when I wasn't doing anything wrong. After all, what else *should* I have been doing? Instagramming pictures of clouds with the Hacky Sack kids? Wandering around the mall with Keely and Emily?

Laugh lines crinkled around Mr. Klish's eyes as his face cracked into a smile. "You'll sleep when you're dead, huh? Well, I hope you get a little shut-eye before then. And while we're talking, I wanted to make sure you're aware that the committee for the Ainsworth semifinals doesn't only look at the application and recommendations. It does some background research on the World Wide Web. You know, looking into your FaceSpace, your Tweeter, any of that stuff," he said, awkwardly tripping over the social networking terms.

"You don't have to worry about that. I don't do that stuff." Yes, I occasionally creeped into Keely's prom-dress-covered Pinterest page and Ingrid's Instagram feed full of pictures of her, her nose piercing, and European landmarks. I checked Matt's Twitter feed. It was mostly baseball stats, unintelligible

LOLing about inside jokes, and one time, a sentence that made me think maybe, wildly, that we could somehow be something together: *Psyched to make the yearbook's sport section mad good!* It was stupid, one of his stream-of-consciousness comments. It wasn't like he was trying to impress me. I *knew* that. And yet, I kept checking back, hoping for more comments that somehow, indirectly, related to me.

"Good. Keep it that way. I won't have someone's scholarship chances in jeopardy because of this so-called social media nonsense. Seems a lot more trouble than it's worth." He rose to his feet, a sign that our meeting was over. "And keep up the good work. They should announce the semifinalists for the state in a week. And then, it'll be an interview in front of a board and your competition —"

"I know," I interrupted. I'd studied the Ainsworth protocol for weeks. The semifinals were modeled after the interviews done at Oxford and Cambridge, where the interviewers would ask random questions that you were supposed to answer off the top of your head. Past topics had been connecting Lady Gaga's music to Mozart's, how *The Decameron* and *Jersey Shore* were similar, and the Ophelia trope as exemplified by Miley Cyrus. They were bizarre questions, and that was the point — if you were Ainsworth material, you'd figure out a way to answer them that drew on your knowledge from a broad range of subjects.

"All right, well, I'm glad to hear you've done your homework. Just don't get cocky. Keep your head down and keep studying."

"That's what I always do," I said, heading into the waiting area. There, sitting on a bench and eating a piece of pie, was

Adam. I immediately noticed the way he jiggled his foot up and down, as if he were a toddler who really, really had to pee.

"I see you're enjoying your breakfast of champions." I directed my gaze to his knee, which was still uncontrollably bouncing up and down. It was another trick, courtesy of debate: *Let your enemy see you know his weak spot.*

Immediately, the jostling stopped. "And I see you're still being Miss Congeniality. So, what's up with the Ainsworth?"

"Do you honestly think I'm going to tell you?"

"Are you scared I'm going to win?" Adam countered. His tone was jokey, but the look in his eyes told me he was dead serious.

"I'm not afraid of anything," I said, turning on my heel.

"Hayley Has-No-Fear Westin," Adam mocked. "That doesn't seem like an Ainsworth-worthy attitude."

I ignored him and let the guidance door close behind me.

As I entered the crush of students in the hallway, I noticed that Matt Hartnett's arm was casually slung across the bony shoulders of Erin Carlson, a pretty sophomore theater girl. I felt a sting of betrayal, as sharp and sudden as the snap of a rubber band against my wrist. He wasn't *supposed* to have a girlfriend.

I shook my head. It didn't matter. Soon, I'd have a UPenn boy — or maybe even a Parisian dude, if I wanted one. It'd be worth the wait.

CHAPTER 3

That evening, I walked out of school just as the sun was setting. I'd meant to make it an early day, but then I got caught up in a conversation with my debate instructor, Mr. Greenberg. Debate didn't officially begin until December, when my fate with the Ainsworth and UPenn would be decided, so it wasn't like it was essential to my college apps. But even though I'd never admit it, I was still psyched about it.

"I just want to have fun," I'd explained to Mr. Greenberg. "I don't think I'll even care about winning. I just want to do it."

"Whatever you say, Hayley," he'd said drily, shaking his head. "You can't turn off that competitive streak. Whether you like it or not, you're a warrior. Trust me, when the season starts, you'll want to win."

Warrior. I liked it. It sounded way better than *mathlete* or any of the stupid terms teachers used to make academic stuff sound hard. And it was accurate. To me, the Ainsworth *was* life or death — or at least the ticket to *having* an actual life in college, instead of another four years devoted to pushing myself.

Outside, the air smelled like burning leaves, and my car — the tan 1988 Cougar I'd bought from my eighty-five-year-old neighbor after he accidentally drove up the walkway of the town library, thinking it was the parking lot — was one of the few left in the lot.

I slid into the driver's seat and made my way past the single-story Victorian-style shops and restaurants that surrounded the U. The farther I drove, the bumpier the road became. Houses were more spread out, and horses peered curiously over wooden fences at my car as I made my way to the ramshackle farmhouse my mom and I lived in. At one point, it had belonged to one of the owners of The Sound and the Story, the used bookstore where my mom worked. It was an unexpected inheritance from a relative who hadn't had the time or the energy to give it the overhaul it needed. Or at least that's what she said when she offered it to my mom as a rent-free place to live, but I was pretty sure it was because she felt sorry for her.

Or, not sorry. That was the wrong word. More like *entranced*. People always gave my mother things, but it wasn't because she was a poor single mom. It was because she was still beautiful, and had an aura of fragility surrounding her. She could recite all of William Blake's poems, but I wasn't entirely sure she knew how to reset the circuit breaker or when to put out trash for collection. I always did that stuff. I didn't mind. She was the dreamer, the one who'd first given me a sense of possibility. And I was a worker, the one who made everything fall into place.

I walked up the steps and put my key in the lock, jostling the door until it banged loudly against the wooden frame.

"Hello?" I called, my voice echoing in the drafty kitchen. Sadie, my dog, a poodle-and-terrier mix whose floppy body and oversized eyes made her look more Muppet than anything, nuzzled my knee.

"In here!" my mom yelled. I walked into the living room. My mom was curled up on the lumpy yellow sofa, a mug of tea clutched in her hand. Her dark blond hair was pulled back into a messy ponytail, and her makeup-free skin made the smattering of sun-freckles on her nose and cheeks extra prominent. She was wearing an oversized button-down shirt and a pair of leggings, and looked interchangeable with any of the college students who hung out at the Ugly Mug. The only thing that made her different was the fact that her boyfriend, Geoff, was at her side. Overweight, red-faced, with salt-and-pepper hair, Geoff looked more like her dad than her boyfriend. He was a real-estate developer from Boston. He was pretty much the opposite of how I always pictured my father — James, the academic my mother had the misfortune of falling for all those years ago. I couldn't stand Geoff, and also couldn't understand what my mom saw in him.

"Hey," I said to both of them, averting my eyes from Geoff's beefy hand on Mom's leg.

"Hayley bunny," she said in her soft voice as she stood up from the couch and pulled me into an embrace. "Geoff was in town and decided to stop by to say hi. Wasn't that nice of him?"

"Hi," I said shortly.

"Comet!" he said jovially, using the stupid nickname he'd come up with the first time he met me. Because my name is *Hayley*, and no one had ever thought of that before. His insistence on calling me that was almost as annoying as his insistence on using business acronyms, like EOD and ETA, all the time.

"Geoff and I were waiting for you to see if you wanted to grab dinner."

I shook my head. I doubted Geoff wanted to rally the troops to get dinner, or whatever stupid catchphrase he'd use. He didn't care about me. He wanted to spend time with my mom, and even though I tried to give her the benefit of the doubt, it was hard to grasp what she could possibly *see* in Geoff. I worried that her main motivation was his well-padded wallet, and I hated the idea of Mom dating guys based on their cash potential. She said that she found him *grounding*, especially after the string of philosophy PhD students, winter ski instructors, and professional baristas she'd dated. She said she needed to date a grown-up. But I wondered if it didn't have more than a little bit to do with the fact that Geofferson could easily supply tuition money to anywhere in the country — and Mom knew he'd fallen for her enough to do it in a heartbeat, if she asked him.

"Hayley? What do you want for dinner?" Mom pressed.

"I'm fine. You guys go ahead. I'll just make a sandwich or something," I said.

"You sure, baby?" Mom asked, tilting her head quizzically. "It's the first day of senior year. You should celebrate. *We* should celebrate," she clarified.

There's not much to celebrate, I wanted to say. My Yearbook meeting had been shaky, Jess was attempting to undermine me, and I still allowed Keely, Ingrid, and Emily to get under my skin. I mashed my lips together to keep myself from saying anything. I'd stopped confiding in Mom in ninth grade, right after I'd stopped being friends with Keely, Ingrid, and Emily. I'd come home crying, and Mom had begun crying, too. It had terrified me.

"I just hate seeing you sad. I want your life to be as easy as possible," she'd said, hugging me tightly. I felt like I'd let her down. And I didn't want to feel like that ever again.

"I'm fine," I said. I smiled brightly to try to ease the worry evident in Mom's eyes.

"Great!" Geoff said. "See, I knew Comet would be wiped. The first day of school would kick anyone's butt!"

I watched my mom's face for any sign of annoyance. She loved *poetry*. How could she love a guy who used the phrase *kick butt*? It embarrassed me for him. But Mom was oblivious.

Instead of engaging in conversation, I hurried to the kitchen and made a PB and J sandwich. It was one of the few meals I could count on. PB and J was reliable, simple. Grabbing a soda from the fridge, I headed up the creaky stairs into my attic-turned-bedroom. I pulled off my black cardigan and red skirt and threw on a pair of old gray Bainbridge sweats and a white cotton tank. Then, I flopped onto my bed and exhaled. Sadie jumped up close to me, nosing her way toward my sandwich.

"No!" I pushed her away. I took a quick bite and picked up my laptop from the floor and turned it on. As it whirred to life, I thought back to Mr. Klish's social media rant. Of course, he didn't know that I Googled myself almost constantly, and I always knew exactly what would show up: lists of debate wins, honor roll mentions, and academic awards. I typed my name in the search box.

I scrolled through the first page — as expected, it was filled with debate transcripts, Bell Award for Excellence nominees, and absolutely nothing from Keely's freshman year Tumblr. Then, something on the bottom of the third page caught my eye.

Hayley Kathryn Westin Facebook.

I clicked the link. Probably it was just another Hayley Kathryn.

I blinked.

It was a full-body picture of a girl covered in whipped cream, a rainbow-colored bikini barely visible beneath the white swirls of frosting. She was smiling proudly at the camera, pleased to be caught in the act. Her eyes were slate gray, and her dark brown hair skimmed her angular shoulders. I clicked. Instantly, the picture magnified to fill the screen. I gasped, clasping my hand to my mouth. Sensing opportunity, Sadie grabbed the sandwich and jumped off the bed, but I didn't stop her. I couldn't tear my eyes away from the chin dimple, the bangs-covered widow's peak, the freckles dotting her long arms. *Monkey arms.* The phrase popped into my head. It was what Keely used to call me on the playground.

The profile was open to the public, so I frantically scrolled down, trying to figure out how this *image*, this girl who was me but was not — could not — be me, could exist. It didn't make sense; it was like a philosophy problem that my mind couldn't wrap itself around. There *had* to be an explanation.

There was a status update written at 9:02 a.m., the same time I was in AP English, discussing the meaning of magic and superstition in *Macbeth*.

> Nothing better than midweek madness. Bonus points if it's with college hotties!

Below the status were two comments, including one from Keely.

> I thought you were good at math? Apparently not, cuz Hayley does not equal hotties in any way.

> More like midweek sadness . . . for the dudes who have to hang out with you.

That had been Keely's contribution. My cheeks burned as I frantically clicked on photos. The same girl wearing a pair of red short shorts and a white furry crop top, a Santa hat perched on top of her shoulder-length hair, dark except for subtle streaks of blonde. *I've never used hair dye.* The girl canoodling with a muscly dude. *I've never been kissed.*

But it didn't matter, because it was me. I looked at the picture of her — me — making out with the guy again. Instead of looking at him, she was looking at the camera, her eyes wide, her smile toothpaste-commercial perfect. My tongue poked my own teeth, noticing the way that my own incisor stuck out, despite years of orthodontia.

It wasn't me. I knew that. I *knew* that. And yet . . .

I closed my eyes and massaged my temples. Then, my mind flashed to the image of Adam waiting outside Mr. Klish's office. Of course. He'd gotten the same speech about the Ainsworth and the Internet and had come up with a way to sabotage me. He knew I didn't have Facebook. He knew I probably never would have come across the page. And he knew that there was no way he'd have a chance at the Ainsworth if I were also a candidate.

My hands unclenched, and I realized I'd etched fingernail marks into my palms. *Breathe.* I'd print out the offending page, march it into Mr. Klish's office, explain the situation, and demand Adam's suspension. It would be *fine.*

Now that I knew exactly what was happening, I allowed myself to click through the entire profile. It had already amassed forty friends, and seventeen pictures had been uploaded. Fake Hayley at what seemed to be a frat party. Another image of her and a guy kissing, her bra strap clearly visible as her tank top slipped off her shoulder.

Tears pricked my eyes. This wasn't *funny*.

A memory sprang to my mind.

Ninth grade, the first day I'd gotten anything below a B. It was a C-minus on a geometry project, and I knew it was because I'd barely studied. I'd snuck a glance at Adam's paper. He'd gotten an A.

And then, I'd known: I had to quit field hockey. I *needed* to focus on academics. It had already become clear that fall that I couldn't compete with Keely, Ingrid, or Emily when it came to our social lives. Academics were all I had. And if it meant I had to give up social stuff entirely, then I would. I'd gone in to Coach Smith to discuss it with her, but instead of allowing me to quit privately, she'd made me come to Saturday practice and turn in my uniform. I'd tried to explain why I was quitting to Keely, Emily, and Ingrid — that I *needed* to focus on school, I couldn't be okay with mediocre grades the way they were — but I don't think they realized I was actually going to follow through.

Everything was fine until later that afternoon, when I realized I hadn't heard from any of them. We always hung out on Saturday afternoons, either at the mall or the movies or walking aimlessly up and down Main Street. But I didn't have any missed calls or texts, and when I checked my e-mail, the only messages I had were from the most popular guys in school, telling me just how much of a loser I was.

When I checked my Facebook page, I found out why. They'd scanned every single stupid HIKE list I'd ever written and put them up as a note on my Facebook wall, under the heading *Guys I Love*. And the worst part was, I hadn't even *liked* any of the guys I'd written about. I didn't think Jon Weber was *hotter than a Hemsworth brother*, I didn't believe Seth Koen was *first-kiss worthy*, and I certainly didn't want to make out with Max White. I'd just written that because those were the guys Keely was always talking about, and I'd been trying to fit in.

Back then, I'd ran out of the house, gotten on my bike, and gone to Adam's. He was the one who had managed to trace the IP address. The next morning, I'd taken down my Facebook, blocked my e-mail, and gradually scrubbed away any personality from my Internet presence.

I'd never let Keely see how much it bothered me. *That* would have given her satisfaction. Instead, I'd reinvented myself. I'd gotten rid of my brightly colored camisoles and skinny jeans. I'd ripped the pictures from my bulletin board. Even my handwriting had changed, from bubbly, oversized script often written in purple ink to small, neat print.

No one knew that I was vulnerable — except Adam. He'd been the only one to see me cry. The next day, I'd gone to school and ignored the comments flying around me. Eventually, they'd died down — but the anger and hurt hadn't. I'd never be seen as normal. I'd always be a grade-grubbing freak that no guy would admit to liking — even if, by some miracle, they did.

I grabbed my phone from my bag, hating that Adam was the first person in my address book. I *hated* him. I wanted him to be expelled. To have to move somewhere where I'd never, *ever* see him again.

He answered on the first ring. "Hayley, what's up?"

"You know exactly what's up," I said in a low voice.

"I have many talents, but mind reading isn't one of them. At least, not yet," Adam drawled. "What do you need? Help with Osborn's homework?"

"I'm not talking about this on the phone. Meet me at the Ugly Mug in half an hour," I demanded, my voice shaking.

"Wait, what?" Adam asked. "I'm doing homework. Can we talk tomorrow?"

"No!" I exploded. "You have to talk to me tonight. I know what you did, and you need to fix it. Or else I'm calling the police. It's harassment, you know. It's not funny."

"Hayley, what are you talking about? I haven't harassed you. I haven't talked to you all freaking summer."

"Stop it!" I screeched. "Just shut up and listen. It's not a joke, and I need to talk to you. Now."

"I know you're not kidding, I just don't know what you're talking about. And I don't know why you're yelling at me."

"Will I see you at the Ugly Mug?" I asked, trying to contain the hysteria in my voice.

"Yes. Fine. Ugly Mug, half an hour, full-on Hayley freak-out. Can't wait," he said sarcastically.

I didn't bother responding. I hung up, slammed my laptop closed, and ran down the stairs.

"Heading to town to study!" I yelled. But it didn't matter. Mom and Geoff had already left for dinner.

I made it to the Ugly Mug in record time. I gazed around. No Adam. Just Percy, a philosophy-major barista, a few lone students wearing oversized headphones, and a couple in the corner feeding each other forkfuls of chocolate cake.

"What's up, Hayley?" Percy asked, leaning on the counter.

"Nothing," I said shortly. The clock above the door read seven twenty-five. If Adam wasn't here by seven thirty, I was going to call the police. Which meant I had four and a half minutes to figure out how to explain to the Bainbridge police department why a fake Facebook profile was a legitimate emergency.

"Want the usual?" Percy asked companionably, already turning to the espresso machine.

"Sure." I was way too keyed up for coffee, much less the double-shot latte Percy was whipping up, but I knew if I said no, he'd ask questions, and questions were the last thing I wanted right now. I perched on the edge of a moth-eaten purple velvet loveseat in the back of the shop. Who the hell did Adam think he was, and didn't he *know* that I was smarter than that? I couldn't believe he thought it'd be so easy to take me down.

The front door opened. As soon as I saw Adam, clad in his Varsity Debate jacket, I wanted to snap, run toward him, and claw his eyes out. How the hell could a guy who thought a *Varsity Debate jacket* was a remotely appropriate fashion choice even dare try to sabotage me?

"Over here," I called sharply, annoyed as I said it.

Adam nodded at me, then headed up to the counter to order.

"Not now," I growled.

Adam walked toward me. "Seriously, you're not even letting me get coffee? Okay, this is way more serious than I thought." His voice was jokey, but his brow was furrowed in concern. "What's up?" He didn't bother to sit down.

"You know," I said, struggling to maintain an even tone of voice as I looked into his eyes. I could vaguely make out my reflection in his glasses, and I tried to appear calmer. If he saw I was upset, then he'd win. "The Facebook page."

Confusion crossed his face as he peered down at me. "Is that what you wanted to tell me? That you finally joined the twenty-first century? Well, congratulations, and I'll be sure to not friend you, so you won't scream at me for harassment."

"No." I stood up so I could look him in the eye. "The. Fake. Facebook. Page. That. You. Made. To Sabotage. Me," I said through clenched teeth.

"Hayley, what are you talking about? I don't have time for this."

"You think I do?" I practically shrieked. Percy, who was walking toward us with my latte, paused midstep.

I lowered my voice. "Look." I pulled out my laptop and logged on to the site. "I found it, Adam."

Adam grabbed my computer as Percy hurriedly made his way to our table and practically threw my latte in front of me. I took a large gulp, feeling even more anger when the liquid burned the roof of my mouth.

"I didn't make that. And it's not even you." Adam shook his head and passed the laptop toward me.

"What do you mean?" I'd expected him to deny that he'd made the page, but not deny that it was me. "Who else would it be?"

"Well, you're not exactly the Queen of Frat Parties, are you? It could mean someone did a decent Photoshop job. They might have found an image of a girl who looked similar to you and morphed some features together."

"Is that possible?" I asked in a small voice, beginning to doubt my suspicions.

"I don't know," Adam admitted. "But I didn't do it, Hayley. I'd never cheat my way into something. Look, I want to win the Ainsworth. So do you. But we've always been pretty decent about separating friendship and competition, don't you think?"

"Yeah, but . . ." I trailed off as I realized that I'd wanted it to have been him.

Adam sighed. "Then it's going to be a really long year for you."

I narrowed my eyes. "What does *that* mean?"

"Nothing. Hayley, listen, you're under a ton of stress. I get it. So am I. But you can't let everything get under your skin. I mean, this sucks, but I didn't do it. And it's just a stupid prank. You need perspective. It's not like a million people are Googling you."

I stared at him. Was he kidding? "The Ainsworth committee is," I said flatly.

Recognition dawned on his face. "You think someone's trying to sabotage you?"

"Yes!" I snapped. I didn't want to be here anymore, playing amateur detective.

"Hayley." Adam's voice was firm. He reached toward my hand. I yanked it away.

"Sorry." Adam let his hand fall into his lap. "Hayley, look at me."

"What?" I asked flatly.

"I know you probably think I did this to win the Ainsworth. And I don't know what I can say to make you believe me, except I didn't do it. I'd never hurt you. I know we have fun being competitive, but I wouldn't . . . I wouldn't . . ." He trailed off.

"It's fine." I squeezed my eyes shut to stop tears from falling. I wasn't crying at what Adam said. But I wanted to cry because even if he didn't do it, the fact remained that someone did. Someone hated me enough to sabotage me.

Adam looked at me quizzically. "It's not fine."

"No," I agreed. "But there's nothing you can do about it." I stared at the coffee-ringed table. If I looked at him, I'd lose it, and that would give him even more of an upper hand than he already had. And the thing I hated most of all was the realization that no one would have done this to him. He didn't have a ton of friends, but he wasn't actively disliked the way I seemed to be. And I didn't need him feeling sorry for me.

"I can at least sit with you until you stop doing that shaky-hand thing," he said.

I squeezed my hands together, realizing it looked like I was praying. I slid them into my pockets, instead. "I'm fine. Freaking amazing. *Je suis très bien*," I practically shouted, realizing that my slipping into French meant I was seriously losing it.

Adam's eyes widened. "Whoa, Hayley, don't freak. It's *fine*. It's just some joke that got out of hand. Bet you anything that it'll be taken down as soon as you tell Klish. It seems like the only people who've even seen it are Keely and her clique. I doubt the Ainsworth committee is doing any recon right now. I mean, no offense, but you don't even know if you're a finalist. *I* don't even know if I'm a finalist."

"I know. But . . ."

"Listen, if you want, I can hack into Keely's e-mail and see if I find anything. I bet you anything her password is *spray tan*."

"Do you think she did it?" I asked, ignoring Adam's joke. I thought back to her comment this morning. *Even the losers are joining Facebook.* Had that been a dig at me, one so subtle I hadn't even caught it? Probably.

"She could have. But it could also have been someone from that debate camp you went to. Did you talk to them about the Ainsworth?"

Fury shot through my body and I clutched my knees to keep from reaching up and strangling Adam. "Really? Do you really think that I'm running around, bragging to everyone? I'm just trying to be the best I can be, and no one will leave me alone." My voice had taken on a high-pitched, hysterical quality. "Even *Jess* is trying to sabotage me."

"Really?" Adam wrinkled his nose.

"What?"

"She doesn't seem to be the sabotage type, is all." Adam shrugged and I remembered that they'd worked on a physics project together last fall.

"Maybe not to you. But maybe she did it. She tried to get me kicked off the editorial board of Yearbook."

Adam shook his head. "This has Keely written all over it. Jess plays by the rules. She was pissed that you were EIC of Yearbook and Newspaper, so she went to Klish. Keely's just . . ."

"Just what?"

"Being Keely. Unless you think there's someone else who might be mad at you."

"So you think I just have a million enemies running around New Hampshire?" I asked flatly.

"No, Hayley, I'm just saying that sometimes you can be . . ."

"What?" I challenged.

"Intense." Adam nodded toward the latte I was holding in my hand. "Like, right now, you're holding your coffee like you're gonna throw it at someone. You can be intimidating, and that *attitude* might rub people the wrong way. If they don't know you."

"And you can be an idiot," I retorted, taking a large sip of my latte so he couldn't tell how much he'd hurt me. It was one thing for Keely to think of me as an intense, intimidating weirdo, but it stung coming from Adam. "Anyway, I'm sure you're right. It's just a prank and I'll discuss it with Klish tomorrow. Thank you." I grabbed my bag from beside me, as if I were running late to a very important appointment, which both Adam and I knew was a lie.

Adam stood up. "Right." He shifted from foot to foot, standing over me as if he expected me to say something else. "Well, good luck with everything. And if you need anyone . . ." he trailed off.

I didn't bother to watch him leave. Instead, I stared at the screen when I noticed a response to the latest wall post alert. It was from Keely.

> God, Hayley, if you're actually willing to be normal, then . . .

"Then *what?*" I said out loud. A girl in the corner, furiously highlighting a textbook, glared at me.

I angrily slammed my laptop shut and made my way out of the Ugly Mug. I still had a ton of work to do. I had a problem set due for Calc. I needed to read through Act II of *Macbeth*. I needed an actual agenda for the Yearbook meeting so it wouldn't dissolve into a free-for-all discussion like last time. I had a French conversation topic to prepare, and I should be making cookies for the next Key Club bake sale. But Facebook — which I didn't even belong to for the very reason that it was a total time waster — had ruined all of that for me.

I headed into the still-empty house, crept upstairs, and crawled under the duvet, not bothering to wash my face or brush my teeth. I remembered an article I'd read about the secret to success in some hippie magazine my mom had left lying around. Most of it was about channeling your inner goddess and making a vision board, but one piece of advice had stuck with me. It said that the biggest mistake you could make in a crisis was to do something immediately. *Sometimes, you need your spirit guides to bring you to a decision in your dreams!* And while I didn't think spirit guides could help me any more than Adam Scott could, I wondered if it might be best to just fall asleep and figure everything out in the morning.

Not like I could fall asleep. My mind felt mushy, like overcooked oatmeal, and I couldn't focus on anything besides the pattern of the shadows of branches on the wall. In the distance, I heard an owl hooting. These sounds normally calmed me down. But now, they only made me feel more jumpy.

I crossed the room to my DVD collection and scanned the titles: *Sleepless in Seattle.* No. *Valentine's Day.* No. *Mean Girls.* That sounded about right. I pulled the disc from the box and pushed it into the DVD player, allowing myself to get lost in the familiar storyline. But now, the plot, about how girls try to plan revenge on one another, just hit too close to home. I turned off the DVD player and slid back under the covers.

I couldn't get the eyes from the photo out of my mind. Silvery and shiny, like the underside of a fish caught from a pond, my eyes had always been my trademark, the one thing I really liked about the way I looked. But now, they didn't feel like *mine*. And now, even though the photo was just an encrypted piece of data lying dormant on my laptop, I imagined the identical eyes, the ones from the picture, watching me.

Toss. I thought of the picture of her and the guy. She was smiling, but she didn't look like she was having fun. Rather, she looked as though she knew some secret.

Turn. I turned my pillow to the fresh side.

This was ridiculous. There was no way I could sleep.

Instead, I pulled up my laptop and opened Word. *Agenda for Yearbook Meeting*, I began. No matter what, at least I always had work.

CHAPTER 4

*H*ayley?"

I woke up to sun dappling my ancient pink-and-purple-striped comforter.

"What?" I blinked, disoriented. I'd fallen asleep on top of my laptop, and one of the keys had indented itself on my cheek. Since my contacts were still in, my eyes felt dry and sandy, and it hurt to blink. I looked at the screen, where I'd fallen asleep midway through my memo writing, the Facebook page still pulled up.

And everything came flooding back.

"Hi." I struggled to sit up.

"Hayley bunny, are you all right?" Mom perched on the side of my bed and peered at my computer.

"Don't do that!" I shrieked, my voice rising. I didn't want her to see the pictures on the profile. It would just make her worry, and that would make *me* worry, and all the Advil in the world wouldn't stop that headache.

Mom pulled back. "I'm sorry," she said quietly. "I was just concerned. I was about to leave when I saw your car in the driveway. Are you sick?"

I shook my head. "What time is it?" I croaked. My throat was sore, and I'd have given anything to just crawl back under the covers and hope everything had been a bad dream.

"Eight."

"Eight? Why didn't you wake me up?" I'd already missed Yearbook and Calc. Not only that, but if Kelsey, Emily, or Ingrid knew about the profile — which they *did*, since their comments were all over the wall, then *everyone* did. And I hadn't even been there to do damage control.

"You look a little feverish." Mom held the back of her hand to my forehead. I swatted her away.

"I'm *fine*. I just have to go. And you need to go to work, Mom." The Sound and the Story opened at eight, and even though I was pretty sure that no one in Bainbridge was seeking their used copies of James Joyce quite that early, I did need her to leave me alone.

"All right. But if you're sick . . ." Mom said uncertainly, concern evident in her large blue eyes.

"I'm fine," I said, more gently this time. I wouldn't bother her with this until I knew what, exactly, *this* was.

"All right." Mom wandered out of the room and closed the door. I didn't even have time to take a shower. Instead, I pulled my hair into a messy bun, pulled a pair of jeans puddled in the corner over my hips, and yanked on an oversized white T-shirt. And then, because my eyes were killing me, I took out my contacts and put on my glasses. I hoped I looked like *tired grad student* but knew when I caught a glimpse of myself in my rearview mirror that I looked more like a hot mess. *Hayley Kathryn Westin, tired party girl.* Just like I appeared on the fake profile.

Once I got to school, I hastily parked in my spot at the far corner near the auditorium. As I sprinted through the doors, I caught sight of six seniors, including Keely, huddled around an iPhone. Before I knew what was happening, Keely and I locked eyes. Then, she turned away, leaning toward Emily. I tried to imagine what they were saying.

Look how easy she is to freak out.

Let's give her a nervous breakdown. Hashtag: funsies!

The imaginary conversations made me run faster, bursting into the main office at eight thirty-seven a.m., gasping until Mrs. Miller, the office secretary, turned from her computer.

"Yes, Hayley?" she asked, her eyebrows rising at the sight of my disheveled self.

"I . . . need . . . a . . . late . . . pass," I heaved, watching the second hand on the office clock jump forward. It was only a few minutes before AP English, and I wanted to get there early to talk to Mrs. Ross and make sure no crucial Yearbook decisions had been made without me.

"No you don't." Mrs. Miller waved me away. "Of course, for most students, we require a parent's note to excuse tardiness, but I think we'll let this one slide. After all, it's nice to know that even Hayley Westin can come down with a case of senioritis."

I didn't bother to correct her. "Thanks," I said miserably, hurrying down the hall to the English wing.

"What's up, Westin?" Matt. I turned, not bothering to break my stride.

"Running late!" I called over my shoulder.

He easily caught up with me, matching my pace.

"What's the rush?"

"I missed the meeting this morning, so I have to . . . Mrs. Ross . . . I need to explain that I was sick. . . ." I panted, catching my breath.

"Oh . . . it wasn't a big thing. Jess led it. I don't think Ross realized you weren't there. She conked out as soon as Jess started dividing the calendar into deadlines."

I stopped in my tracks. "What?" *Deadlines?*

"Yeah, while you were sleeping off your epic evening at the U, she went ahead and gave everyone September deadlines. Hey, it's the way to do things. Get others to do the grunt work, and leave the glory for you."

I barely heard Matt's philosophical rambling. Jess ran the meeting? I was at the U? I felt like I'd been dropped on some alien stage, unsure of my lines and even whether or not I was in a drama or a comedy.

"What are you talking about?"

"Your Facebook. If you want to rage, you should really think about changing your privacy settings." Matt nodded sagely.

"What did I say I was doing?" I asked, simultaneously not wanting to hear the answer and knowing I needed to.

"Chillin' with some dudes at the U. So you go from no partying at all to, like, partying with the big guys? That's bold."

"Chillin' at the U?" I repeated. I cringed as the words left my mouth. I *hated* the word *chillin'* almost as much as the word *dope*. I'd never use those terms.

Matt nodded. "That's what your status said. So tonight, want to hang at Alyssa's barn? Everyone's going to be there."

I barely heard him. Alyssa's barn was legendary. It was the site of pretty much every makeout, breakup, and scandalous Facebook photo that occurred in high school. I probably couldn't have picked Alyssa out of a lineup, but even *I* knew what went down in her barn . . . and the hayloft . . . and the bank of the lake.

"Um . . ." If I *did* go, as myself, how would they post fake status updates? But if I went, then I'd have to face Keely. On her turf. My stomach churned. All I'd had was the PB and J from last night, and I could sense that was approximately ten seconds away from coming back up.

I gagged, clapped my hand over my mouth, and ran toward the bathroom, not caring how it looked or what Matt thought.

"Man, if you don't remember, it must have been a *really* good time." Matt laughed as I stumbled into the girls' room. "Seriously, come to the barn! I promise it'll make the U parties look lame!" he called to my retreating back.

"Move!" I yelled to a trio of freshmen huddling around the mirror, blocking the stalls.

"Um, say please?" one giggled.

"Shh, that's a *senior*!" another whispered.

The three of them burst into snorts of laughter as I rested my head on the metal stall door. In there, the air was cooler and I didn't feel like I had to throw up. But I didn't exactly feel good. I'd always had a nervous stomach, and I hated the way it betrayed my nerves. Usually, the nausea would go away once I'd participated in a debate or given a speech. But now, it seemed like I was stuck with it. I took a few deep breaths, trying to ready myself to go back to class.

"She's the girl who parties with frat guys at the U," one of the freshmen said admiringly on her way out. My stomach dropped again.

I stumbled out of the stall and looked at myself in the mirror. Behind my glasses, my eyes were bloodshot and watery. My face was pale. *At least I didn't look like the profile anymore.* That was the ironic upside. Profile Hayley was tan, confident, always smiling, a girl with a glint in her eye who made it clear, even to the camera, that she didn't give a damn about anything.

Get it together. I'd said it to myself a million times in the past few days, and now it was even more essential. I was comparing myself to someone who didn't exist. Shaking my head, I pulled my shoulders back, marched out of the bathroom, and headed across the hallway to the guidance office.

"Hayley!" Miss Marsted cooed, but I didn't say hi. I walked straight for Mr. Klish's office, not caring if I was interrupting another appointment. I wasn't some random tenth-grader who'd decided he could no longer handle Honors Geometry or a sad junior who wrote depressed poems for the literary journal.

I opened the door and immediately saw the oh-so-familiar logo for Varsity Debate on the jacket slung on the back of the chair.

Adam was already here.

What the hell? My mouth felt cottony. Had this been his plan all along? To make me suspect him, then confide in him, and *then* use my moment of weakness to move ahead in the Ainsworth finals?

"Adam," I croaked.

"Hayley, good, I'm glad you came down!" Mr. Klish grinned.

"I'm sorry?" I said. I felt like I was outside my body, watching everything. This was the guidance office. This was my guidance counselor. This was my academic counterpart. The pieces, separately, made sense, but once they were together, I couldn't figure out what I was supposed to do or what I was supposed to think.

"I'd called you down last period, but Dr. Osborn said you weren't in class. I'm glad someone gave you the message, and I am delighted to be the first to inform you that both you and Mr. Scott are officially invited to the New Hampshire round of Ainsworth semifinals. Now, this is one of the few times that our school has had one candidate, let alone two, and I am confident you both will do our school proud," he finished, smiling broadly.

"Wait . . . *what*?" I asked. It was taking too long for his words to reach my brain, for them to click into meaning. "I'm . . . a *finalist*?" I whispered. I clutched the back of Adam's chair.

"Yes! And you look like you're going to faint!" Mr. Klish said jovially. He hauled himself from his chair and shuffled to my side. "Take a deep breath." He rested his hand on my shoulder.

Mr. Klish lumbered back to his desk. After shuffling through an enormous pile of papers, he pulled out a single sheet. He pushed his glasses up the bridge of his nose, scanned the paper, and settled heavily into his chair.

"Now, kids, the semifinals are next weekend in Concord. I'd bring you, but unfortunately, that's when the Renaissance festival is and . . ." Mr. Klish shook his head.

"It's fine," Adam said. "We can get there by ourselves."

"Yeah," I murmured, not really paying attention. All I could think of was the profile. Because now that Adam and I were both going to the semifinals, the fake Facebook profile would definitely be found and scrutinized.

"All right. So you two will get yourselves to Concord. They're holding the interviews at the Vintage Plaza downtown. You'll check in, grab one of those minimuffins they always have at those types of events, get your coffee, maybe you'll have time to read the paper, something to de-stress . . ." Mr. Klish babbled.

"And then when does the actual competition *start*?" Adam interrupted.

"Oh! Well, as you know, the semifinals are conducted as an Oxford-style interview, done in front of an audience of your fellow competitors. You'll share what you know, be charming, and put Bainbridge on the map." He smiled encouragingly at both of us. "Any questions?" he added.

Adam's hand shot into the air. "What did they ask last year?"

Mr. Klish's grin widened even farther. "Excellent question. Well, last year one of the more colorful prompts was to explain how Shakespeare would use social media to interact with his critics, and another topic was whether teenage popularity was innate or could be learned. Any other questions?"

"No," I said, shooting a death stare toward Adam before he could come up with something else. For all I knew, he was just asking inane questions to waste time. After all, the longer the profile was up, the more chances the judges had to see it. "I have something I'd like to discuss *in private*," I blurted out.

"Okay," Mr. Klish said.

"I'll leave," Adam offered, as though it were a question. As soon as he brushed past me, I took a seat opposite Mr. Klish. I didn't allow my eyes to wander toward Ian-or-Morris, who was gazing down dolefully from the UPenn poster. I didn't want him to have to hear what was happening. He'd be above the high school drama.

"I know you said that the Ainsworth committee would be looking carefully at any online presence." I shifted uncomfortably. "My online identity is being impersonated."

Mr. Klish narrowed his eyes. "How so?"

"Well, someone has created a Facebook profile with a picture that looks like me. It's *not* me. It's clearly a Photoshop job," I said hurriedly. "But it looks like me. And it's not good."

"How is it not you, if the photo is *of* you?" Mr. Klish's voice was cold, accusatory, and I shrugged miserably. I wanted him to tell me that it didn't matter, that he'd just been trying to scare me yesterday and the Ainsworth committee was entirely made up of people even more computer illiterate than he was. But he didn't.

"I think maybe they were able to Photoshop the picture or . . . I don't know. And I don't know who did it. But I have my suspicions." *Adam.* Keely wouldn't have been smart enough to change the IP address.

"Can you please show me, Miss Westin?" Mr. Klish said, standing up from his chair and stepping aside.

"Of course," I said, typing my name onto his crumb-covered keyboard. He breathed heavily behind my shoulder. Facebook took forever to load on his computer.

But instead of the profile popping up, a blank page with a single sentence appeared: *No user exists by this name.*

"Maybe it's in another browser," I murmured, quickly typing *facebook.com* into Firefox. Again, the same message. Mr. Klish leaned even closer and I could smell the scent of stale coffee on his breath. I mashed my lips together, trying not to gag.

"Where is it?" he asked again.

I pushed the chair away from the desk. "I must have made a mistake," I said. "I'm sorry. Sorry!" I grabbed my bag and slung it over my shoulder and hurried out of the office, without saying good-bye to Miss Marsted. Matt's words bubbled back up in my brain: *If you can't remember, you must have had a really good night.*

A shiver rode up my spine.

What had "Hayley" done last night?

Adam was waiting outside the guidance office, shifting from one foot to the other. I paused. Every fiber of my being wanted to hate Adam, wanted to accuse him, but he looked concerned. Vulnerable.

"Everything okay?" he asked uncertainly.

"Yeah . . ." I trailed off, looking up and down the hallway. Empty. "Last night, you saw the profile, right?"

"In the coffee shop, when you showed it to me, of course," he said. "Actually, I looked when I got home, too. She really looks like you, Hayley. But . . ." He let the sentence hang, but I knew what he wanted to say. That he didn't do it. And I wanted to believe him, but I couldn't bring myself to say the words. Even if he hadn't, he was still my competition, and I had to remember that.

I sighed. "It doesn't matter. It's not there anymore."

Adam wrinkled his nose. "You mean it disappeared?"

"Yeah. It's not there."

"Well, that's good, isn't it?" Adam asked.

I nodded and turned on my heel just as the bell rang. Almost eleven, and I still hadn't gone to class. I felt like my brain was ready to burst from my skull. After all the emotional drama of the morning, spending forty minutes talking about the Treaty of Utrecht, or whatever was on the schedule for AP Euro, sounded like a vacation.

"Wait!" Adam called.

"What?" Students were streaming around us and I felt claustrophobic, unsure what people knew about me or were thinking about me. I pressed my back against the wall.

"Want to study together sometime this weekend? For the interview? I mean, we may as well. It could be helpful for both of us."

I thought about it. On one hand, Adam was smart, incisive, and, from years of being debate partners, I knew he could come up with killer on-point criticism. On the other hand, we weren't partners in the Ainsworth. And even if he didn't create the profile, telling him about it showed my weakness. I didn't need to do that again.

"Tonight?" he pressed.

I shook my head. "Not tonight." I was still thinking of Matt's invite to Alyssa's barn. Not like I would go. Or could go. And yet . . .

"Tomorrow?" he asked.

I nodded. "Tomorrow's fine. Like seven at the Ugly Mug?"

"Sure," Adam agreed. He pulled out his phone and began punching in the time, as though it was a real appointment and not just a casual study date.

"Listen, Adam . . ." I began, then trailed off as I saw Keely, Ingrid, and Emily saunter down the hall. But instead of ignoring me or offering a snide comment, I saw Emily offer the slightest hint of a smile.

"See you tonight," she said under her breath as she walked by.

Clearly, Matt had told them I was coming. And I'd surprise them. I would show up. If I was at Alyssa's, that meant that no one would believe it if the profile did resurface, saying fake Hayley was somewhere else. Somehow, being surrounded by my enemies in their element seemed less scary than sitting alone, in my room, waiting for their next move.

CHAPTER 5

J knew exactly where Alyssa lived — just a mile down the road from me. I'd been to her house before, back when her hayloft was for art projects and not truth-or-dare sessions. Back in second grade, our Girl Scout troop had come to fulfill some type of nature badge requirement. I wasn't sure what we were supposed to learn or do. We'd spent the majority of the afternoon playing hide-and-seek in the hayloft, splashing in the stream that trickled behind Alyssa's house, and trying to make the goats that wandered around the property eat our math textbooks. Back then, we all had the same goal: to have fun. It was so different now.

I recognized Keely's sky-blue Prius in the line of cars along the side of the road. I wasn't exactly sure where I was going, but I saw a few kids were wandering down to a collection of trees where a cooler was half-hidden beneath a bush. Keely was in a far corner with Garret Evans. Kayla and her best friend, Alana, were huddled around one of their phones, and a few guys were sitting in a semicircle outside the barn, playing cards and talking. Their baseball caps were pulled low over their faces, making them impossible to identify.

I self-consciously tugged on my shirt. It was a plain gray V-neck underneath a Bainbridge hoodie. Based on what the pictures of the Photoshopped me was wearing, I thought I'd be underdressed, but everyone was wearing similar outfits. Weird.

From the way I'd overheard Keely, Emily, and Ingrid talking about barn parties in the past, I'd assumed that they were epic. This was tiny. It'd be impossible to talk to Keely without everyone listening.

I stepped back, my foot landing on a branch. At the crack, one of the guys looked up.

Matt.

"Westin, what are you doing here?" he asked quizzically, as if he hadn't invited me here fewer than twelve hours ago. His tone made it sound like we'd run into each other in the guys' locker room or somewhere similarly random.

"Hayley?" Keely pried herself away from Garret and put her hands on her hips.

No backing down.

"I need to talk to you," I said, aware that every pair of eyes was on me.

Something — Amusement? Confusion? Fear? — flickered across her face. She shrugged, then snapped her gum.

"Okay."

Okay? Was it really that easy?

Keely stalked toward me, stopping several paces away from me before nodding.

"Come on," she said finally. At that, the party resumed its low hum as Keely walked across the lawn toward the stream. Finally, she stopped near a cluster of willow trees. A few wicker lawn chairs were scattered around. Keely perched in one, then rustled through her bag and pulled out an iced tea bottle. She pried the cap open with her teeth, then took a sip. I smiled. She used to insist on buying old-fashioned Coke bottles just so she could do that trick when we were kids.

"Want one?" Keely asked in a flat voice.

"I guess?" Grabbing another, Keely repeated the process and handed it to me.

"So, I wanted to talk to you about my Facebook profile," I said finally.

Keely wrinkled her nose. "What about it?"

"Well . . . it's not me," I said.

"Okay . . . do you want me to, like, defriend it or something? What's the problem?" Keely asked, her voice edged with annoyance.

"No, it's not online anymore. It was taken down. But I was wondering if you put it up," I said in a rush of words. "Because it's embarrassing. It had those pictures . . . and the status updates . . . and I feel like someone's sabotaging me."

"*No!*" Keely said. "No . . . I mean, I wouldn't do something like *that*. I thought you'd loosened up over the summer. And I didn't think it was embarrassing, I thought it was kind of fun. And I deleted that midweek sadness comment." She bit her lip and shrugged. "I don't want to, like, torment you. And I'd never have made the whole thing up. I barely have time to keep my own profile up to date. How would I have time to think up a whole, like, new life for someone I don't even care about?"

"Right," I said.

"No, I don't mean it like that . . . I mean, I know we've gone through a ton of stuff, and I know you hate me, because you're always *glaring* at me, but I wouldn't, like, ruin your life."

"You did once," I said.

"You mean the HIKE thing?" Keely shook her head. "That was when we were, like, children. I was mad at you. Are you seriously still hung up on that?"

"It just seems like something you'd do. And I wanted to ask you directly. Because if it was you, and you tell me, I won't press charges," I said definitively.

"Press charges?" Keely raised one blond eyebrow. I remembered: I hadn't learned the eyebrow trick from debate. I'd learned it from her. "It sounds like a stupid prank. But people liked it. Everyone was talking about it. Like, you could get rid of the sexy Santa outfit picture, but the other ones were cute. It's not bad to be noticed for stuff beyond, like, debate skills. I mean, you aren't ugly, you used to be fun, and probably could be again if you tried to . . . just live a little." Her tone wasn't mocking. Instead, it sounded vaguely friendly.

In the distance, an owl hooted, and then I heard a crash. Keely and I both whirled around, but nothing was there.

Keely shrugged. "Anyway, I'm sorry. And I'm sorry you're still mad about that HIKE thing. I didn't mean to hurt you. I was just mad at you."

"Why were you mad at me?" The way I'd remembered it, she'd been so busy talking about which guys liked her, I was surprised she'd even cared whether or not I'd quit the team.

"Because . . ." Keely chewed on her lip. "It was like you thought you were better than all of us. And you hadn't even told us that you were going to quit field hockey. I guess it just felt like you turned your back on us. So we turned our backs on you. But I mean, it was kid stuff. And I wouldn't do that now. I mean, I saw that profile and thought it was cool. Like, finally, you're chilling with the masses, you know?"

I appraised her. In the almost-darkness, her profile seemed different from that of the girl who'd spent the last three years glaring at me every chance she could get. She was biting her lip with her front teeth, her gaze off in the distance, and I couldn't help but wonder what it would have been like if we'd stayed friends. Would we still have sleepovers and make s'mores in the microwave or would we have naturally drifted apart?

"Pinky swear you didn't do it?" I held my hand out toward her. It was shaking slightly. It was our childhood oath, one we never backed down on.

A trace of a smile flickered across her face as she reached her hand toward mine. Her pinky hooked with mine and she squeezed.

"I wouldn't do that. I think you know that. Or at least I hope you do." She kept her finger entwined with mine. Silence fell between us again. But the quiet felt warmer, friendlier, like when we'd finally snuggle into our sleeping bags at five a.m. after eight hours of endless conversation. I was about to bring up an old memory, but just then, Keely shifted and turned toward me. And just like that, the spell was broken. Too much time had passed.

"Is that all you needed from me?" Keely looked over her shoulder toward the barn.

I nodded. I felt more confused than ever.

"Cool." Keely stood up, pulling her long hair into a high ponytail on the top of her head. I couldn't help but watch her every move. "Anyway, good luck with the profile thing. But it's not bad for people to see you as human. It's not, like, a scandal. It's high school." She cracked her knuckles and stood up. After a few steps, she looked over her shoulder. "Well, since you're here, you might as well stay. Have fun for once."

"Thanks." I slowly stood up and made my way back to the kids clustered around the barn. I felt like I was an anthropologist, learning about the rituals of the American teenager.

Matt was standing by the cooler. Despite myself, I made my way over to him.

"Need another?" he asked, unearthing two bottles from the cooler. He pushed them toward me and I reflexively grabbed them.

"No!" I held the bottles as far away from me as I could, watching condensation sweat down their sides as he rooted on the ground for an opener. I didn't want anyone to think I was drinking.

"Lighten up," I whispered to myself.

"What?"

"Nothing!" I said, bending to put the bottles on the ground just as Matt stood up with the opener. His head collided with my chin. And then, a flash from the bushes, but I wasn't sure if it was coming from a camera or from the pain radiating from my face. It *hurt*.

"Ow!" I gently held my hand on my chin.

"Sorry!" Matt took a few steps back.

"It's not a big deal," I mumbled.

"What?" he asked.

My face still hurt. "I'm fine," I whispered under my breath, trying to convince myself.

Matt paused, then put his drink down next to mine. A half smile crossed his face.

"You do that a lot, you know?" he said finally.

"What?"

"Talk to yourself. It makes me feel left out. It's very rude to have conversations in front of other people."

I grinned as I tried to come up with an appropriately flirty response. But I didn't have anything. I had no problem coming up with things to say *to myself*, but I was fundamentally incapable of having a conversation with someone else. Awesome.

Just then, my phone quacked to signal that I'd gotten a text. *Shoot.* I'd always meant to change the sound, but I kept forgetting. Not like it mattered. It wasn't like my phone was usually blowing up with texts.

I put one of the bottles on the ground, then slid my phone from my pocket.

It was from Adam.

> What's up? I know we're doing Ainsworth stuff
> tomorrow, but I started going through the materi-
> als now. Wanna come over?

"Who was that?" Matt asked curiously.

"Oh, just a friend," I said.

"You should tell them to come!" Matt grabbed my phone as I yanked it back.

"Whoa, sorry!" Matt let go of the phone. "I didn't realize you were texting your boyfriend."

"What, Adam? He's not my boyfriend!" I said quickly.

"Good for me."

My stomach flipped. "What did you say?" I wanted to hear it again.

"He seemed to be."

Oh. Disappointment sliced through my stomach. "Nope, just a friend."

"Cool," Matt said.

"So . . ." I desperately racked my brain for something to say that *didn't* involve Yearbook or Adam or the Facebook profile.

Just then, Erin hurried up to Matt and threw her skinny arms around his waist.

"I was looking for you *everywhere*. We're about to play flip cup and you know I need your help."

"I have to go," I mumbled, even though it wasn't necessary. Matt was oblivious to my presence. I put my drink down and headed home.

Once I got there, I popped *Love Actually* into the DVD player. That was why romantic comedies existed — so people could remind themselves that meet-cute situations never, ever happened in real life. Of course Matt had the attention span of a gnat. Of course he didn't care that I left. And of course it never would have occurred to him to follow me. And the only person I should have been mad at was myself for having wanted it.

CHAPTER 6

"What's the similarity between the American Liberty Movement of 1934 and the Tea Party of today?" Adam asked, glancing up from his laptop.

It was Saturday evening, and Adam and I were studying like rock stars, eyeballs deep in American history. Adam, clad in his dad's Harvard Law hoodie, was chugging down chai lattes like it was his job. I was similarly dressed in an old Harvard shirt of my mom's, drinking my third cup of black coffee.

"We're totally twins!" Adam had noticed.

"I wouldn't say that. I'd say we're both guilty of raiding our parents' closets, which makes us both kind of pathetic," I'd cracked. Even though Adam hadn't done or said anything wrong, just the fact that he wasn't Matt was enough to put me in a weird mood. I couldn't help but wonder what was going on at Alyssa's barn tonight. I knew it was more of the same: gossiping. Flirting. But for whatever reason, part of me wanted to be there.

"Hayley?" Adam asked, snapping me back to my Saturday night studying reality.

"Um, well, I think that the similarity is the idea of states' rights." I chewed on the edge of my sweatshirt. "But this question isn't hard. Think of something weirder. The Tea Party question is just to make sure that people are up on current events."

"That question was one of the ones Klish gave us," he said defensively, flipping through a thick packet.

"Okay, well, I'll think about it later. I'll give you one." I looked around the almost-empty café, finally noticing a guy in the corner, bobbing his head back and forth to the beat from his headphones. He was wearing a checkered scarf knotted tightly just below his bearded chin, and his head was covered by a newsboy cap. His jeans were skinny and tapered into a pair of polished brown loafers. He was probably a student at the U. "If a hipster's in a coffee shop, but there are no hipsters around, is he still a hipster?"

"What?" Adam asked irritatedly, causing the is-he-or-isn't-he-a-hipster to glance up. "That's a ridiculous question. Ask me something real!"

"Um, okay . . ." I shuffled through the packet Mr. Klish gave us. *Trace how the industrial revolution is responsible for social media.* Maybe. *In a century, what national or international event will most likely be artistically commemorated on a continual basis?* Maybe.

"Come on!" Adam urged. "I want to get at least three more questions."

"All right. Um, is it possible for someone to suddenly find him or herself attracted to someone they'd never noticed before? And compare the concept to, uh, the theory of relativity," I finished lamely.

Adam peered at me dubiously over his glasses. "Is that question in the packet?"

"No," I admitted.

"Come on. Give me a real one!" Adam took one of the cookies from the plate in the center of the table. I grabbed one as well. "Arts and Sciences, please."

"Okay, Mr. Trivial Pursuit." I flipped through the packet. He chuckled. We were acting just like we had when we were debate partners, before all the Ainsworth stuff had come between us. It was weird. It was nice.

Just then, my phone buzzed, skittering across the table.

There was a text, from an unfamiliar number.

> All work and no play. . . . It won't make me go away.

My heart thudded against my rib cage.

> PS: You give Keely way too much credit.

I quickly pressed delete.

"What was that?"

I shook my head. "Nothing."

"Really? It doesn't seem like nothing."

"It was just a random text. Like an automated spam thing." I shoved my phone into my bag.

"Anyway, here's one. If ancient Rome had television, what would the top five reality programs be, and why?" I asked quickly.

"Well, clearly, the Colosseum was a cultural center, so there'd be something about that. But do you think the committee wants to subdivide within gladiator programs? Like, *Soldiers of Style* could work, since that would speak to Rome's interest in textiles," Adam said, allowing me to zone out.

But just then, the door to the café opened and Jess walked in with her boyfriend, Robbie. Robbie was a skinny, bearded junior whose interests seemed to be Hacky Sack, incense, and Phish.

Instead of heading to the counter, Jess came up to my table.

"Hey," she said, but not in a friendly way.

"Hey, Jess," I said coolly.

"I'm surprised you're here," she said.

"Really?" I asked, immediately on edge. "Where did you think I'd be?" I could sense Robbie and Adam both looking back and forth between us, as though we were playing an invisible tennis match.

"Partying," Jessica said smoothly. "You certainly talk about it a lot, at least. And I wonder what Mr. Klish would think of your extracurricular activities," she said.

My blood turned to ice.

"What do you mean?" I asked, forcing my voice to stay calm.

"Your Facebook page," she said. She pulled out her iPhone and quickly scrolled, then shoved the phone in my face.

The profile was back. Or rather, *I* was back. It was a photo from last night, where I was standing next to Matt, one bottle in each hand. Except this time, it was *me*. It was taken in the half a second before I'd put the drinks on the ground, before the collision, before he'd asked if Adam was my boyfriend, before Erin had led him away. The flash from the bushes. The pain radiating behind my eye sockets. That moment.

"You took that picture," I realized slowly. "You'd been watching me." *Of course.* I'd been so focused on Keely that I hadn't even thought about Jessica. And I'd walked right into a trap of my own making. I took a deep breath and looked down at my hands, noticing the way my fingers were trembling ever so slightly.

"No, I just looked at your profile pic and saw that you were partying with your Yearbook staffers. Which, to me, seems kind of sketchy. But I guess we can find out whether Mr. Klish is cool with it, right?" Jess asked, barely able to conceal the glee in her voice.

Adam took the phone from Jessica's hands. "That's you," he said in a flat voice. "It's what you were wearing yesterday."

"I know, but you don't understand. It's . . ." I shook my head. Jess had gotten something even better than a Photoshopped image. She'd caught me, red-handed. And it wasn't like I could deny it, because everyone had seen me. And even though a lot of high school kids spent weekends partying, I was held to a different standard. Mr. Klish had pretty much spelled it out for me in our meeting in the guidance office the other day. And I'd blown it.

"What do you want?" I asked, panic edging into my voice.

"Step down from the editor-in-chief position and allow me to take over. I won't tell anyone about the Facebook page. I mean, if I were you, I'd take down the pictures immediately. But if you don't give me the editor position, then I'll have no choice but to demand your resignation. After all, I don't feel comfortable being led by an editor who clearly has such dubious judgment."

"Hey, Jess, do you want a chai?" Robbie called loudly from the counter. He looked almost as miserable as I felt.

"Yeah. Soy milk. And make sure it's not watered down," she commanded. Robbie turned on his heel and practically ran to the counter.

"Up to you." She shrugged as she slid her phone into her pocket.

I desperately glanced over at Adam. He and I were a team.

He'd come up with *something*. But instead, he was packing his papers into his backpack.

"Adam?" I croaked, hating the way I sounded so desperate. So scared. He may not have been my best friend, but he was the only person I had. And I needed him on my side.

"Hayley, for all I know, you're starting all this drama. And I don't want to be a part of it. I need to study," he said coldly. "I'll see you on Monday."

Jess smirked as Adam walked out. I closed my eyes, hoping this was some terrible stress dream. I opened them. Nope. Jess was still standing in front of me, her smirk growing wider with every second that I stayed silent. I knew she knew I was trying not to cry.

Robbie walked gingerly toward us, holding out his chai toward Jess like an offering. *Sorry*, he mouthed to me. I turned away. I didn't want his hippie pity.

"Thanks, honey!" Jess cooed as she grabbed the drink. She perched next to me on the love seat. "Anyway, Hayley, how you live is your choice. I'm not judging you for partying. I mean, if I were under all the stress of senior year and the Ainsworth . . ." She sighed. "Well, I think stepping down from Yearbook makes sense on so many levels, don't you agree?" she asked brightly.

I stood up so quickly I jostled the love seat and caused Jess's drink to splash onto her jeans. As she hurried to dab the spot with a napkin, I ran out of the coffee shop. And it was only when I got to my car that I allowed myself to cry.

I put the key in the ignition and turned on the radio. A cheesy Madonna song from the eighties filled the car, its techno-pop beat at odds with my mood.

I'm a failure. The thought came, unbidden, to my mind. I'd worked so hard, for so long. I'd missed out on field hockey, on friendships, on parties, on everything. And now, because of *holding* a drink, not even sipping it — the one time in my life that I'd acted like a normal high schooler — everything was falling apart. I wasn't like my mom, who people just *liked*. People didn't like me. They respected me. But they wouldn't, not anymore.

I cried harder, resting my head against the steering wheel. Then, the song "Forever Young" came on. I recognized it from the soundtrack to the movie *Listen to Me*. It's one of those movies hardly anyone knows, about a group of college debaters whose hyperambition serves as the basis for their friendships. Of course, it's full of eighties hairstyles and earnest dialogue, but it was one of my favorites. Before I knew about the Ainsworth or about UPenn, I knew that was what I wanted my future to be like — full of fiercely intelligent people having all-night conversations and pushing themselves to be the best they could be. But now, the future was so close to slipping from my grasp. Losing the Yearbook job chipped away at my identity as the girl who did everything.

A sob of self-pity escaped my lips.

Pull it together, Westin. I was still in the game.

For now. A voice inside my head responded. It wasn't my voice. It was small, scared, full of self-doubt. And I knew that from now on, that voice would be a part of me.

CHAPTER 7

By Sunday, the Facebook profile had once again disappeared into the Internet ether. If that didn't prove Jess's guilt, I wasn't sure what would. But at least she could put her well-honed Photoshop skills to good use on Yearbook, I thought grimly, as I made my way to Monday morning's meeting, where I was about to follow Jess's blackmail instructions and resign. I'd even practiced a resignation speech. That was just the type of person I was. I couldn't even be *blackmailed* without significant prep.

I felt like I was marching to my execution as I walked up the stairs to room 201. And the worst thing was that none of the other Yearbook staffers seemed to notice or care. They climbed up the stairs in groups of two or three. None of them said hi to me.

I caught a glance of myself in the glass that surrounded the stairwell. I was wearing a black knee-length skirt, a white sweater, and my knee-high leather boots. It was professional, but not over-the-top, and somber without being ridiculous. Focusing on my outfit was the only way I could face the task ahead of me. Inside, I might have been falling apart, but at least I looked pulled together.

I walked to the podium at the front of the classroom, surveying the staff. Some girls, like Andrea Faville and Marisa Ollins, were animatedly talking and laughing while others, like Pauline

Millard and Kristen McGonigle, shuffled into the room in their Uggs and sweatpants, their eyes glued to their tiny iPhone screens. They wouldn't care. Which only made me feel worse.

The bell rang, and Mrs. Ross nodded at me. So did Jess. I turned away from her. As if I needed her permission to speak.

"Okay, let's start," I said in a small voice, not making eye contact with anyone.

"So, I think, personally, that we should do, like, a shirtless soccer spread," Pauline said loudly, ignoring me.

Marisa wrinkled her nose. "Isn't that kind of sexist? Besides, I don't think any of them are that hot. I'd prefer doing a shirtless spread of the marching band. At least that's making a statement, you know? Some of them are pretty hot."

"Um, guys?" I tried again.

Just then, the door opened and Matt sauntered in.

"Sorry, Westin!" he stage-whispered as he walked in front of me.

"It's fine. So, like I was saying," I tried again.

"Is everyone listening?" Mrs. Ross interrupted. I glared at her, annoyed at her help. I had this. Or, I would.

The room quieted down. To avoid eye contact, I looked at the poster across the room. It was of a mountain at sunset, with one lone hiker at the top. SOMETIMES, WHEN YOU FEEL LIKE DARKNESS IS APPROACHING, ALL YOU NEED IS A SHIFT IN PERSPECTIVE. Thank you, inspirational poster. I shifted my focus to Matt, who was gazing at me curiously.

I took a deep breath. "After much consideration, I've decided to step down from my role as editor in chief of the *Spectrum*. Thank you so much for the opportunity, and I look forward to enjoying the *Spectrum* as a reader. I'm sure it'll be great."

Silence. I wasn't sure what I'd expected. A protest? A walkout?

Finally, Mrs. Ross spoke up. "Well, this is unexpected, Miss Westin. Do you have a successor?"

I nodded. "AndJessicaAdamsonisthenewreditorinchiefpleasedirectquestionstoher," I said in a rush of words. Then, I bolted out the door. A group of junior girls were clapping for Jess, and she was eagerly making her way up to the front of the classroom as though she'd just won an Oscar. I didn't need to watch.

I sat down on the dirty linoleum floor and rested my cheek against a metal locker. I could hear Jess's saccharine voice seeping underneath the doorway, talking reelections for class-section editors. Hearing her made everything worse. I knew I should stand up and get out, but I was so *tired*.

Just then, I heard footfalls. I glanced up at Matt peering down at me.

"Hey," he said.

"I'm fine," I said mechanically.

"I didn't ask how you were. I assume it's somewhere between crappy and sucky. Am I right?"

I took a deep breath and nodded.

"Here." Matt offered his hand to me. I scrambled up on my own, not wanting his help. Then, he pulled me toward him into a hug. I could feel his heart pounding inside his chest. When I pulled away, there was a wet splotch on his blue-and-green button-down.

Matt took a step back.

"Sorry I got your shirt wet." I bit my lip to keep it from trembling. "It's just . . . a tough morning."

"No worries," Matt said, a crooked grin crossing his face. "It's good to see that you're human."

"I'm really fine," I said stiffly. "You should go back to the meeting."

"Nah." Matt shook his head. "Yearbook's for losers."

"Are you quitting?" I asked.

"No . . ." Matt trailed off.

"Well, you shouldn't!" I said quickly, hating how presumptuous I must have sounded. Of course he wasn't quitting just because I'd resigned. "Anyway, thanks for checking on me!" I said quickly.

"Wait!" Matt called. "Where are you going?"

"Coffee." The word hung between us, not quite an invitation. "You can come if you want," I added awkwardly.

"Cool. Let's do it," Matt said. And even though I'd suggested it, it was clear he was in charge. I didn't mind. It was nice to finally follow someone else's lead.

Together, we walked down the stairs and into the bright September sunshine. The air smelled like wood smoke, burning leaves, and freshly cut grass. I took a deep breath. I already felt better.

"Where's your ride?" Matt asked, scanning the parking lot.

"Over there," I admitted, pointing to my ugly brown Cougar. I'd kind of hoped Matt would drive.

He let himself into the passenger door, throwing my pile of books and binders into the backseat. "Ugly Mug?" he asked expectedly.

"Nah." Memories of Jess's blackmail were still too fresh. "Coffee Hut." It was a generic chain in the strip mall at the other end of town. The coffee tasted like sugary dirt, but at least it wouldn't lead to some post-traumatic episode.

"Cool," he said. I started the ignition and he turned on the radio, jumping back when Bon Jovi blasted over the ancient sound system.

"Someone loves their eighties rock," he murmured, fiddling with the dials until he came across an acoustic rock guitar song.

"Yeah, sorry about that." I hadn't adjusted the radio since my Saturday night cry fest.

"It's so weird that you have, like, a tape player in your car. It's like, beyond retro," he said, examining the ancient dashboard and piles of mix tapes left over from my mother's own adolescence that were spread across the floor.

"It's a retro car," I said awkwardly. I knew he was just trying to make conversation, but it was hard not to take his comment as an attack against the Cougar.

"Cool." Matt drummed his fingers along to the beat.

We parked and walked into the Coffee Hut together. It was in the middle of the early-morning rush. As we got in line, part of me hoped the customers surrounding us would look at Matt and me and assume we were a couple.

When it was our turn to order, Matt stepped in front of me.

"I'll get a hot chocolate. And it'd be awesome if the whipped cream was epic," he said, immediately moving to the coffee pickup area.

"You?" the barista asked.

"A vanilla latte," I decided. I deserved it.

"That'll be ten dollars even," she said. Clearly, Matt's epic hot chocolate came with an epic price tag.

But Matt was at the other end of the store, and I didn't want to call him out to pay. "Fine." I pulled out a ten, passed it to the cashier, then headed over to wait with Matt.

"Yo," Matt said. Clearly, the fact that he had to pay hadn't even crossed his mind. And while it wasn't like I was going to bring it up or anything, I couldn't help but note that our coffees were the equivalent of an hour and a half of my own barista-ing.

As soon as we got our drinks, we went outside. Matt sat on the bench and I joined him, even though I was worried about being late for first period. How didn't *he* worry?

"You know, I didn't get captain of the hockey team last year," Matt said out of the blue.

"Oh?" I glanced sharply at him. His seemingly random conversation made it feel like he'd read my mind.

"Yup. I was bummed. Coach gave it to Dave Fowler. He told me that I was more talented, but Dave wanted it more. And according to Coach, passion always wins. Of course, that's what they always tell the losers, right?"

"Well, I guess that's good for Dave," I said, not quite willing to explain the real situation about what had gone down between me and Jess.

"Wasn't that what happened with you? Ross made you give it to Jess?"

"Not exactly." I paused. "I just have a lot of stuff going on. I'm applying for this scholarship, and it's kind of a big deal. . . ."

"Yeah," Matt interrupted. "Well, whatever, at least now you get to sleep in, right?"

"I guess so," I hedged.

"Meanwhile, I'll be toiling away at the crack of dawn, brib-ing Jess for more sports pages and trying to sneak party photos past Ross." He took another sip of his hot chocolate, then wiped away his whipped cream mustache. It was so weird how Matt was, like, the big man on campus and he didn't drink coffee. I thought *everyone* did.

"Am I supposed to feel sorry for you?" I asked, laughing a little despite myself.

"Maybe." Matt stretched his arms to the sky, and I caught a glimpse of his tan, buff abs. "Depends on what you do for guys you feel sorry for."

I stiffened. Was he *flirting* with me? He couldn't be. And yet everything — his smile, his abs, his easygoing attitude — made everything extremely confusing. I averted my gaze up to his watch. It was already seven forty.

"We should go." I took a few final gulps of my coffee and threw the empty cup toward the metal trashcan at the edge of the curb. *If I make this shot, then everything will be all right.* The paper cup hit the rim before rolling onto the pavement.

"Damn it," I exhaled, before I realized that I'd spoken out loud to myself — again. I glanced up, and saw Matt giving me a knowing smile. I shrugged as he picked up the cup from the pavement and threw it away.

"Thanks," I said.

"Dude, I wouldn't let you litter," he laughed.

"No." I shook my head. "I mean, for everything. You kinda saved the day."

"Just call me Superman," he said as he let himself into my car.

And something *had* shifted. I was still hurt, but I no longer felt like I was on the verge of tears. I was able to take notes in class and go over a few Ainsworth questions during lunch. I was okay.

Or, I would have been okay if Jessica hadn't appeared at my locker at the end of the day.

"Hey," she said in a small voice.

"What?" I snapped.

"Um . . . I was just supposed to ask you for the budget stuff. Mrs. Ross told me to."

"I'll give it to you tomorrow. Is that all?" I asked crisply, slamming my locker shut.

"You don't have to hate me, you know. If anything, I did you a favor."

"Right. Because setting up a fake profile, then stalking someone until she does something incriminating is really philanthropic. Don't have time to volunteer at an animal shelter? Ruin someone's life! It all helps save the world," I said sarcastically.

"What are you talking about?" Jess asked. "Your profile had public settings. All I did was find it."

Around us a cluster of kids had paused to listen. Even Dr. Osborn had stopped in the middle of the hallway.

I lowered my voice. "Don't play *dumb*, Jess. You made the Facebook profile, and you framed me. You took the picture, you uploaded it, and you smeared my character. Yes, I was at the party. And yes, I was holding a drink. Was that a bad decision? Yes. Do I regret it? Yes. Was it normal teenage behavior? Yes. Meanwhile you were hiding in the woods, spying and taking pictures of me. That is insane." I was shouting now, but I didn't care.

Her freckled face drained of color and she took a few steps back. She was afraid of me. I felt a sliver of satisfaction.

"Hayley, listen. I didn't upload anything. I found your profile, and felt it was inappropriate. But the picture was there. I didn't take it. Do I look like a girl who would run around the woods when I have a boyfriend to hang out with?"

"I don't know. You look like a blackmailing backstabber," I said tightly.

"Oooh!" a freshman yelled.

"Catfight!" another cheered.

Jessica shook her head. "You're calling me crazy, but I really think you should listen to yourself, Hayley. Look, I care about the *Spectrum*. But not enough to, like, sabotage you."

I looked into her eyes. They were small and narrow and her face was birdlike, with a thin, pointy nose and eyebrows that sloped upward, giving her a permanently suspicious look. She stared back at me.

I mashed my lips together. "I'll give the budget and the other materials to Mrs. Ross tomorrow," I said for the benefit of our audience.

When I got home, I immediately went to my bedroom and flopped onto my bed. Then, I abruptly sat up. The faintest trace of smoke seemed to waft through the air. It wasn't fiery; it was as if someone who'd just smoked a cigarette had walked through the room very recently. But Mom and Geoff were out. And neither were smokers.

"Sadie?" I called.

Immediately, I heard her running up the stairs. She paused at the threshold, panting hard and staring at me.

"Sadie!" I clapped my hands against the tops of my thighs. At this, she ran toward me, hurling herself into my lap before licking my face.

"Everything all right, girl?" I whispered. I glanced around the room. From the neat shelf of DVDs to the framed *Starry*

Night print to my open closet, where all my clothes hung in order of color and length, everything was the same.

"I'm fine," I whispered, as if answering myself. Sadie cocked her head, as though she were agreeing with me.

I opened the window to get rid of the scent, then pulled out my laptop, sat cross-legged on my bed, and began to work on my Ainsworth bio. Now that I didn't have the *Spectrum* editor position to talk up, I needed to make sure it was perfect; that every sentence painted me as the serious, ambitious student who was going places.

Hayley Kathryn Westin has always looked around the corner for answers, I began. I chewed my lip, erased the sentence, then wrote it again. But I wasn't stressed out. This was something I could control.

CHAPTER 8

The profile remained down. But there were a few small things — an all-out search for my Bainbridge student card, a mysterious "no ID available" missed call, and a temporary lockout to my e-mail address — that made me feel like I was going crazy.

"Have you seen my bracelet?" I yelled to my mom before I combed my fingers through my jewelry tray. It was the Friday night before the Ainsworth interview, my clothes were all laid out, and the only thing I was missing was my — or rather, my mom's — bracelet. A thin chain with an engraved silver-plated ID, it had been a present from her parents upon her acceptance to Harvard. She'd given it to me when I'd advanced to the state finals of the fourth-grade spelling bee. Ever since then, I'd always worn it for luck. But now, it was nowhere to be found.

From the doorway, Mom cocked her head in concern. "No. Is it missing?" Mom was wearing a sky-blue cocktail dress that hit midknee and hugged her curves. I knew that she was going out with Geoffferson tonight. I knew she'd cancel that in a heartbeat if she thought I needed her to stay home with me. And I didn't want her to have to do that.

"I'm sure it's somewhere," I mumbled. It was just one more not-quite-right thing to add to the list of odd occurences. The Facebook profile hadn't come back. There hadn't been any random texts. But there'd been the vaguely smoky scent that seemed to linger in my bedroom coupled with the feeling that *something* wasn't right.

"Things always turn up," Mom agreed. She let her gaze linger on me. I knew she wanted me to open up and tell her what was wrong. But what could I say when I wasn't even sure myself?

"Anyway . . . good night. I'm just going to read, then try to fall asleep early," I said, as if I was talking to a stranger.

"All right. I'll just be in town with Geoff, but I'll be coming home tonight. I love you, Hayley bunny." She walked into the room and planted a kiss on top of my head. "Think about the bracelet before you go to bed. Maybe you'll dream about where you left it." She nodded as if she were willing herself to believe her hippie-tastic rhetoric.

"Really?" I gave her a hard look. After all, at one point, Mom had been intelligent. Skeptical. And there were some things that dreams just couldn't solve.

"It can't hurt." Mom opened her mouth as if to say something else, then closed it, sighed, and padded down the stairs. I heard the front door click closed.

Abandoning my bracelet search, I set my regular alarm clock and my phone alarm clock, and opened the blinds to my window so if all else failed, I'd be woken up by the sunrise. It was something I did before every major competition.

I took a swig of water from the bottle on my nightstand, climbed under the covers, and somehow fell asleep, only to wake up at four o'clock, when the creak of a stair step made it clear Mom had come home. At six a.m., I heard the low strains of a Nina Simone song coming from the kitchen, meaning Mom was making breakfast for me. Just like always.

I padded down the stairs, trying to seem perky. I felt awful. My stomach was swirling, my head was pounding, and I knew I was getting sick. *Great.*

Mom glanced up from the counter. Cooking wasn't one of her strong suits, but she always made an effort to make me a spinach-and-egg-white omelette on the morning of a major academic event. Today, the thought of it made my stomach churn in protest.

"Hayley, you should still be sleeping!" Mom admonished, waving a wooden spoon at me. "Did you find the bracelet?"

"Nope." I crossed over to the coffeepot and poured a cup. I may have felt like death, but that didn't mean I didn't want coffee. "Couldn't sleep."

"Because you're nervous or because you're excited?" Mom asked, pouring the egg mixture she'd concocted into a pan on the stove.

"Both." When I was younger, Mom would always tell me to *have fun* at debate tournaments, instead of saying *good luck*. She wanted to raise me to be noncompetitive. Clearly, the method backfired. But really, I felt sick. I wasn't going to tell her. It wasn't as if she could prevent me from going, but she could — and would — worry.

Mom ran her fingers through my tangled hair. "Hayley, I wish you wouldn't drink so much caffeine," she clucked.

"I could be doing worse stuff," I said, my voice muffled by a cough.

"I know, but I just hate thinking of so much caffeine in your system," she fretted. "And are you getting sick?"

"I'm fine," I lied.

Mom gave me a hard look, but luckily, any further questions were interrupted by the fire alarm beeping.

"Shoot!" Mom rushed to the oven, sliding a blackened mess onto a plate.

"It's fine," I said, grateful that I didn't have to force it down. "Adam and I will grab something on the way. Or something."

"If you're sure . . ." Mom hedged.

"I am!" I said quickly, grabbing the plate and throwing the omelette into the trash. "You can go, I'm fine." She had the opening shift at The Sound and the Story on Saturday mornings.

"Okay, so I'll see you tonight. We'll go out to dinner?" she asked. We used to always get pizza after competitions.

"Sure." I shrugged. Hopefully, by then my stomach wouldn't feel as awful as it did now.

"Good. And I hope you don't mind, but I've invited Geofferson. He and I are spending next week in Boston, and I think it'll be good for you and him to get to know each other a bit. He's a good person, Hayley."

"I never said he wasn't. It's just . . ." I sighed.

"What?" Mom's normally aqua eyes darkened into a stormy indigo.

I held my head in my hands and massaged my temples with the pads of my fingers. The last thing I wanted to do was get in a fight with Mom.

"He's great," I said, lying through my teeth.

Mom mashed her lips together into a firm line before she spoke. "He is. Someday you'll understand. Everything isn't as simple as it seems."

With that, she grabbed her purse and headed out the door.

*　　*　　*

Everything isn't as simple as it seems.

The sentence tugged into my head, interrupting any thoughts I had about how the Renaissance influenced hip-hop or how Facebook proved the theory of relativity. What the hell did Mom mean? That there were underlying reasons for her hanging out with mouth-breathing, ugly-tie-wearing Geofferson? Again, my mind turned to money. It wasn't something I could exactly ask . . . but at least if I won the Ainsworth, that would be out of the equation. And then, if she kept dating Geoff, I'd be better able to accept it. It was only the idea that she was dating him to make life easier for *me* that I couldn't stand.

I took another large sip of my travel mug of coffee. The caffeine was already sharpening the edges of my brain and calming the butterflies in my stomach. Now I just had to focus. I turned and inspected my reflection in the window. At least I looked the part. My dark hair was pulled into a low chignon with all the annoying flyaways bobby-pinned back. I had clear mascara on my eyelashes, a peachy gloss on my lips, and the subtlest hint of bronzer dusting my cheekbones. I'd decided how to do my makeup after Googling what lawyers are expected to wear on a job interview.

At eight, Adam rolled up to the curb. As soon as I opened the door, I was hit with a blast of hot air, coupled with the sound of a 1970s-style guitar riff. Adam always listened to Jethro Tull before debates. Usually, I made fun of his vaguely hippie-ish leanings. But I felt too awful to say anything today.

"Hey." Adam drummed his fingers on the wheel and pulled away from the curb. He was wearing a dark suit with a blue-checked shirt. He looked older. Self-assured. We hadn't really talked since last week, when he'd seen the pictures of me and Matt in Alyssa's barn. There had been a few times when I'd been about to call him, but I'd resisted. Right now, it was easier not to trust anyone.

"Ready for donuts?" Adam asked, once we'd turned onto the highway.

"I guess so," I said, even though I wasn't anything close to hungry. But tradition was tradition. Ever since a seventh-grade field trip, when I'd discovered that a sugar rush could subdue my car-induced nausea, it had been tradition for us to stop and get as many donuts as possible from the rest stop right after the entrance to the highway.

Inside, Adam headed to the coffee stand while I waited in line for donuts. This was a well-choreographed part of our routine. He was in charge of picking out the most caffeinated beverages while I always went for the gooiest, weirdest donuts. It was nice to know that some things didn't change.

I picked out two cream-stuffed ones, two chocolate-flavored, and two bear claws, then stepped up to the counter. I looked at my haul, remembering how Adam and I used to make jokes about our donut binges compared to our classmates' booze binges. Now it didn't seem that funny.

"Five fifty," said the bored-looking cashier.

I pulled out my wallet. *Weird.* Where I'd once had at least two twenties, now I had nothing but my Coffee Hut receipt from when I'd gotten my latte the other day.

"Miss?"

I glanced up sharply at the cashier.

"Um . . ." I fished around the bottom of my purse and pulled out a few dollar bills. Then, I tipped it all the way to the side to come up with a handful of change.

"Here you go." Behind me, Adam slid a five across the counter.

"Sorry," I said in a small voice as I guiltily grabbed the donut bag. "I thought that I had cash."

"No prob," Adam said, but his voice was tight.

We got back into the car and turned onto the highway. The ride to Concord would take about an hour, so I pulled out acupressure bands from my bag and slipped them over my wrists as insurance against throwing up. Then, I took out a donut and gingerly took a bite. My nausea was worse than ever.

To distract myself, I looked out the window and visualized myself walking onstage to participate in my interview. The rules were easy: *Shoulders back, eye contact, pause after each sentence. Take your time walking to the podium; choose one judge you can connect with. Recognize they know you're nervous and aren't looking for an automaton. They're looking for a human to root for. Make it a conversation.*

Don't throw up. It wasn't on the list, but it should have been. Because the sugar-and-acupressure combo wasn't making anything better.

"Perfect," I whispered under my breath, even though I felt the cardboard, sickly-sweet taste of the bear claw on the roof of my mouth. My teeth felt slick, and I felt bile rising in my throat.

"You need to pull over!" I burst out, just as Adam had gotten off the expressway and into the winding streets on the outskirts of Concord.

"Can't you wait?"

"No!" I yelped. I held my hand to my mouth, frantically looking for somewhere — anywhere — to park.

"Gas station!" I panted, viewing a run-down structure at the corner.

I didn't even wait for Adam to fully stop the car before I ran into the convenience store, grabbed the key to the restroom, and retched, over and over again.

I splashed cold water on my face, not caring that some droplets dripped on my silk blouse, and headed straight for the soda aisle.

Once I was there, I opened the door to one of the refrigerated cases and allowed the cold air to wash over me. The car had been too hot, the music too loud. I felt my body temperature begin to lower and exhaled in a sigh of relief.

I kept the door open for another minute, pretending to be supremely interested in debating the pros and cons of ginger ale versus orange soda.

I headed to the front of the store and slid the key across the counter.

"Huh," the cashier appraised me. "I thought you'd already left."

"Leaving now," I said. I could see Adam pacing in the parking lot and knew he was freaking out about our unanticipated delay.

"Well, we should get going," Adam announced as soon as I walked into the parking lot. As if I'd just been hanging out in the gas station for fun. If I'd felt better, I'd have called him out on it.

"I know," I said sulkily. "And, FYI, I no longer feel like I'm gonna die."

"Oh, sorry," Adam said.

"It's fine. I'm getting in the back." I stretched out in the backseat, pushing aside a pile of library books. I popped in my earbuds and closed my eyes, hoping that even a ten-minute nap could restore me to normalcy. Lulled by the swaying of the car, I fell into a fitful sleep.

"Hayley!" Adam's voice woke me up from a fever-fueled half sleep. My throat was dry, my shirt was sticking to my back, and my heart was hammering, even though I hadn't had any more caffeine than usual. I felt sick. And Adam was standing above me, blinking down in concern.

"You were freaking out. But I couldn't stop in the middle of nowhere. I had to drive with you screaming in the backseat. I thought we'd get pulled over. Seriously, it was awful," Adam said. "Are you sure you're okay?"

"I have a temperature. I'll be fine." I gingerly swung my legs out of the car and struggled to my feet. My legs were shaky, as if my knees were about to buckle, and my skirt was wrinkled from tossing and turning. "You drove too fast," I accused. It wasn't true, and we both knew it.

"Are you sure you can do this?" Adam asked skeptically.

"Do I have a choice?" I asked. "I'll be fine. Just . . . go ahead. I need fresh air."

"All right," Adam said uncertainly, walking toward the all-glass convention center that jutted awkwardly from the hotel. Around us, suit-clad kids were streaming through the entrance. All were carrying briefcases. Mr. Klish had said that only the best and the brightest were going to be at the semifinals. When he'd said that, I'd assumed he meant ten or so kids. But there had to be at least one hundred contenders.

I shakily walked toward the double doors.

"Welcome!" a doorman said grandly, opening the door and gesturing me inside.

What was wrong with me? I didn't get sick. I'd barely eaten a peanut-butter-and-jelly sandwich last night, so it couldn't have been been food poisoning. I'd only drunk water and coffee. Was it my subconscious sabotaging me? And since it wasn't like I could find a shrink in the next ten minutes, how could I make it stop?

I wove my way toward the registration table. I didn't feel any better, and neither the swirly, dizziness-inducing carpet pattern nor the stale scent of deodorant combined with the clinging odor of salmon dinners from conferences past were doing me any favors. I wasn't sure where to look. If I looked down, I felt nauseous; if I looked up, I felt nervous. I concentrated on the red EXIT sign over the ballroom and made my way to the front of the line.

"Hello?" A woman with a neat blond bob and black-framed glasses glanced up at me expectantly. Farther down the table, I noticed Adam checking in. I yanked my gaze away. I couldn't worry about him. I needed to focus on myself.

"Hayley . . ." I croaked, then swallowed. "Sorry. I'm Hayley Westin," I said.

"Ah, the infamous Hayley." The woman nodded and checked my name off in red pen. "You're at twelve thirty. You can head into the auditorium now, and if you need to leave, please make sure you do so after someone has finished their interview. Here's the program with the biographical notes."

I stiffened. What had she meant by *infamous*?

I sat in the back of the auditorium, paging through the program. Adam was scheduled at one, just a few candidates after me. I hunched down in my seat, hoping he wasn't looking for me. I didn't want to have to make conversation or pretend everything was fine.

Quickly, I flipped to the bios, relieved that even though it had looked crowded, there really weren't more than fifty students. I could beat fifty. I flipped to my bio, anxious to see how it would read compared to the rest of the competition.

Hayley Kathryn Westin: In addition to striving to be the best in everything she does, including latte drinking and pantyhose wearing, Hayley also finds time to watch and collect chick flicks — the cheesier, the better. Her greatest ambition is to head to an Ivy League university. There, she'll continue to pad her résumé with impressive-sounding activities and acting like she's better than everyone else.

I blinked. This wasn't my bio. Not even close. How had the Ainsworth committee allowed this? Didn't they *realize* it was a cruel joke? That someone had hacked into my e-mail and sent this to sabotage me?

I stood up, ready to march out of the auditorium and explain to the glasses-wearing lady at the registration desk that there was a *major* problem, when a short suspenders-wearing man strode onstage. The lights dimmed. I was stuck.

"Welcome to the semifinals of the state Ainsworth competition. I'm Dr. Peter Schorr, chancellor at the University of New Hampshire and a proud member of the Ainsworth selection committee. It goes without saying that all of you have made significant achievements and are a credit to your homes, schools, and communities. It is the goal of the Ainsworth Institute to recognize the individuals who have the most potential to achieve . . ."

Seriously? How could everything be proceeding normally? Didn't anyone realize or care that there was a *major* problem? I felt like I was in a nightmare. I dug my fingernails into my wrist, feeling a jab of pain. Nope. Definitely wasn't in a dream.

Around me, people burst into applause, indicating that Dr. Schorr's speech was done. My head snapped up. Down the row, I noticed a blond girl looking curiously at me.

Are you okay? she mouthed.

I nodded, even though I was in full-on crisis mode. I scanned the crowd for Adam, but I couldn't make out his head in the sea of people in front of me. He'd done this. He had to have. It had been him all along, seeming sympathetic, pretending we were in this together. I would kill him. I would rip his head from his skinny neck. But before I destroyed him, I needed to save myself.

"Jane Jensen, can you please come up?" Peter Schorr asked, naming the first candidate as he headed to his place at the long table reserved for the ten judges.

From the middle of the auditorium, a small girl sprang up and practically skipped down the aisle. Once onstage, she adjusted the microphone and blinked out at us, her huge eyes covered by a heavy curtain of brown bangs.

"Hi there. I'm Jane Jensen from the Meadow School, right here in Concord," she said in a babyish voice. The Meadow School was a notorious private school, famous for classes like Honors Improv and History According to Jon Stewart. Students weren't called by their first names, but rather chose a moniker that described their inner lives, like Peace, Tranquility, or Chaos. The school had no admissions policy, and was some-place I'd joke about with people from debate camp. Whenever someone made a mistake, we'd ask if they came from the Meadow School. But even Meadow School students didn't have a bio as stupid as mine.

"I was going to sing a song I wrote?" Jane's voice lifted into a question.

The room exploded into laughter and I felt my jaw unclench slightly.

"This isn't a talent competition," an angular judge said.

"I know, but it is my talent. And I know the Ainsworth is about creativity and intellectual freedom, so I thought it would be acceptable," the girl argued.

"Is that Hayley Westin?" I heard a girl whisper in front of me.

"I thought they said her name was Jane. I guess we have two idiots in the competition."

They laughed and I felt my face burn. But what could I do? Leaving would admit defeat. I couldn't argue the bio when I had the interview coming up. All I could do was wait.

"No song," the judge said firmly. "Instead, I want you to discuss the trope of the stranger in nineteenth-century fiction."

"Well, fiction is all about strangers, because the characters aren't real. So because the characters aren't real, that means none of us know them. . . ." The girl trailed off and blinked again. The audience rustled in their seats. Jane was bombing, big-time, but it didn't comfort me. I'd already looked at her bio, and despite the fact that she preferred if people called her Willow, the paragraph made her sound normal enough. When it came time to make decisions, of course the committee would look back to the bio. No matter what, my words would be seared into their memory.

Finally, after Jane mumbled a few more things about imaginary friends, she wandered offstage. A few more people went, talking about technology, history, and what social media had in common with eighteenth-century yellow journalism. They were all topics I could speak to, but I was getting more and more panicked with every student. What would I say when I went up there? Should I pretend no one had read my bio, even though I knew everyone had? Admit that someone had tried to sabotage me? It was the most obvious choice, but it came with risks, not the least of which was the committee wondering what type of person would prompt someone else to sabotage them. It would be hard to paint myself as sympathetic.

I glanced up at the stage. A blond girl was gesticulating wildly as she explained how some complicated physics principle related to why people were obsessed with cute kitten photos. Ordinarily, she would have been my competition. But now, I barely cared, drifting back to my feverish thoughts — until she edged back into my row.

"Was I all right?" she asked breathlessly.

"Yeah."

"Well, I'm sure I won't be worse than that Hayley girl. So there's that," she said, clearly eager to gossip now that her interview was over.

"Hayley Westin?" the judge called.

A hush fell over the auditorium. I took a deep breath, stood up, gave my blond seatmate an ice-princess stare, and threw my shoulders back as I walked toward the stage.

"Oh, God, that's her!" I heard a few people whisper as I walked by. I stared straight ahead, stepped onto the stage, and centered myself in front of the microphone. I didn't have any other option but perfect. And I was ready.

"Miss Westin, we're thrilled to meet you in person, especially after reading your colorful biography," Dr. Schorr said, not even bothering to look at me. Instead, he glanced at the audience, where he was rewarded with a wave of laughter. I smiled politely.

"Dr. O'Connell, the question?" He nodded to a frizzy-haired woman at the end of the table.

"Yes. Hayley, what does it mean to 'take' someone's car?" she asked, enunciating each word.

I paused, allowing the question to sink in. It was similar to the ones Adam and I had discussed. On the surface they were simple, but they became complicated once you tried to actually intellectualize the answer.

And then, I had a genius idea.

"I'm so glad you asked that question. As many of you noticed, and as Dr. Schorr so kindly mentioned, my biography is colorful. Everyone who's seen it assumes that's who I am, and I'd assume that, too, if I read it. As humans, we take information at face value and assign ownership based on assumption. If someone is in a car, we assume they have ownership, or, at least temporary custody of the vehicle. If someone has biographical information attached to their name, that's *their* identity. And this is a system that worked for a long time, when there could be a one-to-one relationship. But now, we've become a society of shape-shifters," I ad-libbed, noticing how some of the professors were nodding appreciatively. My stomach had stopped rumbling. Was this *working*?

I continued to talk about ownership being fleeting in our Wikipedia- and Pinterest-obsessed society. I couldn't help smiling at the committee. And then, I took a step forward to directly address the panel.

"Finally, I hope I didn't interrupt the Ainsworth process with the biographical submission. While it's not one that I wrote, I will take responsibility for it. . . ." At this, I made eye contact with Dr. Schorr. *Witty remark. Bring it home,* coached the calm, detached debate-champ voice in my head. "But I'd prefer to take the car."

The room erupted into applause and I smiled into the crowd. The house lights came up, and all of a sudden, I froze.

In the semidarkness, the entire audience had been fuzzy. But now, everyone was thrown into crystal-clear relief. And my eyes landed on me, or at least a girl who looked exactly like me: the doppelgänger that had been haunting my Facebook page and my dreams. She was sitting on the aisle seat in an empty rear row, wearing a pair of jeans and resting her feet on the seat in front of her. Her hair was pulled into a messy ponytail that skimmed her shoulders. She looked half-bored, half-amused.

I blinked again, but the figure had stood up and was hurrying out of the auditorium. Not bothering with another thank you, I barreled down the stairs, up the aisle, and into the lobby. The only people there were a few name tag–wearing greeters.

"Did a girl just leave?" I demanded.

A woman looked up and shrugged. "Lots of people have been in and out. Haven't noticed anyone in particular."

But I had.

I ran out into the parking lot. No one.

"You okay?" the doorman asked, glancing at me.

"Did you see . . ." I trailed off. What was I supposed to ask? *Did you see me?* No. Because what if the girl *wasn't* real? What if she was a figment of my imagination, a sign that my grip on reality was becoming less and less firm? The headache and stomachache, which had disappeared due to adrenaline, had returned in full force. My knee buckled. I knew Adam had his interview coming up, but I couldn't wait for him. I needed to leave *now*.

"Can you get me a cab?" I asked.

"Sure." The doorman pulled a phone from his pocket and I sat on the edge of the curb. *Don't think.* The more I thought, the crazier I felt. I needed to hang on to whatever sanity I had. I tried to remember the first and last names of every character Reese Witherspoon had ever played. Tried to count how many kisses in the rain occurred in Nicholas Sparks movies. Tried to think of anything *but* the obvious.

"Hey." I looked over my shoulder. It was the blond girl from the auditorium. "I'm Leah," she said.

"Hi," I said tightly. Couldn't she tell I was in the middle of a breakdown?

"I just wanted to say good job. And I'm sorry about that comment. It was just . . . you know. Anyway, I just mean that we're all in it together. So —"

"It's fine." I cut her off.

"Cool. Well, good luck," she said dubiously as she shifted from one foot to the other. Her hair was blowing in the breeze and a few golden strands were sticking to her ChapStick-stained lip. Outside the auditorium, she didn't look like a threat. She looked scared.

"Thanks." I pulled out my phone so we wouldn't have to keep talking.

"Listen, I was thinking about getting lunch. There's a bagel place down the street that I passed when I came. Do you want something . . . or want to come? You look pale," she said, biting her lip.

I shook my head.

"Okay." She looked like she wanted to say something else, but just then, a white car pulled up to the curb, BUDDY'S LIMO SERVICE emblazoned on its side. I climbed in and fell into a dreamless sleep, not waking until we reached my house.

"That'll be a hundred bucks," the driver said.

"Hold on," I said. I ran into the house and to my room, crossing my fingers that my cash — the money I'd saved from hours of thankless shifts at the Ugly Mug when I was a sophomore — would be there.

It was.

I flew back down the stairs, paid the driver, and collapsed on the couch.

CHAPTER 9

W ell, I'd like to raise a toast to Comet!" Geofferson said loudly.

"Thanks." I shifted to the side in the cracked red vinyl booth at Armenio's, the pizza place in the center of town. Around us, babies were shrieking, and the waiters were dodging knee-high kids who were too antsy to sit still. My five-hour nap had been filled with bad dreams: me in a mental hospital, me losing the Ainsworth, a weird mash-up of cars and unicorns that I think came from all the Ainsworth answers. Awake wasn't better. Now, I was worried I was losing my mind, and unsure whether I should tell someone, or keep it a secret until it became all too apparent. You know, just the normal concerns every seventeen-year-old worries about.

"You haven't told us anything about it, Bunny," Mom pressed as she hooked her blond hair behind her ears. "What was it like?"

"There's not much to say." I picked at a ragged cuticle. "I mean, I won't know anything until they announce the finalists, so it doesn't seem like there's much of a point in discussing it." I'd had a few missed calls from Adam, but I'd ignored them. I didn't want to compare how we'd done or pick apart judge observations. I didn't want to lie about why I hadn't watched him. And I didn't want to hear any congratulations. What I'd done up there had been good. I knew that. But it had also been a stroke of dumb luck. And dumb luck didn't win competitions.

"Well, tell me everything. Was it fun? Did you enjoy yourself? How was Adam?" my mom asked. "Geoff, these academic competitions are always so fascinating. And Hayley always seems to have the best stories!"

I stared down at the menu, refusing to engage. Not like I needed to look at the menu. We always ordered a half-mushroom, half-peppers pizza.

A skinny waiter wearing a red Armenio's T-shirt glanced at us expectantly. I put down the menu.

"I'd like the —"

"I think I'll have the shrimp dish, and, Wendy, what do you think about sharing that with me?" Geoff asked.

I shot a disbelieving look at my mom. What had happened to this being *my* dinner? Besides, *no one* ordered actual entrees at Armenio's. Most people were tipped off by the four-foot-tall fiberglass sculpture of a pizza slice out front. Or by the fact that the menus were circular and dotted with smiling cartoon pepperoni slices. But not Geofferson.

"All right," the waiter said. "And you?" he asked, staring at me.

"Hayley, are you planning to eat with us?" Mom asked, enunciating each word as though she were speaking to a toddler.

"I thought we were having pizza," I enunciated back to her.

"Well, if you'd like pizza, by all means order it," Mom said, smiling through her teeth.

"Never mind. I'm not hungry anymore."

"Shall I come back when you folks sort out what you'd like?" the server asked, looking confused.

"No, it's fine," Mom said. "I'm sorry. We'll get the shrimp dish and then a pizza with mushrooms and peppers."

"All right, then." The server practically sprinted away from the table.

"I said I wasn't hungry!" I snapped. I knew that I was behaving irrationally, but I was far too on edge to stop myself.

Geofferson cleared his throat, one of those eh-eh sounds that's shorthand for *I will do anything, including stage a fake choking attack, to remove myself from this situation.* "It's fine. She's had a long day. I think the best thing we can do is give Comet her privacy and let her sleep," Geofferson announced. He scraped his chair back and hurried off to flag down our waiter to make it to go.

"What's wrong with you, Hayley?" Mom hissed, grabbing my wrist.

I yanked my hand away. "I don't know." I sounded like a belligerent teenager and I knew it.

Mom glanced at me, as though she were going to say something, but simply set her lips in a firm line and shook her head slightly.

"Let's get Hayley back home and settled," Geoff pressed. "I canceled the order. We can just get something on our own and let Comet chill out."

I didn't bother to say anything as I trailed behind them to Geoff's BMW. He pushed down the front seat so I could squeeze into the back.

"Maybe she really is sick," Mom murmured up front, sure that I couldn't hear her, even though we were only separated by a few feet.

"Maybe," Geoff said disinterestedly. "I'll tell you what, I'd have gotten sick if we stayed at that pizza joint. My wine tasted like turpentine. I get that they want to be homey, but do they want to poison their guests?" he boomed.

Just then, my phone quacked, startling me so much that I dropped it. I groped the floor mat with my fingers, finally picking up the phone from under Geoff's seat.

I had a new text from a blocked number.

> That was a good show today. Maybe too good. Ever heard the phrase 'on thin ice'? Better lace up . . .

I gasped.

"Hayley?" Mom craned her neck to glance back at me.

"Fine!" I said in a high, artificial voice.

"You know, she had to get up so early and she was studying all week. She's been pushing herself a lot. And she's never really been rebellious. It could be a stage. Let's just give her some space." Mom murmured to Geofferson in the front seat, as if I weren't sitting two feet behind them.

Her words swam through my mind as I stared at the text. The screen darkened. I pressed the button on my phone and, again, the text lit up, as shocking as the first time I'd seen it.

"Sounds like those academic types gave you the smackdown, Comet. I thought I had it tough with football. I never knew the nerds . . . uh, I mean, the smart kids . . . were the real warriors," Geoff boomed from the front seat.

"Right," I said faintly. He had no idea. I'd been through a battle today, but this was war. And I had no idea who I was fighting.

Once we came inside, Sadie began barking and jumping all over me.

"What's going on, girl?" I ruffled her fur as I surveyed

the kitchen. The messy pile of mail on the edge of the table, the breakfast dishes from this morning, the falling-apart cabinet door. All the same. I felt my breathing begin to return to normal for the first time since the car ride home.

Mom and Geoff were standing in the breezeway, their coats still on. Geoff had his arm slung protectively around Mom's shoulders.

"Mom?" I asked, noticing she hadn't moved.

"Oh, honey, I'm going to stay with Geoff tonight. You need your rest," Mom clucked.

"No, I'm fine," I said. I took a few steps toward the refrigerator and squinted at a photograph of a girl — me — fastened near the ice dispenser with a magnet. The refrigerator door had always been covered with photos of me as a child. But this one was new. The girl's face was turned up, pink plastic sunglasses glinting in a beam of light. She looked like she was five or six, but she had long, tangled, sun-highlighted hair that fell past her shoulders.

That wasn't correct. When I was six, Keely and I had played endless hours of beauty parlor, meaning that both of us had uneven, bowl-shaped haircuts that hadn't grown out until the third grade.

"Are you hungry now?" Mom asked, following my line of vision. There was a slight edge to her voice.

"Yeah, Comet, you should eat," Geoff concurred. "And so should we," he added, placing his hand on my mother's waist and pulling her toward him.

"No. I'm fine." I redirected my attention toward the cabinets, Sadie's crate, somewhere, anywhere else. Now, I was questioning my own sanity. *Someone* had put that photograph there. It hadn't been there this morning. *Had it?* I remembered how tired and achy I felt, how it seemed I was moving in a foglike dream state, how I had to spend most of my energy convincing my mother I was okay. But *this* wasn't. I wasn't.

"Hayley, you're exhausted. I respect that. We'll give you some quiet time and you and I will talk in the morning. I don't leave for Boston until Monday." I waited for her to come over toward me and ruffle my hair or kiss the top of my head, but she didn't.

"Mom . . ." I trailed off. At least Sadie had stopped barking. I sniffed the air, but the only scent was the wood smoke–tinged wind from outside. Still, my missing bracelet from this morning and the photograph on the fridge made it clear that someone had been inside the house.

Or they were still here.

I gasped, despite myself, a strangled cry that got stuck in my throat and caused my hand to fly to my neck.

"Hayley?" Mom asked. Sadie barked from the corner.

"I'm fine. I'm sorry, I just got . . . something stuck in my throat," I lied. I didn't want them to leave, but I didn't know how to explain what was wrong. "You guys should go. Seriously, go," I said, my voice taking on an urgent edge.

"Wendy, come on," Geoff urged, his hand on the small of her back.

"If you're sure," Mom hesitated, and I saw her gaze flick over to the refrigerator.

"Go!" I practically pushed Mom out the door, feeling simultaneously relieved and terrified when the door clicked closed.

I heard the ignition of Geoff's car and saw the swath of lights pan across the living room as he drove down the road. I was alone.

Or maybe I wasn't.

"Hello?" I yelled. Sadie barked in response. My heart beat in my ears. I raced up the stairs to my bedroom. I glanced around wildly, not sure what — or *who* — I was expecting to see. My bedroom looked the same as always. The window seat below the eave was covered with rejected blouses and tights from the morning. The hardwood floor was scattered with notebooks and highlighters, and socks that Sadie had dug from the hamper. I opened my drawer, but everything was exactly where it had been when I'd come in earlier.

I looked at the tray where I kept my jewelry.

And then, I screamed.

The bracelet was back, the ID plate glinting toward me like it was winking. I grabbed it with one hand, realizing I was holding my cell in a death grip with the other.

Grabbing my bag, I raced down the stairs, up the gravel path, and into the street. My legs were pumping, my eyes were flicking back and forth, and I wasn't sure where I was going, only that I needed to get away, as far and as fast as possible.

Finally, at the corner, I stopped, resting my hands above my knees as I caught my breath. As my gasps slowed to uneven pants, I began to sort through the thoughts swirling through my mind.

I was safe. No one was chasing me. Around me, everything was normal. It wasn't even nine o'clock. Down the street, an elderly couple was walking a shaggy golden retriever. The house on top of the hill had all its lights on, looking warm and inviting. In contrast, the only light on in our house was the one in my bedroom.

I squinted at it. The room was empty.

And yet I knew I couldn't go back inside. I needed to go somewhere with lights and people and noise where I could actually figure out just how crazy I was going.

And the only place I could think of was Alyssa's barn party.

CHAPTER 10

J shivered as I walked through the split-post fence gate and around to the barn. Even from a distance, I could see that this party was far more crowded than the one last week. The speakers seemed to echo through the damp ground, and the tiki torches that lit the path to the barn made me feel like I was entering into a tribal ritual.

I threw my shoulders back and walked into the barn, which was lit only by large white candles held in hurricane lanterns. The flickering flames cast shadows across the wall, and I had to squint to make out individual faces in the crowd. I saw Keely, Ingrid, and Emily huddled by the ladder to the hayloft and was about to head over to them when someone lumbered over to me.

"Hayley!" Matt flung his arms around me, catching me off guard. I took a step back and he let go.

"You need a drink!" He took an uneven step toward the cooler set up in the corner of the barn.

"No, that's fine." I wanted to redo the hug. *That* had been where I'd felt safe. But he'd already unsteadily lurched away.

I was about to follow him when Alyssa grabbed my arm.

I whirled around, ready to explain that I wasn't crashing her party, at least, not really, but she had a huge smile on her face. "Thanks for coming!" she squeaked in her high-pitched voice.

"Oh, thanks for inviting me!" I said hurriedly.

"It's just . . . you were *so* stuck-up and annoying for so long, and now you're actually becoming fun! Like, normal fun," Alyssa explained, her eyes widening. "It's nice."

Keely, Ingrid, and Emily glanced in our direction. Keely looked at me, then at them, then at me again, before heading over, like a lioness stalking her prey.

"Hayley, you *beast*!" Keely called by way of greeting, her voice ensuring that everyone was now looking at us.

"Hey!" I called uncertainly. Was *beast* a term of hatred or one of endearment? It was impossible to tell. I felt like I'd fallen into an alternate universe where nothing was what it seemed. What would be next? Would I not get the Ainsworth but win Homecoming queen? Would I discover that my subconscious actually had been posting the status updates, give up on excellence, and find satisfaction in some random skill like cake decorating or basket weaving? I hugged my arms tightly around my body, as if preparing for an attack from Keely.

"Hiiiiii!" Keely drew the word into six syllables. Clearly, *beast*=friend. I mentally filed away the information. "It's, like, so awesome to see you. Except why are you wearing *that*?" She wrinkled her nose at my still-Ainsworth outfit, which included a pair of pantyhose that were digging into my waist.

"Because . . ." I was about to explain the Ainsworth, Geofferson, how freaked I'd felt alone in my house, but I'd stopped myself. What good would that do?

"Well, whatever. You should change. Will's been asking about you *all night*." She rolled her large gray eyes conspiratorially, as though she were sharing inside info.

"Will?" I repeated.

"Yeah. I guess he's looking for a repeat performance from last night. He's over there if you want to say hi, or . . . you know." She burst into giggles while I blinked curiously at her. I glanced over her shoulder at Will Thorn. A hulking junior, Will was a goalie on the hockey team. He'd had a full beard since seventh grade, around the same time that he probably read his last chapter book. He was funny, loud, and had once hosted an impromptu barbecue in the parking lot by wiring a George Foreman grill under the hood of his car. He and I had nothing in common. I didn't even think he knew who I was. There was *no way* any interaction between us — an *excuse me* in the hallway or accidental eye contact across the cafeteria — could ever be construed as a sign we were *together*.

I blinked. "I think you're confused," I said carefully.

Keely shook her head adamantly, her blond hair whipping across her thin shoulders. "No! You and he were, like, intense last night. You guys are kinda cute together, actually."

"Wait. So, you mean, you saw Will and me together last night?" I'd been asleep. *Hadn't I?* I remembered the woozy, out-of-it feeling I'd had when I'd woken up. The way it had felt like I'd been walking through a fog. Could I have sleepwalked to a party and hung out with Will? It didn't seem likely. And yet when nothing made sense, this seemed to at least be a hypothesis that *could* work.

Keely laughed, a single snort.

"What?" I asked.

"You and Will."

"What about us? I mean, what are you talking about?"

"Nothing. Just that you guys looked like you were having a good time. Look, it's cool. It's just . . . weird."

She had no idea how weird it was. And before I could ask any more questions, Kendra wandered over to us.

"Hey, honey!" she cooed. I stiffened as she grabbed my shoulders and kissed me on both cheeks. "So, you know the pictures from last night? I know there were a ton of inappropriate ones, but can you send me the kind of okay ones for *Spectrum*? It might be cool to intersperse them with the profesh ones. I mean, I guess? I should probably go to a meeting, right?" Kendra muttered to herself as she pulled a can of Red Bull from her bag and cracked it open.

"Pictures," I repeated numbly, not even bothering to tell her that I wasn't even the editor in chief anymore. I glanced over at Will, who now had two forty-ounce energy drinks taped to each of his hands. *Oh my God.* "There are pictures from last night?"

"Obvi." Kendra shrugged and wandered into the barn.

"'There are pictures from last night?'" Keely asked in a sing-song voice, imitating me. "Hello, of course there are! You can ask her not to *share* them or show them but it's just weird to totally pretend like they didn't happen." Her eyes flashed accusingly.

"Right . . ." I trailed off. "I'm sorry, it's just . . ."

"That scholarship thing?" Keely asked knowledgeably. "Look, whatever. You can have fun and be smart. You don't have to choose. You do know that, right?"

"I guess so." The way I was interacting with Keely made *me* feel like an imposter. Why was I just going along with whatever she said as if it were true? The old Hayley, the real Hayley, would have done *something* by now. So why was I just going along with everything?

I remembered a movie we'd seen in Psych class last year. It was called *Sybil*, about a woman who had multiple personalities and literally didn't remember who she was or what she'd done. Could *that* be what was happening to me? And if so, what did it mean that one of my personalities was attracted to Will?

Keely stared at me, unblinking. "Good. I'm glad you've learned your lesson."

Learned your lesson. The words tugged at my brain. But before I could ask what she'd meant, Matt lumbered toward both of us from the cooler in the corner, holding a bottle aloft as though it were a trophy.

"Look, Keely . . ." I said desperately as Matt stood in between us.

"You don't need to, like, analyze!" Keely interrupted. "Just have fun. With whoever you want," she added meaningfully, jutting her chin toward Matt as she wove her way through the crowd and toward the cooler in the back of the barn. Matt and I were alone. I shivered.

"You have a problem," Matt said, interrupting my thoughts.

"What do you mean?" I asked sharply.

"Whoa!" He held up his hands and took two steps away. "You don't need to attack. It's not a bad problem."

"Well, then what *is* it?" I asked.

"You look thirsty." His voice sounded almost deflated as he pressed the cold bottle into my hands.

"Thanks." I took the drink and held it against my forehead.

"You okay?" Matt asked.

"I guess. It's just . . . long day." It was ridiculous to try to have a conversation when I felt I was only moments from throwing up, having a heart attack, or both. But what else could I do? My house was haunted. I was either possessed or sleepwalking or had an undiagnosed case of multiple personality disorder. At this point, maybe trying to act normal was crazy, but it was the only thing stopping me from snapping.

"Yeah." Matt shifted from side to side. A whoop of laughter emerged from the barn. "This party's kind of lame, isn't it?" he asked finally.

Was it? The conversations drifting from the barn were about school, TV, and Instagram filters — the same stuff that was discussed in the hallway at school. Everyone was wearing jeans and fleece pullovers. The scent of incense wafted through the air, mixing with the scent of burning leaves. I was surrounded by people I'd known since kindergarten. It felt *safe*, a word I'd never imagined using to describe being surrounded by Keely and her crew.

"I like it here," I admitted quietly. I thought of my empty house. Booting up my laptop and not knowing what I'd find on the screen. The intermittent text messages from a blocked number, never threatening *enough* that I could go to the police.

"Are you sure? You seem kind of shaky." Matt gazed down pointedly at the hand holding my drink. Drops of liquid were jetting from the top like a broken fountain.

He put his hand on top of mine to steady it. I placed the bottle down and wiped my hand on my skirt.

"Do you want to go somewhere to talk?" he asked.

"I don't know," I said quietly.

Matt glanced toward the barn. "Let's go. You aren't missing anything. I saw Keely giving you kind of a hard time. Girls are tough, right?"

"Yeah." I nodded meekly.

"Look, where do you live? I'll drive you home, then we can talk. If you want. Cool?"

I didn't say anything. I was so tired of talking, of saying things that didn't make sense. I just wanted someone to tell me what to do.

Matt set down his drink. "My car's just up the road."

I expected Matt to poke his head into the barn to say good-bye to everyone, but instead, he began walking, taking the gravel path that led around the house. This was happening, Matt and I were going home together. Two weeks ago, this would have only happened in a too-much-coffee dream. Unless *this* was a dream. I stopped midstep and held my hand in front of my face. I'd once read that hands never looked right in dreams. They'd either have extra fingers or be oddly shaped. I blinked, noticing my pale fingers and the thin ribbon of dirt crusted under my nails from when I'd fallen during my run over here. Definitely mine.

All of a sudden, Matt stopped and turned around.

I dropped my hands to my sides.

"What are you doing?"

Just making sure I'm not sleepwalking.

"Just . . . doing that thing. You know, how if you hold your thumb out, the moon looks like it's the size of half your thumb-nail? It's a perspective thing," I invented.

"Really?" Matt held his own large hockey-player hand over his eye and squinted. "That's so weird. I knew you were smart, but that's, like, freaky smart. Did you learn that in, like, *Physics for Geniuses?*"

I shook my head. It had been a scene in some movie, but I couldn't remember which one. I was sure that after the characters discussed the phenomenon, they kissed.

In the distance, a dog barked. The streetlights cast an amber glow onto the dry, dead leaves beneath our feet. I could see my breath and shivered.

Matt looped his arm around my shoulders and began walking. It had begun to rain, so lightly I barely noticed until I looked at Matt and saw his damp shirt clinging to his arms.

"You're funny, Westin."

"Thanks." I wanted him to pull me into his arms, tilt my chin toward his face, lean down and . . . Instead, I fell back and allowed him to take the lead toward his car. He unlocked the doors and I slid in, directing him toward my house.

"Very . . . country," Matt said as he stepped out of the driver's side, taking in the sagging porch, the unfinished woodshed, and the random rockers and wheelbarrows and oversized farm tools that were randomly scattered around the lawn. Mom collected them because, in her words, she felt sorry for them. But in the darkness, they looked hulking and ominous.

"You were expecting a high-rise?" I asked, hurrying to unlock the back door. Immediately, Sadie emitted a low growl that changed into joyful yelps as I opened the door. As she jumped on me, I was accosted by the scent of gardenias and jasmine, a vaguely floral scent that was out of place in the cold fall night.

"No, it's cool. I just didn't know what type of place you lived in. It's hard to picture you anywhere but school." Matt blinked in the semidarkness before settling at the kitchen table.

"It smells nice," he noted. Sadie sniffed him disinterestedly before turning back toward me and barking again.

"Sadie, girl, over here!" I called just as a crack of thunder sounded. The rain then started in earnest, drops hitting the porch and creating a steady beat against the roof.

Sadie barked again, then bounded toward me. The scent was cloying, and I wondered whether she'd somehow managed to tip over one of the perfumes in Mom's room. That had to be it. Intruders didn't wear perfume. Intruders didn't rearrange pictures and leave everything else in place. And intruders certainly didn't come into a house without the dog realizing something was up.

I reached down and scratched Sadie's ears. She whined happily, her tail thumping loudly on the floor. Everything was *fine*.

"Have anything to drink?" Matt asked finally.

"Oh yeah. Sure. Sorry!" I headed toward the fridge, then stopped.

The photo was gone.

I blinked. The metal surface held the same collection of photos as always: Mom and me in New York City for my sixteenth birthday; me onstage at school, holding up an Academic Excellence in the Sciences trophy; a picture of me, age five, wearing a kangaroo costume, the headband ears perched atop a short, blunt haircut.

"Drinks!" I announced loudly, hoping Matt didn't see my skin turning red and blotchy. "Coming right up!" I added, pushing past the carton of eggs and the container of soy milk until I found an ancient bottle of soda Mom had brought home from some Sound and the Story party. I grabbed two jam jars — what we always used instead of regular glassware — and poured for both of us.

"So, what's it like?" Matt asked, draining his glass and gazing at me expectantly.

"What is what like?" I took a sip of the soda. It was flat and tasteless. I pushed it toward him.

"Being Hayley Westin. Being the brilliant scholar in the making? Being perfect?" He took a sip from my glass.

"I'm not perfect," I scoffed. He had no idea. I was a nervous-breakdown-suffering weirdo with enough enemies — not to mention personalities — to fill a volleyball team. "Remember, I resigned from Yearbook?"

"That's not exactly a criminal offense, you know. I've quit a lot of stuff. Piano lessons, lifeguard training, Spanish, Halo 3, spelling bees . . ."

Spelling bees? Matt could barely put together five words. Was he a secret genius? And did everyone have hidden personalities?

"You're kidding, right?"

Matt shook his head. "Nope. First in the state, nationals, everything."

"So what happened?"

Matt smiled. "I turned eight. And we moved here. I wanted to be someone different. I didn't want to be stressed about whether *obsequious* had an *i* in it or whatever. I just wanted to chill, you know?"

"Wow. All that potential, wasted."

Matt's mouth became a tight line. "That's what my parents always say, too."

"I didn't mean to . . ."

"No, it's cool. But what I mean, is . . . quitting is awesome. Quitting is *the best*. Without quitting, you never really know what you want to do. You just get stuck with a schedule full of *stuff*."

"But what's the alternative?" Even though this was my house, and my kitchen, I felt like Matt was running the show. Like we were two actors playing high school students, only he knew the script and I didn't, so it was in my best interest to follow his lead.

"I mean, we're young. We're supposed to be driving fast cars and playing Never Have I Ever in barns and stumbling around on weekends, making stupid decisions. And then, you're all like little Ms. Serious. Why, Westin?"

A full-body shiver started in my scalp and ran down my back when he said my last name. It was so weird. I always called myself Westin when I was doing my stupid debate-mandated self pep talks. But hearing the name come from Matt's lips, especially when it was just the two of us in my kitchen, felt really, really good — like he might even have the potential to know me as well as I knew myself.

"I don't really have a choice," I said finally.

"Can I ask another question?" he asked.

"Fine." I was disappointed. I wanted him to dig farther, so I could talk about the pressure, the endless expectation to always be the best, everything I'd been keeping inside for so long.

"So, if you're all serious and stuff, then what's the deal with Will?"

"There is no deal," I said angrily. Clearly, he didn't know me very well after all. "I don't even know . . . I mean, there's nothing."

"Good. Because I'm only saying, as a friend . . . Will's not right for you. He's not going to make you happy."

"Like Erin makes you happy?" I asked before I even knew what I was saying. It wasn't something I'd have ever said if I weren't desperate to change the subject.

"A lot of people could make me happy," he said noncommittally. "Erin's a nice girl. But all I meant was that you don't need to date a random guy just because Keely says you should. Or whatever." His eyes flicked from me to the refrigerator. "Do you have any food?"

"Um . . ." The conversation was jumping around too quickly, and I couldn't latch on. Did Keely spread the Will rumor? Did Keely tell sleepwalking me to make out with Will and did I do it because of some weird subconscious thing? Did Matt like Erin? I didn't even know which question to focus on, so I decided to start with the easiest: food. "I think there's, like, eggs and stuff. But, seriously, the Will thing is just . . . it's nothing." *At least nothing I can explain.*

Without prompting, Matt opened the fridge. "I need pancakes," he announced.

"Um, okay . . ." *Pancakes?* What was *that* teen code for?

But Matt had already reached toward the cabinet with the broken hinge and pulled out sugar, flour, and the carob chips Mom insisted tasted just the same as chocolate.

"This is fine," he murmured as he spread the ingredients along the cracked laminate counter. "Just a warning. I make shapes, but I don't take requests. Just respect my vision."

"Wait, you're making pancakes? Like, for real?"

Matt turned and gave me a crooked smile. "Isn't that what I said I was going to do?"

"Yeah . . . it's just . . . Nothing. Cool." All right. So this was how normal teens spent normal Saturday nights. Or, at least, how a secret child spelling champ and a valedictorian wannabe spent a Saturday night. I kind of wished I'd known that earlier. As Matt got to work, I pulled open my laptop. I went to my e-mail inbox. There was one lone e-mail.

Important Announcement from the Ainsworth Committee

I eagerly clicked on the message.

To: All Ainsworth semifinalists (New Hampshire)
From: Ainsworth Committee, Northeast Chapter
Re: Sad news

It is with deep sadness that we inform you of the death of Leah Kirkpatrick. Leah, 18, from Grand Falls, was a senior at Grand Falls Regional High School. A National Merit Finalist who was, at the time of her death, ranked #1 in her class, Leah's academic ambition was matched only by her personal passions. An accomplished swimmer and equestrian, Leah also founded a club to raise money for the pediatric unit of the Grand Falls Children's Hospital. Her family and friends will remain in all of our

thoughts. For those who would like to pay
their respects, a memorial viewing will be
held tomorrow, Sunday the 18th, at Bradley
Family Funeral Home in Kennilworth, New
Hampshire, from 2 p.m. to 8 p.m.

Please note that in light of this trag-
edy, the committee will not be releasing
rankings from the Ainsworth interviews,
but will be privately contacting the
schools of those winners who've moved on
to the next level.

A picture of a smiling girl leaning against a tree was attached
to the e-mail. I instantly knew who it was. It was the blonde
from the parking lot who'd wanted us to have lunch together.

The image swam to my memory. Her hair blowing around
her face, the way she'd caught her lip with her front teeth. I
quickly Googled her, recoiling when the autofill added *car
crash* after her name.

Car crash. I thought of the way she'd asked me to lunch and
I'd brushed her off. If I'd agreed, would she still be alive? Or
would we both be dead?

Plane crash theory. The term floated into my head. It was the
idea that, for something horrible to go wrong, a million tiny
things — the exact amount of rainfall, the time you left the
house — had to click into place. I wondered if I'd been one of
the links in the chain that had led to Leah's death — if I hadn't
looked upset, she wouldn't have talked to me, and would have

made her way to her car two minutes earlier. And those two minutes could have meant the difference between life and death for her.

A shiver crept up my spine, causing my entire body to shake uncontrollably.

"You okay?" Matt turned away from the stove and faced me, spatula in hand.

"Yeah." I sat heavily down at the wooden table, cradling my head in my hands. "I'm fine. It's just . . . this girl. I met her at the scholarship competition. And she died."

"No way." Matt walked behind me and draped his arms around my shoulders.

I quickly shrugged off his arms and turned the computer to face him, so he could read the e-mail. He read quickly, his eyes darting across the screen.

"How did it happen?" Matt asked.

I shrugged. "It didn't say. It's fine. It was a car accident, I guess. Those things happen. I didn't know her at all. It's just sad." I slammed the laptop shut and scraped my chair back under the pretense of examining the pancakes. "How's it going over there?"

"Don't look!" Matt raced me toward the stove, outstretching his arms to barricade my view.

"Hey!" I squealed a little too loudly. But the noise seemed to break the mood, and Matt turned to me with a wide grin on his face.

"What did I tell you about my vision? You can't peek!" Matt poked me in the center of the chest with the spatula, the touch feeling like lightning running up my spine. For the second time in fewer than five minutes, I gave in to a full-body shiver.

"Now, sit back down and let me do my work."

I perched on the counter, swinging my legs back and forth, trying to push any thoughts of Leah out of my mind. Outside, the wind was howling, and condensation on the windows made the glass steam up, but the stove was warm, and for the first time in a while, despite everything, I felt safe. I wanted to stay here, with him, forever. I picked up his iPod from the counter, clicking through until I found his Bob Marley playlist. I plugged it into the dock on the counter and reggae music filled the air.

"Nice." He bopped his head to the beat, but didn't look back at me. I watched him work, ultra-aware of the sinewy muscles moving between the thin fabric of his still-damp Bainbridge Soccer T-shirt.

"Thanks for doing this," I said.

"It's cool. I like getting my Anthony Bourdain on." Matt walked to the table, holding the still-steaming pan in front of him. "All right, dinner is served."

"I'll get plates." Hastily, I grabbed two chipped red dinner plates and put them down on the table.

"Cool." Matt put three misshapen pancakes on my plate, then four on his. After dumping the pan in the sink, he sat opposite me. He wordlessly picked up a pancake and held it up in a mock toast.

"Here's to . . . carpe diem. Or whatever we should toast to. The girl who died. Your scholarship. The fact that we're finally hanging out. Whatever you want."

"Nice. You know, I do have forks. If you want one." I hastily went to the silverware drawer and grabbed two.

"Unnecessary." He took a large bite of his pancake.

"Gross." I wrinkled my nose.

"Sorry." Matt grinned. "So, what are you thinking?"

"That I'm going to use a fork," I shot back, avoiding the question.

"What else?" he prompted. "You know what I'm thinking?" Matt asked, not waiting for an answer. "What it'd be like if I died today. You know? Like, that Leah chick had no idea what was coming."

"None of us do, really," I said. "Anyway, isn't this kind of heavy stuff to talk about over breakfast? Or . . . whatever this is?" I asked when I realized the time blinking above the stove read two a.m.

Matt picked up another pancake and ripped it apart with his fingers. "Nah, you *need* to talk about heavy stuff over breakfast. Carbs make everything go down easier. And it's heady stuff. I feel like if I died, I'd be all right. I mean, I'd be dead, but I'd have lived a pretty sweet life. No complaints. Listened to some good tunes, had some fun, made friends. I don't think I'd regret anything."

"Then you're lucky," I murmured. Would I be happy with myself or proud of my life if I'd died today? No. No one would remember me, not really. I'd be an *almost*. She *almost* won the Ainsworth. She *almost* was valedictorian. She *almost* was starting to have friends. She *almost* learned to lighten up. *Almost* wasn't enough. Ever. *Almost* was a sign I was slipping. Once I was valedictorian, once I was an Ainsworth scholar . . . *that* was when I'd let myself be happy.

"Anyway . . ." I trailed off, unsure how to change the subject from life and death to something even a tiny bit more typical. "So, have you started your college apps yet?" *Ugh.*

"Not really." Matt shrugged. "I mean, I guess I'll just go to the U, if I get in. Does it really matter?"

"Does it really matter?" I repeated. "Um, *yeah* it does."

"Why? It's still college. Harvard or wherever doesn't own knowledge. You get whatever you put into it. And I feel like they'll be plenty of good people and good times at the U. And in the end, isn't that all that really matters?"

"Not really. College isn't like high school. It's not about good times. It's about . . . finding yourself." I sounded like a lame college brochure and I knew it. "I mean, it's about challenging yourself and pushing yourself and becoming better."

"Becoming better?" Matt raised an eyebrow skeptically. "What does that mean? The way I see it, I'm me no matter what, and as long as I'm chilling and having a good time and not hurting anyone, then what's the big deal? I don't think getting, like, an A makes me a better person. Do you really think that it does?"

I shrugged. "It's not a bad thing, either."

"Right. But there's so much other stuff, is all I'm saying. And if you don't take the opportunities when they present themselves, then you miss out. And I don't want to miss out on anything. Especially the important things."

"So what's an example of an important thing?"

But Matt didn't speak. Instead, he leaned toward me and pressed his thumb against my chin. I tilted my head as my heart started thumping against my chest so loudly that I was sure Matt could hear it.

Our lips touched, then he slowly pulled away.

"That," he said, smiling.

I touched my mouth, then self-consciously dropped my hand to my lap.

I leaned toward him. "Carpe diem," I whispered. Our lips met, and already I felt like his mouth was familiar. I tilted my head, feeling his breath on the side of my neck.

I wasn't sure if it was the ticklish sensation of his breath or just the entire situation, but suddenly, I had the uncontrollable urge to giggle. I pulled away.

"What?" Matt asked.

"It's just funny. You and me here. It's weird."

"I'll take weird." Matt leaned toward me again, this time weaving his fingers through my hair.

We kissed again. I wanted the moment to last forever, but I also knew how dangerous that would be.

I pulled away a third time.

"We need to stop."

A cloud of confusion crossed Matt's face.

"Why?"

"It's getting late. I need to go to bed. You can sleep over. I mean, not *sleep* sleep over, but stay over. If that makes sense?" I stood up and hurried into the cluttered living room. He could sleep on our enormous purple couch.

Matt trailed behind me.

"You can sleep there. It's comfortable," I chattered.

Matt plopped onto the lumpy cushion, his eyes glazed. He pulled one shoe off, then another, and swung his long legs onto the couch.

"This feels good. Come join me?"

"Okay." My heart pounding, I slipped onto the couch next to him. He gently threw his arm over my waist. I expected to have to explain to him why we couldn't kiss anymore, but he didn't try. Instead, his breathing got deeper and deeper until I realized that he'd fallen asleep.

And soon, I did, too, realizing just before I lost consciousness that I hadn't thought once about the profile, the weird comments from the party, or the now-I-saw-it-now-I-didn't photo.

I woke up to a raging headache, a cramp in my shoulder, and a realization that I was entirely dressed — and the elastic from the pantyhose I'd selected to wear to the Ainsworth over twenty-four hours ago were *still* digging uncomfortably into my hip.

And, of course, Matt Hartnett was snoring next to me.

I wiggled out of his arms, causing him to stir. His eyes opened, and a sleepy smile crossed his face. He stretched, revealing an irresistible sliver of skin at his waist, and smiled up at me.

"Westin." He blinked his eyes at me and I took a step backward.

"How did you sleep?" I perched back on the edge of the lumpy couch, but that felt too oddly intimate. I slipped onto the floor and hugged my knees to my chest. Much safer.

"Oh man." He blearily rubbed his eyes. "That couch is my friend. Seriously, I slept awesome."

"We call it the Purple People Seater. My mom named it." I glanced around our tiny living room and imagined what it looked like to him: the lumpy, mismatched furniture. The haphazard stacks of used books. The tumbleweed-like tangle of dog fur under one of the blond wood shelves. Last night, he'd made me feel like *I'd* been the one he was missing out on, the one he'd do anything to kiss. Today, I wondered if he felt like he'd settled. I was the girl who'd freaked out twice in front of him, who'd only offered him flat soda, who'd pulled away from a kiss. I wasn't giggly and energetic like Erin Carlson. I was nervous and weird. And if he hadn't noticed last night, there was no way he wouldn't notice now.

"Cool. Purple People Seater, you've done well." He caressed the couch with his hand and blinked sleepily up at me. "So, is anyone else here?"

I shook my head. "We came here after Alyssa's. . . ." *Remember?* I wanted to say. But I didn't. Because what if it hadn't happened? What if this was another weird half-waking *thing* and he was only here because I'd fainted or dragged him or who even *knows* what.

"Yeah. Yeah. Of course. Fun times." He swung his legs off the couch, stood up, and stretched. "Well, I guess I should go, huh? Don't want to get in your way. I'm sure you've got a ton of stuff to do."

"I don't. Not really." I was surprised by how much I wanted him to stay.

"Oh. Well, I mean, I have to go. Soccer practice." He leaned down to grab his shoes.

"Right!" I stood up so quickly that the top of my head collided into his chin.

"Ouch!" I yelped, more for show than anything. I hoped he'd remember how we'd had a similar collision the first time I went to Alyssa's barn. I wanted him to make a joke about how we had to stop bumping into each other like this, anything that would bring back the quirky guy who'd been in my kitchen the night before. But he didn't.

Instead, he leaned toward me. "You okay?" His eyes widened, and for a second, I thought he was going to kiss me. Instead, he gently brushed my cheek with his index finger and held up an eyelash.

"You know how you're supposed to make a wish on these?" Matt asked.

"You want me to?" I asked.

"Yeah."

I closed my eyes and blew, but there were too many thoughts circling my mind to focus. I opened my eyes, noticing the eyelash still sitting on his finger.

"Better luck next time, right?" I shook my head and walked toward the kitchen to let him out. As I opened the door, I noticed the pancakes on the table, a sign that at least *that* hadn't been a dream.

I opened the door to the back porch.

"Bye," I said.

"See you around, Westin."

CHAPTER 11

I didn't go inside after Matt left. Instead, I sat on the porch steps, hugging my knees to my chest and staring out toward the pastures in the distance. The rain had stopped, but the air still felt heavy with dampness. Usually, rain made me feel refreshed, like everything bad had been washed away, but now I felt empty and sad and exhausted, as if every all-nighter, every early morning spent studying, every stressed-out Saturday night had piled on top of me.

I grabbed a rock and threw it as hard as I could into a bush, imagining I was aiming at Matt's head. But that didn't make me feel any better. I was angry with myself. I'd driven myself to an almost nervous breakdown. I'd stayed out and partied and *for what*? I was still alone. I was still the ex–*Spectrum* editor. And I still had to deal with this ghost or my subconscious or whatever was haunting me. If anything, I'd given it even more ammo than it had before.

Stupid. I stood up and brushed the dirt off the back of my jeans, then walked into the house.

And then, I screamed.

On the table, in between the two jam jars we'd used for our drinks, was one single, tiny, pink baby shoe, sitting there as though it had been there all night.

Underneath it was a Sound and the Story Post-it, placed carefully on top of a yellowing envelope.

Don't worry, Hayley. Some of us don't ever find our soul mates. And some of us need to search a little harder. You need to get a clue. But for now, I'm giving you one.

I screamed.

Then, the doorbell rang. I screamed again.

"Hayley? Hayley!" It was a male voice.

"Go away!" I yelled. My heart thumped in my chest as I grabbed a fork and the envelope from the table.

"Hayley, it's Adam!"

Adam?

I edged toward the back door, holding the fork in front of me like a weapon, and peered through the window.

It was Adam, shuffling from one foot to another, a book in his hand.

"What are you doing?" I opened the door a crack.

"I came to talk. I saw you on the porch, I tried to call for you, then you went inside and started screaming. What's going on?"

"Nothing. Just . . . a bug. What are you doing here?" I croaked.

"I was worried about you," he continued. "I wanted to see if everything was all right. You weren't answering your phone, and then I thought, with that e-mail we got . . . that you might be freaked out," Adam said finally.

"About the girl dying?" I asked, opening the door and standing in front of him on the porch. The envelope crackled between my fingers. *He'd called?* I tried to remember the last time I'd checked my phone.

"Yeah, because it pushes the Ainsworth date back a week, and I know you've got this whole schedule. I don't know, you just seemed really on edge yesterday. So I feel like that news could have pushed you over the edge. And no offense, but I feel like it kind of did. I thought you were going to kill me with that fork."

"Well, you shouldn't have scared me," I said.

"Right. So . . . do you want to go talk? Or get breakfast?" Adam asked.

I shook my head. "I can't."

"Why not?"

"Because I can't. I just need to . . . do stuff by myself." The envelope crackled in my hand.

It's just a prank. Just a dumb Keely prank, I reminded myself. Maybe she'd put Matt up to it. I wouldn't put it past her. It would be embarrassing and humiliating but I'd survive, just like I'd survived before. I'd be fine. And this time, I wouldn't ask Adam for help. I wouldn't ask anyone. Help equaled weakness. Help was drama-fueled and overrated.

"I need to be *alone*," I said to Adam.

Hurt flickered in his eyes, then he nodded. He jammed his hands into his pockets.

"Seriously, I'm fine. Thanks for coming, but everything's cool." I said it loudly, in case Matt or Keely or anyone was hiding in the woods, watching and ready to laugh. Well, they could watch all they wanted. They wouldn't see me break down.

"Okay," Adam said after a pause. He turned and headed down the steps. And finally, when I was alone, I headed back inside, opened the envelope, and saw my mother's handwriting looping and slanting in front of me.

What was this?

I'd expected some lame journal entry Keely had salvaged from her bedroom from back when we used to do sleepovers.

Another old HIKE list. Maybe even an old draft of my Ainsworth essay she'd fished out from Klish's office. But how would she have access to my *mother's* stuff?

Smoothing the paper on my knee, I began to read.

It was a letter, written in my mother's bubbly, slanted script.

Dear Mom and Dad,

I don't expect you to understand about the babies, or about the adoption arrangements. And I'm not asking you to. I'm also not asking for forgiveness, as I've done nothing wrong, or for understanding, as I doubt it's something you're capable of. What I ask is that you realize that I'm done with both of you. I'm giving my children up for adoption, and I hope they know that it's not because I don't love them. Because I do. It's because I am scared of what it would be like for James and me to be parents. I don't want us to be like you. I don't want my children growing up in a large, silent house afraid to touch or say the wrong thing. I don't want them always being afraid. I want them to learn that life is messy and big and raw and real. And I know this will give them what they need. I always thought

The letter trailed off. It was obviously just one page of many, but it didn't matter. The proof was in the page.

Children.

I thought of the picture on the refrigerator. The girl smiling, eyes wide. Me, except not. Was that . . . *her*? Was she my *sister*?

*   *   *

The bell above the door at The Sound and the Story rang, and the fifteen or so members of the Sunday afternoon book club looked up at me. I waved, trying to seem casual.

"Your mom isn't on the schedule today, love," Joanna Fenton, the store owner, said. She was English and a retired philosophy professor and normally I loved talking with her.

"I know. I had to grab something from downstairs," I said shortly.

"All right, love," she said. Thankfully, she turned back to the group.

"I think Jane Eyre only *thinks* she hears things. She's being haunted by her own psyche. The voice in the attic is a metaphor for the voice in her own head," I heard one woman say knowingly as the rest of the group murmured in agreement.

If only she knew.

Downstairs was the so-called rare book section, although it was usually more of a repository for the water-stained, ink-marked, paged-through volumes that were periodically discarded by the U. With each step, the air smelled mustier, although there was the scent of lingering lavender — the scent of my mother — as well.

Downstairs was her domain, where she cataloged the books, shipped orders, and spent hours reading and daydreaming. Walking into her office felt like stepping into her private sanctuary, even if it was open and owned by Ms. Fenton.

I gently stepped over the black-and-white cat named Cow and picked up the book on top of a messy stack. *Growing Up and Moving On: A Guide for Almost Empty Nesters.* Underneath it:

Debt U: How to Save for College Without Losing Your Savings.
My heart twisted when I read the title. My mother used to read
dense philosophy books and oversized anthologies. Now, all
she seemed to read were self-help books geared toward dealing
with me.

And then, I found a book at the bottom of the stack, the one
that had caught my eye the last time I came down. My mother
had tried to push it away without me noticing, although at the
time, I hadn't thought much about it. *Chaucer and Philosophy,*
by James Thomson-Thurm.

James. Like my father. I picked up the book, fingers trembling, and turned it over. On the back was an author picture of
a handsome man with a trim beard. He was sitting in what
seemed to be an office, his gaze off in the distance.

He was my father. He *had* to be. There was something about
his half smile, the way he pushed his lower jaw out slightly, that
reminded me of me. My mother always said that I smiled like
a Lhasa apso puppy. And in this picture, I could see it.

I had my father's smile.

I shoved the book in my bag and began looking more fer-
vently, sure there were more clues. I yanked open the bottom
drawer of my mom's desk. It was scattered with old bills and
programs from previous bookstore events. I shuffled through
them until I found a single lockbox.

I picked it up. Shook it. I heard a soft thud.

The box had been locked at one point, but years had caused
the metal to rust, and the lock practically crumbled in my
hands.

Inside was just one picture: a sonogram photo. I squinted,
held it to the light. It looked like a photograph of the universe.

But then, I saw the writing. *Baby Girl A* with a hand-drawn white arrow.

And then, *Baby Girl B*.

Baby Girl B was underneath Baby Girl A, stacked as though they were sleeping on bunk beds.

Upstairs, applause broke out, abrupt as last night's surprise storm.

I slid the photo into my pocket and raced up the stairs two at a time.

"Hayley, darling, did you find what you were looking for?" Ms. Fenton called. "And would you like to join the discussion? A young person like you would provide a great counterpoint."

"Nope!" I said too loudly. My voice was strained and sweat was collecting at the back of my T-shirt. "I'm fine."

"Would you like to stay for coffee?" she pressed.

"I really can't," I said. I headed off in the rain toward the car.

I had a sister.

I had a sister.

I couldn't. I didn't. I was Hayley Kathryn Westin, an only child and part of a team with my mother. She'd told me everything: Five years ago, she'd found out her father had died, from one of the periodic Google searches. She'd been sitting at the kitchen table, flicking between her horoscope and the search engine, when her face had crumpled and she'd begun crying slow, long moans that filled the house and caused Sadie to growl. I'd held her tightly, patting her back and telling her it would be okay, even though I'd only been twelve and couldn't understand why the news affected her so profoundly. Shouldn't she have been happy he was dead? He was the one who'd shunned her.

Another snapshot: six months ago, my bedroom, when she'd woken me up to whisper urgently that Geofferson had said *I love you*. That she hadn't heard the words since . . . *since who*? Had she said the name? Had it been James? I had too many details swirling through my mind, making it impossible to pick which ones were essential. Why had my sister been kept a secret? It wasn't fair. For years, I'd felt all alone. I wondered if she'd felt the same way. And then, another thought: What if my sister had been at the Ainsworth because she'd been a semifinalist? Or because she was friends with one of the other candidates? Leah had said that she and "I" had spoken before. . . .

My phone beeped.

> Hayley, honey — Geoff and I decided to head to
> Boston for the day. Back tomorrow. Love you. oxo

OXO. It was the way we'd always signed off on texts, ever since the sixth grade when I'd realized the combination of letters looked similar to the symbol for infinity.

Ordinarily, I'd type it back.

Now, I didn't.

I pulled up the Ainsworth e-mail detailing the memorial viewing for Leah. Kennilworth was about an hour away. I didn't have to go. After all, I hadn't known her at all. *But maybe my sister had.* It was a long shot, but it was something I hadn't had before.

My heart surged as I started the car. The rain started again, a heavy downpour that required me to turn my windshield wipers up high. My hands were clammy on the steering wheel. This was crazy. I knew that. But so was everything.

The funeral home was on the outskirts of what looked like an industrial mill town. The rain hadn't let up and was streaming on the windshield as I slowed the car to a ten-mile-an-hour crawl.

I parked down the block and walked into the funeral home, aware that my jeans and T-shirt weren't exactly appropriate.

The inside of the building smelled like dead roses and too much air freshener and I felt claustrophobic as soon as I entered. Mourners, clad in black, were clustered in tight circles. A group of teenagers, about my age, were standing near the entrance. Their hands were in their pockets, and they were shuffling from one foot to the other. No one was talking.

In the center of the room was a casket. It was polished oak, and looked almost like a grand piano, the way the lid was standing open on one end. I hesitantly walked toward it, taking halting steps as I moved between different guests. I wondered where Leah's parents were. Whether she'd had a boyfriend. Whether anyone would look at me and know that I shouldn't be here, not really.

Ten steps. Nine steps. And all of a sudden, I felt someone tug on the crook of my arm.

I whirled around. It was an elderly woman, gazing up at me. She was almost a foot shorter than me, and probably weighed fewer than ninety pounds, but her fingers dug into my skin.

"You," she hissed. "What are you doing here?"

"I — I don't know," I stammered. "Leah and I were up for the same scholarship. I met her once. I just wanted to pay my respects."

"You've done enough," she said.

"I . . . don't understand," I squeaked.

"You were the last one with her."

"I . . . don't understand," I said again.

"You were in the hospital. I saw you."

People turned to stare, and I shook my head.

"I'm sorry," I said.

Just then, a blond woman with dark shadows under her eyes walked over to us and clamped her hand on the woman's bony shoulder. "That's enough, Mother. You're upset. You should lie down."

I'm sorry, she mouthed toward me.

"I saw you. At the hospital. You were there. You heard her scream," the woman said.

I turned and walked out, my face burning and my ears ringing.

She — my sister, my twin — had been there. And maybe she'd killed Leah. Or maybe she hadn't. Maybe Leah's grandmother was just confused, her brain overpowered by grief.

I drove aimlessly. I kept thinking of a book my mother had read to me over and over again when I was little. It was called *Are You My Mother?*, about a baby bird who hatches while his mother is away from the nest. He hops all over, assuming each person is his mother.

I knew how that bird felt. Except right now, I *didn't* have a mother I could depend on. Why had she kept my sister a secret? And now, when I needed her more than ever, she was with Geofferson. It wasn't something I could ask on the phone. I needed her. Here. Now.

But I didn't have her. I didn't have anyone.

I had myself.

And somewhere, maybe, a girl who shared my DNA.

CHAPTER 12

I woke up with a start. Sun streamed through the windows, creating a light-dappling pattern on the linoleum floor. My neck had cramped, and my shoulders felt uneven. I blinked up at the fluorescent lights, trying to figure out where I was. I was in Mrs. Ross's classroom, curled up on the small orange love seat in the back of the room. The clock above the door read seven a.m.

I'd slept at school.

It was a new low for me. I'd come here after the funeral home, not wanting to go home and desperate to do research on James Thomson-Thurm. Having spent the past three years in and out of school at all hours, I knew that the door behind the auditorium always remained unlocked, so it was easy to sneak in. The Yearbook room felt safe, and unlike my computer at home, I was confident I wasn't being watched. But I couldn't find much. All I knew was that he was a scholar of medieval history, an adjunct professor, and had written countless articles on Chaucer. I'd found a faculty home page with a brief bio. He had two children. He lived in Brookline, Massachusetts. I'd found an address. But beyond that, nothing. He didn't have a listed phone number. And I wasn't sure whether I should contact him.

I didn't want to. There had to have been a reason why Mom was so adamant about never communicating with him. Plus, what would I say? He knew he had a daughter. The fact that he'd never looked me up made it clear he wasn't interested. And if Mom wouldn't talk about the fact that she'd had twins, how could I trust some guy I'd never met to tell me my history? It was better to just figure it out on my own.

Feeling exhausted, I managed to shuffle toward the gym locker room. I splashed cold water on my face. I didn't recognize the girl blinking back at me in the mirror.

I felt outside of myself as the hallway filled with students. I scuffed down the hall, feeling shorter than I ever had before. I was wearing jeans and a hoodie and my hair was pulled into a messy ponytail. I looked like a girl on the run, which was exactly how I felt.

I shuffled to homeroom, staring at my feet.

The intercom crackled.

I glanced up at the speaker, my stomach churning.

"Will Miss Westin please report to the guidance office?"

"Ooooh!"

"You're in trouble!"

I wasn't even sure who was saying what. It didn't matter. It was the same stuff everyone said when someone was called to the office. In a way, I was glad to be called out. It was obvious I'd snapped. *This* was the moment I'd been worried about: when it would become clear that I was mentally falling apart. Except now, I knew I wasn't. I had the sonogram photo. I had proof.

The white-noise machine whirred inside the guidance suite, and a plate of peanut-butter-chocolate-chip cookies was sitting on the counter. The room seemed so cheerful and innocent that I wanted to cry.

"Oh, sugar, how are you?" Miss Marsted asked, looking up at me.

"Fine." *Not fine.* My stomach involuntarily rumbled, and I had to steady myself on the counter. "Why am I here?" I asked, trying to sound as polite as possible.

"Well, we all just wanted to check on you. We heard that you might be a bit stressed out about the Ainsworth. And we want to make sure everything's okay."

"Everything's *fine*," I repeated. "Who said I was stressed about the Ainsworth?"

"Well, one of your friends popped by. Said you wouldn't do it on your own, but that he was worried."

"I don't have friends," I said tightly.

"Well, that's something you can discuss with Miss Keeshan. She'd love to see you and make sure everything's all right. These types of competitions can do all sorts of funny things to people. I don't know how you do it," Miss Marsted said, swooping out from her spot behind the desk and practically pushing me into Miss Keeshan's office.

"Why not Mr. Klish?" I asked.

"Oh, honey, don't worry. Just have a good conversation, you hear?" Miss Marsted said, closing the door with an ominous thud.

Miss Keeshan was twenty-six, and had just gotten her social work degree the year before and was psyched to work with teenagers, which we all knew for a fact because she used the word *psyched* in casual conversation. She also wore clip-in feather extensions in her hair, sported skinny jeans and fluorescent tank tops under her blazers, and tweeted Nicki Minaj lyrics. She had no idea what I was going through. I doubted she could pronounce Ainsworth, let alone spell it. But I was desperate.

"Hayley, welcome!" Miss Keeshan said, spreading her hands wide, as if her office were a grand palace and not slightly bigger than a vending machine. The room was made even more claustrophobic by the oversized hot-pink beanbags strewn on the goldfish-orange shag carpeting. A poster with a sloth hanging on a tree dominated the wall behind her desk. HANG IN THERE! the poster commanded in oversized letters.

"All right, let's talk," Miss Keeshan said. But instead of sitting behind her desk, she collapsed into one of the beanbags, patting the one next to her to motion me to sit.

"You want me to sit down on the floor?" I asked, arching an eyebrow in disbelief.

She nodded. "I feel like it's more conducive to a conversation than sitting with a desk between us, don't you think?" she asked in a way that made it clear it wasn't up for debate.

"All right." I gingerly perched on the beanbag.

"So, I know that the Ainsworth interviews have been a roller coaster, and we all heard the sad story about Leah." Miss Keeshan frowned as if she knew her. As if *I'd* known her. "And I just thought it might be nice to talk. Get things off your chest. What do you think?"

I shrugged. I was so sick of being asked what I thought. The truth was, for the first time in my life, I didn't know. I felt so tired, an aching feeling creeping through my veins. I'd kept everything bottled up for so long, and now, everything seemed so mixed up in my brain. It was as if the Facebook page for the fake Hayley was a purple sock in a load of light-colored laundry. All of a sudden, everything was stained — including my ability to come up with remotely appropriate metaphors.

"Weird things are happening," I said finally. "So I went to this interview for the Ainsworth scholarship over the weekend and . . . it wasn't bad. I think the interview was all right. But there was a program, and every finalist had to submit a bio. I wrote a bio. I bet Mr. Klish has a copy. I sent it in. But . . . that wasn't the bio that was printed," I said in a tumble of words. I knew I should stop myself. But I was too exhausted to hold back.

"What was the bio?" Miss Keeshan pressed.

"It was a joke bio that made fun of me. And it was stuff that no one could have known unless they knew me *really* well. The type of movies I like and . . . just information most people wouldn't know," I said quietly, remembering the phrases from the text: *Acting like she's better than everyone else.* I shook my head as if to shake the words from my brain.

"Mmmhmmm," Miss Keeshan murmured as she stood up, crossed the room, and reached into a drawer and pulled out a notebook with a sparkly pink cover. She flipped to a blank page and began taking notes. "Continue," she said, perching on the edge of her chair, so she was looking down at me. I felt like a kindergarten student, waiting for story time.

"Um . . ." I asked. "I thought we were sitting down here."

"You can. Just keep talking," Miss Keeshan probed.

"Well . . . I'm worried that someone is . . . impersonating me. Or, at the very least, trying to sabotage me. And while I'm trying to figure out who it might be, I thought it was necessary that people . . . be aware." I glanced down at my hands. My fingernails were bitten to the quick; I'd even begun gnawing on my knuckles. I frowned and glanced at Miss Keeshan.

"So you feel like you don't know what's happening," Miss

Keeshan murmured. "Well, senior year is full of transitions, and it's normal to feel not quite like yourself."

"Oh, no!" I said hurriedly, knowing that Miss Keeshan was using her newly minted master's degree to place any blame on adjustment issues. "I mean, I *am* stressed out this year, but it's not that. It's . . . a personal matter. But I need to make sure that everything related to the Ainsworth isn't in jeopardy while I figure everything out. I just need you to make sure my chances haven't been affected. I'll do the rest myself."

"You'll do the rest yourself," Miss Keeshan repeated. "Sounds like you have a lot on your plate."

"I do!" I chirped nervously. "But, I mean, I'm fine. I'm *more than fine*. I just need to make sure everything is okay for the scholarship. For my future."

Miss Keeshan was still scribbling furiously.

"I don't know why I told you all this. I'm fine, really. I just didn't sleep well. With the stuff about Leah . . . and the fake bio . . . well, I'm just scared. I mean, not scared. Just confused. But I'll fix it. Somehow," I said desperately. I'd only revealed a sliver of the stuff I was thinking about, and she already thought I was crazy. I mashed my lips together, trying to keep myself from saying anything else.

Miss Keeshan looked at me, pity evident in her wide, blue, cartoon-Disney-princess eyes. "It sounds like you're pretty stressed out, huh, Hayley?" she said in the same way a newscaster would ask a murder suspect if it was *really hard to kill your whole family*.

I silently stared down. What could I say? That I somehow had a twin who was most likely impersonating me? Who, even if she didn't kill Leah Kirkpatrick, had somehow been at the hospital as Leah died from injuries sustained in a car crash?

Miss Keeshan cleared her throat. "I feel like you're under a lot of pressure, and when we're under pressure, things can happen. I heard about your resignation from the yearbook. And I know that's not like you. So I'm wondering if we'd like to discuss it together?"

"I'm fine," I said, more firmly this time. I hated when teachers used the word *we* when it was clearly all about me.

Miss Keeshan pursed her lips. "Well, all right. But I don't think this is about the scholarship competition, Hayley. I think you're reaching out for help. And I want to help you."

The bell rang and I sprang up as though I'd been bitten by a snake.

"I have to go!" I stormed out, ignoring Miss Keeshan's protests behind me. This time, Miss Marsted didn't offer me a cookie. It was like I had an invisible *C* for crazy affixed to my chest.

Better than K *for killed.*

The thought jolted into my head, as immediate as if it had been one of the creepy texts I'd received. Whether I liked it or not, my sister — or whoever it was — had invaded my thoughts. And she definitely wasn't going away anytime soon.

CHAPTER 13

I was halfway across the parking lot when a loud honk caused me to lurch forward in surprise. My satchel tumbled off my shoulder, spewing out the majority of its contents.

I whirled around. Behind me was Matt's car. He rolled down his window.

"Yo, Westin, what's up? Skipping out like the secret slacker you are?"

"No." I leaned down to grab my books, all too aware that Matt's greeting had given me what Keely always used to term *the tinglies*. Butterflies raced through my stomach, and I couldn't help but think of the way he'd kissed me across the kitchen table on Saturday night.

"Want to grab coffee? We can call it a study date so it won't be like we're really slacking."

I shook my head firmly. "I *can't*," I said, a little too loudly.

"All right. It's cool. No need to bite my head off. Why are you so freaked out?"

"I'm not. I'm just in a rush."

"A rush to where?" Matt asked.

"A doctor's appointment, okay?" I was on edge, and I knew it.

"Okay . . . whoa. It's cool. I won't bother you." Matt rolled up his window and I slid into my own car.

Don't think.

It was odd the way my mind gave me orders. Usually, it was to think more, dig more. Now, it was the opposite. The only way I could possibly make it to the bookstore was to be incredibly detached.

I inched along the traffic-filled road, crowded with SUVs dropping kids off at the elementary school. Even though it was only the third week of September, Main Street was already decorated for Halloween, with cobwebs twined around the iron lampposts and pumpkins sitting outside the Bainbridge Sandwich Shop, the Laughing Lotus Yoga Center, and the Ugly Mug, all ready to be decorated for the community carving contest.

I burst into the empty bookstore and hurried down the stairs two at a time.

"Mom?" I called, bursting into her office. Cow meowed indignantly, and Mom looked up from her laptop, her glasses pushed haphazardly onto the top of her head.

"Hayley, what are you doing here this morning?" she asked as the corners of her mouth turned up into a smile. She stood and crossed toward the coffee-filled French press.

"I'm not here for coffee," I erupted. "Mom, we need to talk. Now."

"About what?" she asked, stopping midstep and turning to stare at me. For the first time, I noticed how different her eyes were from mine. They were bright blue with yellow flecks toward the center. Like the eyes that had locked with mine across the auditorium in that second when the lights had come up.

I shifted, causing the wooden beams beneath me to creak. Cow arched his back and nuzzled my arm, desperate to be petted. The basement felt too haunted-house-creepy for this conversation. We needed people. Sunlight. A place that didn't feel too dark and foreboding.

"Not here," I decided. "Somewhere else. It's important."

"All right." Mom followed me, childlike, out the door, where she flicked the cardboard sign in the window. It read: THERE IS A TIME FOR DEPARTURE, EVEN WHEN THERE'S NO PLACE TO GO. BACK IN A SECOND; 10% OFF IF YOU NAME THE QUOTE AUTHOR! I'd never thought about it before. I don't know if I'd ever even read the quotation, but today, I could only see hidden meanings behind the words. Mom didn't even bother locking the door.

"Let's go to the park," I decided. Years ago, when I was a child and would be forced to accompany her to a shift at the store because she couldn't afford a babysitter, Mom would bribe me by promising to bring me there once she was off. Although it had a small play structure with a slide, swings, and monkey bars, I never wanted to climb. Instead, I loved sitting on the park bench, feeding the ducks that crowded the pond.

Wordlessly, we walked up the street and into the park. This morning, the playground was swarming with toddlers, while their mothers were sitting on the benches around the perimeter of the park, drinking lattes and swapping stories about bad babysitters, annoying things their husbands had done, and how to get their child to sleep through the night. As we walked by, I realized that I had no memories of her ever sitting on one of the benches with these parents. Instead, she'd always be sitting next to me, throwing bread into the water and laughing along with me when two ducks began fighting over one crust. She'd been my best friend — my only friend. My heart softened slightly. Maybe the whole time I felt like I was protecting her, she'd been protecting me in her own way.

I sat on the bench and pulled my knees to my chest. A few ducks waddled over.

"We should have brought food," Mom said thoughtfully. I wondered if she had the same memory as I did. Her hair blew in the September wind, and, except for the slight lines around her eyes, she looked like she could have been my age.

"Do I have a sister?" I blurted. I pulled out the letter and smoothed it on my knee, followed by the sonogram photo.

She snatched the photo from me, causing a rip down the corner.

"You looked through my things. They're *private. Private*, Hayley."

"I need to know. Because she's here. I've seen her. And so have other people. I know she's around. *She's* the one who's been going through your things. She put up a photo on the refrigerator, and she found a letter you wrote to your parents. She's been spying on me . . . been spying on us! And I need to know who she is. I need to meet her. Do you think you can find out where she is through James?"

At the name, Mom's eyes widened. She blinked, looked down. Blinked again. Clenched her fingers so tightly around the paper I thought for sure she was going to crumple it, but she didn't.

"What else did you find?" Mom said quietly.

"I need to know the truth," I pressed. "I need to know. Why did he . . . leave? What happened? And were you really planning on giving me . . . us . . . up?" I tried to soften my voice, to try to get my mother to react, to stop clenching and unclenching her fist. I needed her to take care of me, to let me know the truth.

I reached toward her hand. She snatched it away, then interlaced her fingers together, the oversized silver ring she always wore on her middle finger catching the light and causing rainbow patterns to dapple on the faded denim of her jeans. She closed her eyes and looked as if she were praying. But she wasn't religious.

"Mommy?" I prompted in a small voice. *Mommy?* It'd been years since I'd called her that.

"Clearly, the adoption didn't happen." She puffed out her cheeks and slumped down farther on the bench. "And yes. You did have a twin." Her voice was devoid of emotion.

"Tell me her name. Tell me something," I demanded. "Where does she live? With James? With my dad?" The word felt foreign in my mouth, with the *d*'s bumping against each other. I imagined a man with slate-gray eyes and a love of literature, someone who could connect all the unknowns about me until they made sense.

"She's dead," Mom said shortly.

"What?" The word *dead* rang in my ears, my stomach twisted in horror. "How can she be dead? She's not! She can't be!" My voice rose, more and more hysterical.

"Hayley, please." Mom put her hand on my hand. It was cold as ice, and I yanked my arm away.

"How did she die?" I asked. "You're lying. She's not dead." *She wasn't. She couldn't be. She's here.* She was at the Ainsworth. She was at the Kennilworth hospital. She was here, in Bainbridge. My brain screamed short, methodical statements, the sentences flashing as urgently as road caution signs on the side of an icy highway. And then, I thought back to the birth story I loved so much: Mom had hitched a ride from the bookstore to the hospital and had been all by herself in the room as I came into the world. Maybe it really had been like a fairy tale — complete with a horrible and bloody death that had been edited out, just like Mom always used to tell me the story of the little mermaid without telling the truth: that she doesn't end up with the prince, but turns into sea foam instead. Had *everything* I believed been a lie?

"What happened?" I pressed again. "I need to know." If my twin was dead, then who was the girl who'd been in the auditorium? Who had been making out with Will?

"We had a couple lined up, ready to adopt a set of twins. It was all planned. You were born first. The doctor hadn't come yet. There was so much pain, and then a cry. And you were perfect."

The word, once so comforting, now felt like a slap. I wanted to scream, to jump into the pond or run into the parking lot in front of a car or throw myself on the ground and kick and pummel my feet into the earth. But I sat still, pinching my wrist with my fingernails to keep from moving.

"What happened?" I asked again, my voice thin and strained.

"It was the hospital. They didn't have the right equipment. And then with the snow, and the roads, and the doctor . . ."

"What happened?" I screamed, desperate to get to the center of the story.

"Hayley, be quiet!" Mom pleaded. She grabbed my arm, and I resisted the urge to squirm away.

"There were a few moments. It was just the two of us. The room was so quiet, and I couldn't believe that you were here.

You stopped crying almost immediately, and you just began to look around, as though you were trying to make sense of where you were. And then, you looked at me."

"Then what?"

"Then she was born."

"And what?" I asked, feeling a deep sense of dread. I knew what Mom would say. But I needed to hear it. The wind whipped up from the water. The ducks quacked contentedly.

"She was dead. Your umbilical cord was wrapped around her neck."

CHAPTER 14

Blood rushed to my brain and thrummed in my ears. I saw spots in front of me, felt my heart and my stomach thud to a halt before jackhammering in double-speed that made me sure I was about to throw up.

I had a twin. My twin was dead. The two ideas bumped up against each other. They didn't make sense. And yet . . .

"You're saying I killed her," I said dully.

"No!" Mom shook her head, but she didn't look at me. "There was nothing that could be done. You were alive, and that's what counted."

"Why didn't you tell me?"

"Why would I have?" Tears streamed down her face, but she didn't make a move to brush them away. She didn't look at me. "What would I have said? It was the worst and best day of my life. The adoption fell through, and I was glad. I wanted you. I wanted both of you. But you were there, and you were alive, and you were mine. And since the moment you were born, I made it my mission to never let you know, to make sure you were raised in happiness and peace. Because what good would the truth do?"

"I don't know," I said quietly. A cloud passed over the sun and I shivered. I had a million questions. *Why didn't you tell me? Why is she haunting me? What can I do now?*

"It's a lot. I didn't want you to know. Don't you see that

sometimes, some secrets are just better left unsaid? And James couldn't deal with any of it. He couldn't handle the fact that she'd died. He couldn't handle a lot," she said bitterly.

I wasn't listening. I couldn't believe that I'd had a twin. And that she *died*. Maybe, even in utero, I'd been jealous, had killed my sister so I could live. And maybe now, my sister was enacting her ghostly revenge.

I twisted my bracelet around and around my wrist. I wanted Mom to hold me, to say everything was all right, to tell me that I was still perfect. Instead, she stood up and pulled her cardigan around her shoulders.

"I haven't thought about this in a long time. It's hard for me. Especially now, with Geofferson . . ." Mom's face twisted. "I have a chance to be really, truly happy. Can you understand why I want to forget the past?"

"Yeah," I said in a strangled voice. *But what if she's haunting me?*

"I care about you so much, Hayley," she said softly.

"Well, you have an odd way of showing it. Lying to me? I can never trust you again! What mother *does* that?"

Mom set her lips into a tight, angry line.

"It's so messed up. *You're* so messed up. You expect me to be okay, after that. What am I supposed to do? I wish I'd been the one to die!"

Mom looked at me as though she'd been slapped. She grimaced, her mouth twisting. Then, as though she had to force herself to do it, she reached toward me.

"No!" I yanked my arm away from her. "Don't touch me! Leave me alone."

Mom nodded. "Fine. Fine, Hayley. I love you. But I can't . . . you need to stop. Before you say something you'll regret."

I didn't look at her. I hugged my arms to my body, wrapping my frame in my sweatshirt. I wanted her to tell me everything would be okay. But it wouldn't be. It wasn't.

I heard the sound of leaves crunching underneath Mom's feet. I didn't look up. Didn't move. And when I finally did, she'd disappeared. The playground had also emptied, and the only sign of life was a group of ducks cutting a V along the dark pond water.

I'd killed my sister. Yes, it was an accident. Yes, it had happened before I was born. But the fact remained that there had been two of us, and I'd survived. That fact was as much a part of me as my drive and determination. It was the dark shadow part of me that woke me up in my sleep, that made me pull away when Matt kissed me. And whether that shadow self was the actual ghost of my twin or the ugly, twisted part of my brain that caused me to go to parties in my sleep or imagine people that weren't there, it didn't matter. This shadow was out to destroy me. And unless I did something fast, it would succeed.

I sat on the bench for hours. There, I didn't have to think or react. I didn't have to run. I could sit.

"Hey," I said, looking up at the sky. I thought back to when I used to go to sleepovers at Keely's house. We'd hold séances and I always was pretty sure Emily was not-so-secretly pushing the planchette so it'd land on *Yes* when she asked if her crush liked her. We'd scare one another, but it was the good kind of scared that made us push our sleeping bags together and giggle into the night. This fear was heavy and made it hard to breathe, made me hope that something would *happen*. "If you're here, you should, you know, show yourself."

I paused. How did you talk to a ghost?

"I know you're here," I tried again. "And I want to say . . . I'm sorry. For anything I did. Just know that. But that doesn't mean you should be punishing me."

Punishing me? I sounded like a kindergarten teacher. I coughed. "Just please tell me what you want me to do. Seriously."

I closed my eyes and waited. Nothing.

Then, I heard footsteps. Felt a tap on my shoulder.

I screamed.

"Whoa! It's all right!"

A police officer shined a light at me. I blinked and realized another cop was standing behind him. I couldn't decide whether to be relieved or annoyed.

"What are you doing? Waiting for your boyfriend?"

"No." I shook my head, my eyes adjusting to the artificial light in my face.

"So you're just sitting here all alone?"

"I was thinking," I said in a small voice.

"Just thinking," he repeated. "All right. Well, the park's closed now. Locks up at dusk. So it's best to do your thinking somewhere else."

I trailed behind the officer. Beside me, the trees lining the winding path formed shadows on the concrete beneath my feet. She — my twin — wasn't here. *Of course she's not, because she's dead.*

"What?" the officer asked.

"Nothing." Had I spoken out loud? I mashed my lips together and stared at the ground.

"Where's your car?" the officer asked as he clicked the padlock in place on the iron gate. The parking lot was empty except for a lone squad car.

"Just down the street. I'll be fine."

He nodded and I headed to where I'd parked, hours earlier, on Main Street. I slid into the front seat and headed toward the house. It was time to face the inevitable.

The lights were on, but Mom's car wasn't in the driveway. There was a note on the rough-hewn table. I grimaced, relieved when I saw my mother's familiar handwriting.

> Dear Hayley,
> I tried calling you a few times, but you didn't answer. I know it was a tough conversation, and it was one that was hard for me, too. I wish I could support you right now with your feelings, but the conversation brought up so much in me as well. I'm going to be staying at Geoff's condo. I'm worried if we're together we both might say or do things we'd regret. And that would destroy me. After all, you're all I have.
> I love you. Remember that.
> Mom

I picked up the paper and crumpled it in a tiny ball. At my feet, Sadie chased her tail in circles, the way she always did when she expected a treat.

I grabbed a dog biscuit from the cupboard, broke it in two, and threw the pieces on the floor. Sadie gobbled them up eagerly, licking the linoleum floor for good measure.

"That's a sweet girl," I murmured. I looked up the stairs to my bedroom. The stairwell looked dark and foreboding and I felt my stomach clench in dread.

It was now or never. If something was going to happen, it would happen. Or it wouldn't. I took a tentative step on the stairs. The wood creaked and I jumped. *It's nothing.* I took another step, and another.

"Hello?" I called loudly as I walked across the threshold into my bedroom. I flipped on the light and glanced around. Everything was the same as it had been on Saturday morning, before the Ainsworth interview. There was a half-drunk mug of coffee. The messy pile of interview outfits. My laptop.

I jostled the trackpad of the laptop and logged into my e-mail, not sure what to expect. But everything was normal. A few messages from the Yearbook listserv that I couldn't unsubscribe from, even though I'd made the list in the first place, an invite to a potential students' weekend at UPenn, a Kendra-sent link to Flickr pictures from Alyssa's party. I read through each quickly, was relieved to see that none of Kendra's pictures included me, and then reached the top of the list.

And then I shrieked.

CONGRATULATIONS! screamed the subject line. But what I noticed was the sender name: *Lucinda Ainsworth.*

I clicked.

Dear Hayley Westin,

We are pleased to inform you that you have been selected to advance to the final round of the Ainsworth scholarship search. As a finalist from New Hampshire, you will need to schedule an interview for Monday the 26th, at the admissions office of the University of New Hampshire: Bainbridge campus. Please contact us at your earliest convenience to confirm.

In Scholarship,

Lucinda Ainsworth, on behalf of Alice Falconer Ainsworth

I blinked at the message, half expecting it to disappear. But it didn't.

Oh my God.

I wanted to celebrate. I wanted to call someone, to scream into the phone, to pop a bottle of champagne and toast to my dreams coming true. I rifled through my purse, but my phone wasn't there. Weird. Then I remembered how I'd dropped my bag in the parking lot. Had my phone fallen out, and I hadn't noticed?

I glanced back at the message, reading it again just to make absolutely sure that I hadn't imagined anything. And then, an instant message popped up on my laptop screen.

You're a lucky girl, aren't you? Future Ainsworth scholar . . . if you stay alive that long.

The avatar next to the message was the same as the one from the original Facebook profile — complete with a bikini, sunglasses, and a flirty, secret-hiding smile. It was her.

"Sadie!" I called sharply. Sadie barked once, then dropped to the ground, continuing to gnaw on a sock. If something was wrong, she certainly didn't know. Couldn't dogs sense ghosts?

I slammed the laptop shut and ran to the kitchen, turning on all the lights along the way. I knew I couldn't run. I *couldn't*. Because she — it — knew who I was. Knew where I was. Still, I grabbed a bread knife from the kitchen and inched upstairs to my computer. A new message was blinking on the screen.

> You can run, but you can't hide, Hayley. I know you too well.

"Where are you?" my voice echoed. The heater hissed in the corner. The wind rattled against the windows.

The green message window flashed. I clutched the bread knife more tightly as another message popped up on the screen.

> Ignoring me won't make me go away.

I took a deep breath, fingers poised over the keyboard, a million thoughts rushing through my head: *I'm sorry. Don't kill me. Did you kill Leah? What is happening?*

Finally, I typed: Are you my sister?

The message box was empty. A minute passed. I placed the knife on the desk. Glanced at the curtains fluttering over the window. Massaged my temples. Repeated *I'm sorry I'm sorry I'm sorry* like a mantra. Then, when the message box stayed dormant, I typed a single question mark.

And then, another message popped up.

> Someone's been doing some research.
> Congratulations, you know who I am. Took you
> long enough.

I paused and took a deep breath. The wind slammed against the windows, louder and harder. I typed back, What do you want?

Instantly, a message appeared. What do I want . . .

"Yes," I said out loud. I clutched the knife again. "Yes!"

It was a shriek that caused the windows to rattle. Sadie barked, three short, raspy, alarm-like sounds.

"Tell me," I said in a quieter voice. I sounded like I was begging.

And then, the words appeared on the screen — slowly and deliberately, as if whoever was typing them knew my heart was pounding, my hands were shaking, and my pupils were dilating with each letter.

> That's for me to know and you to find out.
> Maybe it's time to do another round of detective
> work? You never know what you'll find until you
> look for it ;)

And then, the icon disappeared.

> User has signed out of chat.

"Hello?" I called. Nothing.

Sadie glanced up at me curiously.

"Hello?" My voice was shaky. "What do you want me to do?"

I glanced at the computer screen. Nothing.

"Fine." If this was the game that I was supposed to play, I'd do it. Clearly, the spirit or ghost or whatever expected me to be afraid. It probably expected me to run away. But I wouldn't.

Instead, I took the stairs, two at a time, to my mother's room.

Tucked under the eave of the attic, my mother's oddly shaped room wasn't one I often went in. It wasn't one she often went in, either, preferring to sleep on the couch. It didn't have any sense of her the way that her office did at The Sound and the Story.

I tugged on a drawer and glanced down at piles of folded shirts. The next drawer held ancient notebooks. I picked one up: *Get Motivated to Go Back to College Project* read the lines on the first page. The rest of the pages were blank.

Then, I tugged out the third drawer. It was stuck, the edge of the wood being held back by a yellow swath of fabric.

I tugged harder. The wood creaked and pain shot through my finger. I looked down to see a large splinter sticking out from my skin, blood dripping onto the fabric. Wincing, I yanked out the sliver of wood with my teeth, then resumed pulling.

The drawer fell to the floor with a clatter, causing an eruption of children's clothing from when I was little.

I picked up a frayed blue sundress. It had been my favorite until I'd dropped an ice-cream cone on it at the county fair when I was five. I touched the still-visible stain, remembering how my mother had spent half an hour at the sink in the crowded, hot restroom trying to scrub it out.

My stomach twisted. I couldn't even think of simple memories without wondering whether she'd been missing the daughter who wasn't there.

I balled up the dress and continued to sift through the rest of the clothes. At the bottom of the drawer were a few scattered film negatives, the celluloid cracked. I held one of them up to the dim light.

It was a picture of a newborn. I'd seen photos of me as a baby: They were all red-faced, screaming, as if angry at the indignity of birth. The image of the baby on the film was quiet, placid, staring straight into the camera.

I fanned through the strips, holding the next one to the light. It was the same baby, taken from a slightly different angle. Only there was something else, at the very bottom of the frame. It was a foot. It was grainy and blurry, as if the photo had been snapped midkick. The rest of the body was out of the picture, but it was clear: There had been two children.

Two *live* children.

So why had my mother been lying? And where — or what — was my twin doing now?

"I'm not afraid," I said in a small voice, trying to convince myself.

And in a way, it was true.

I was terrified.

CHAPTER 15

I woke to a loud thud against the window.

My eyes shot open. Through the window, Keely was blinking down at me.

You okay? she mouthed, motioning to me to open the door.

I hastily yanked the handle open and stood up, blinking in the bright sunlight. The parking lot was half-full. I'd slept through the initial zero-period rush and felt like I could sleep for hours longer.

I'd survived. I hadn't been killed. I suppose it should have felt like a victory, but it felt only like the ghost, or whatever she was, was toying with me.

"Um, I know you love school, but sleeping here?" Keely wrinkled her nose and took a few paces back from me. Not like I blamed her. I hadn't showered since Sunday. "That's so not clutch."

"I know it looks weird." *Act normal.* "It's just . . . my mom and I got into a fight, and . . ." I trailed off, hoping my vague explanation would be enough.

Keely winced. "Well, the next time that happens, you could just come over to my house. Seriously. You don't need to be a car-sleeping weirdo." Keely shook her head as Ingrid sidled up to her.

"Yo," Ingrid said in a bored voice. "Sleeping in your car is, like, very Euro. We did that all through Spain to save money."

"Cool," I said tightly.

"Ing, it's gross," Keely said dismissively. "Seriously. Anyway, you should get yourself cleaned up or whatever. Especially before Matt sees you. I'd *wanted* to tell you that I think it's cute you two are hanging out. But it's hard to do that when you're not cute. No offense or anything."

"Yup." Ingrid nodded and took a sip of her iced coffee while Keely beamed at me, clearly expecting me to respond. This must have been what Matt meant by getting Keely's blessing on us dating.

"Thanks, Keely," I said. I forced a smile. "It's great to hear. Really."

"Um, okay . . . don't get all, like, overenthusiastic or anything. I just thought you'd want to know."

"I do! I'm just . . . it's been a weird few days. Hashtag: anticlutch."

A small smile appeared on Keely's face as she raked her fingers through her hair. "No worries. Sometimes people get weird. Like, I got this pedicure on Sunday with this new color called Poison Apple and I thought it'd be, like, all cool-looking. And instead, it looks like dried blood. And, seriously, it's, like, totally messing with me." Keely held up her sandal-clad foot and twirled her ankle in my direction.

"That's intense." I tried to sound interested. Ingrid slurped her iced coffee. Keely leaned down to brush a nonexistent speck of dirt from her toenail.

I coughed. I wanted to say *something*, but wasn't sure where to begin. *So, I think I have a secret twin* wasn't exactly before-school conversation. And it wasn't like I wanted them to know. But I felt like I had to tell *someone*. Someone like . . .

"Yo!" a male voice called.

I whirled around. Matt.

"Skipping again, Westin?"

My stomach clenched. "Not really." Seeing Matt was like grabbing a floating piece of driftwood in an otherwise empty ocean. He wouldn't save me, but seeing him made me feel a teeny bit more supported.

"You were skipping?" Keely raised an eyebrow, clearly impressed.

"You couldn't have had too much fun," Matt teased. "I found your phone. It's in my car. Want to grab it?"

"Yeah. See you guys," I said as I trailed behind Matt. I was grateful to have an excuse to get away from Keely's watchful gaze. How was it possible to actually get to know someone when every conversation was under a microscope?

"I actually have it here," he admitted, reaching into his pocket and pulling out my phone from his shorts. I tried to ignore the jolt of electricity that occurred as our fingers touched.

"Thanks."

"You weirded out on me yesterday. I was wondering if you were mad at me about something," he said shyly.

I shook my head. "Just overwhelmed with stuff." I glanced down at my phone. A bunch of missed calls from Mom. One from Adam. And one unknown number. I'd deal with it all later.

"That's why you should take a break. Another one. Come out with me on Friday night." Matt wiggled his eyebrows up and down.

"Out?" I repeated.

"Yeah. Like, grab some food, walk around, talk. All that

stuff. I mean, we had that heavy conversation at your place. . . . I feel like you need some serious chill time. Like, for real."

"For real," I repeated.

"Yup." Matt nodded. I nodded. I didn't want to be the one to say good-bye first. I wanted the moment to last forever. *This* seemed way more real than my night of terror.

All of a sudden, the bell rang, causing kids to appear from behind trees and slide out of the backseats of cars, as if they were playing some massive game of hide-and-seek. I watched them curiously, as removed as an anthropologist. I wished I could go back to only worrying about school and class schedules. I didn't think I ever could.

"Ready?" Matt asked expectantly.

"Um . . ."

"Westin, skipping *again*?" He clapped his hand to his mouth in mock horror. "I never knew you were such a secret bad girl."

I grimaced at the word *secret*.

"You okay?" Matt's eyes widened.

"Yeah." I nodded. "I'm ready." But I didn't make any move to walk toward the doors.

"Geez, Westin, you're asking for it." He grabbed my waist and threw me over his shoulder.

"Hey!" I shrieked. I knew it was what I was supposed to do. "Put me down!"

"Will you promise you won't skip?"

"Yes! Put me down!" I couldn't shake the sense that I was being watched and that this would all end badly. I was relieved when my feet were back on the pavement. He grabbed my elbow and half dragged me through the doors just as the late bell rang.

"Uh-oh, we're in trouble!" Matt said playfully. But I wasn't listening. My focus was on Adam, standing at the entrance. He was holding a bouquet of forget-me-nots, but as far away from his body as possible.

"Hey," I said. My eyes landed on the bouquet. Were those for me? They were the same flowers he'd gotten me when we'd won a partner debate. *To remind you that together, we're awesome*, he'd said. But now, he seemed anything but happy.

Matt glanced between the two of us. "See you later."

"Hey, *Westin*," Adam said, his voice dripping with sarcasm. "Enjoying your celebration? It's a big day. Here are your flowers, by the way," he said, practically shoving them into my hands. Blooms scattered to the ground, the rose petals reminding me of blood. "I told Klish you were sick. Even though I was watching you in the parking lot the whole time. Do you know how disrespectful it is? Like, we did this thing together, the guidance office is all psyched, Miss Marsted made a freaking *feast*, and you didn't even bother to show up."

"I wasn't invited to anything," I said uncertainly.

"'I wasn't invited to anything,'" Adam said in a nasty, mocking tone I'd never heard before. "Whatever, Hayley. Klish said he called you twice. You knew about it. You were just busy with your new friends."

"I didn't know, Adam. I'm sorry. I don't know who Klish called, but it wasn't me. I didn't even know you were also a finalist. I mean, that's great . . . right?" I asked uncertainly.

"Yeah. Yeah, it's great. Whatever." Adam shook his head. He rolled his shoulders back. "Actually, you know what? I'm done." He kicked at the flowers on the floor.

"Huh?" I asked.

"I'm done with *you*, Hayley. This stupid guidance office thing was the last straw. I mean, here was this huge thing that we'd both been working for, and you couldn't care less. You were mean to Miss Marsted, you could barely form a coherent sentence, and then you disappear to hang out in the parking lot with your *bestie*, Keely, and your boyfriend, Matt."

"Wait, I . . . *she* . . . was in the guidance office?" I grabbed Adam's wrist, then he angrily yanked it away.

"This is what's killing me!" Adam exclaimed. "Your whole innocent act. I mean, you're skipping school because you have exhaustion or whatever, you act like an idiot at the interview and today in the office, and now you're an Ainsworth finalist. Freaking awesome. Hayley Westin wins again." Adam sounded like a stranger — an *angry* stranger.

"You don't understand," I said helplessly.

"Right. Just like no one understood that the Facebook page wasn't you. Or the screwed-up bio wasn't you. Jeez, Hayley, can you *hear* yourself?" Adam shook his head in disbelief.

"Adam, I need —"

"What? A ride? A study partner? A shoulder to cry on? Pick one, Hayley. It doesn't matter, because I'm done."

"Oh." I wasn't sure what else to say. "That's fine." As long as I spoke in monosyllables, I wouldn't cry.

Adam looked straight ahead. "It's just . . . you have no idea what you're doing. Hayley, you're so talented and so smart, and seeing you like this . . . I don't like it."

"I don't either, Adam. I need help." I began crying for real, one tear followed by another landing on my jeans. It was useless to cry. I knew that. But I couldn't stop. *She* had control. And worse, she was here. Or, had been here.

"Adam, something weird is happening," I said.

Adam snorted. "Why don't you tell your new boyfriend?"

"Adam, seriously —" My voice was shaking.

Adam cut me off. "You know what, Hayley? I *liked* you at one point. But now, I feel like you're just manipulating everyone to feel sorry for you. I think that you had a wild summer, the photos surfaced, and you're making up stories and excuses as to why it couldn't possibly be you in the pictures. It's not fair, Hayley. And even though no one else sees through your little game, I do, and I don't want to be part of it. Anyway, Klish told us we could take the day off. And our Ainsworth interviews are on Monday at the U at 10 a.m. In case you even want to show up for it." He kicked the ground. "Have fun."

With that, he turned and angrily walked off, leaving me alone in the center of the lobby.

I glanced at the trophy case. Today, the plaques bearing my name weren't comforting. They reminded me that I was a target. And there was nothing I could do about it.

Turning on my heel, I headed down the hall toward my locker. At least I was safe here.

I opened the dented metal door, and a piece of notebook paper, folded in a complicated square, fell out. The front was covered with a map design. I opened the first flap of paper to find a block-printed question:

WHAT'S AT THE END OF THE TREASURE HUNT?

I opened the second flap and quickly read the words printed on the page.

Wouldn't you like to know? Seems like you're a girl on a mission. Just be careful. We want you alive for the Ainsworth interview . . . and I'd hate for something unfortunate to happen to you before then. Don't worry, I've got your back for now.

Love ya, sis!

PS: I cannot believe you are besties with the guidance counselor and the guidance counselor's secretary. That is beyond lame. Remember that whatever I am doing, I am doing for your own good. Or mine. But isn't it all the same in the end?

PPS: There's a pep rally tonight. And guess what? You're going!

CHAPTER 16

Six p.m. and the sound in the gym was deafening. I couldn't believe that my Bainbridge classmates had so much school spirit, since they certainly hadn't used any of it for the newspaper or yearbook. I also couldn't believe I was actually here. I tried to get inside my sister's head. Would she expect me to follow her orders, or would she expect me to ignore them? Why a pep rally? Was she planning on meeting me? Ambushing me?

Killing me?

I spotted Keely, Ingrid, and Emily on the bleachers at the far side of the gym. I waved to them, but they didn't see me in the sea of people. Some underclassmen bumped into my back. I whirled around, but I couldn't tell who'd done it. Suddenly, I realized that even though the pep rally provided an illusion of safety, it'd be pretty easy to disappear without anyone noticing.

"Keely!" I shouted, my voice impossible to hear over the crowd. On the other side of the bleachers, Jess was sitting on Robbie's lap, surrounded by a few people I recognized from Yearbook. I edged up the steps of the bleachers, elbowing my way past my classmates. I felt dizzy and disoriented, and wished I was back in my own bedroom, watching a DVD under the covers.

"Keely!" I called again. This time, she whirled around and I plastered on a smile. As far as I knew, the only way to stay alive was to stay popular.

She bounded down the bleachers and embraced me.

"This is so fun!" she squealed, ushering me toward the spot where she, Ingrid, and Emily were joined by Caleb and Will. I smiled tightly.

I poked Keely's bicep.

"Yeah?" she asked, snapping her gum.

"So, when I was at Alyssa's party last weekend . . . what was I like?"

Keely cracked her gum. "What do you mean? Normal. Fun. I don't know. Why?"

"Just because . . ." I trailed off. *Because I want to see just how insane my evil twin who is impersonating me can be?* "No reason. That's cool."

Just then, Adam walked to the center of the gym and tapped on the microphone. Because he was the senior class president, he was expected to introduce everything.

"Hey, Bainbridge Warriors!" he yelled into the microphone. His voice cracked slightly.

"God, he's so dorky." Keely rolled her eyes as the crowd slowly began to quiet down. "I thought for the longest time that you and he were, like, this nerdy power couple."

"From HIKE to yikes!" Emily cracked, glancing around for a reaction. Ingrid smiled; Keely shook her head imperceptibly.

Just then, my phone buzzed.

See what a good sister I am? I made friends for you!

I whirled around, but no one was there. It was happening. She was *here*, watching me. And I was totally unprepared. It felt like the walls were closing in.

"I have to go." I elbowed my way down the bleachers. Adam was still talking and I saw the soccer team lined up, ready to be introduced. Matt smiled at me, but I glanced away. My heart hammered in my ears. I was about to confront my sister. I could do this. We were in school. My safe place. She couldn't hurt me.

I glanced around, reaching the bottom of the bleachers just as the entire section stood up to do the wave. Faces blurred together; the gym was hot and I was sweating; the sound of whistling and cheering and stamping was echoing in my head; and all of a sudden, I felt myself falling forward. I clutched in front of me, but grabbed nothing but air.

And then, I fell. And the last thing I remembered was silence.

"I think she fainted."

"Is she on something?"

"Stand clear!" It was Miss Keeshan's high-pitched voice that caused my eyes to snap open.

"I'm fine!" I protested. I shakily sat up. What had happened?

"You're bleeding," Miss Keeshan announced, holding a wad of tissues toward me.

"I am?" I experimentally held my hand toward my nose, surprised when I saw a red smear of blood.

"Yes. Have you been drinking?" Miss Keeshan asked, angling herself away from me so that my blood wouldn't get on her floral-print jeans.

"No." I shook my head. "Just . . . tired."

All of a sudden, I was aware that I was still sitting in the middle of the gym, and every single Bainbridge Secondary School student was peering curiously down at me. I could imagine how it looked: Hayley Kathryn Westin, academic superstar, bleeding and disoriented on the dirty gym floor. If my sister had set out to humiliate me, she'd succeeded. I knew that I was the one who'd fallen, but I couldn't help but wonder if she'd somehow facilitated it. In my mind, she had taken on a godlike quality, getting into my head and twisting everything. I felt tears prick my eyes and I angrily wiped them away.

"Well, if you're feeling all right . . ." Miss Keeshan stood up and offered her hand. I grabbed it, taking a shaky step forward.

"I'm fine. Perfect," I said tightly.

"We'll take care of her," Keely said, her eyes wide.

"Come on," Emily urged, slipping her arm through mine.

"I've got your stuff," Ingrid announced importantly.

Together, the four of us walked out of the gym as the noise cranked back to concert level.

"We're going to the diner," Keely announced. "And then we'll sleep over at Em's. Your parents will understand, Emily," Keely said, arching an eyebrow. "After all, Hayley almost *died*."

"I didn't almost die," I said sharply.

"Well, fainted, whatever." Keely shrugged. "The details don't matter. What matters is that you got a ton of attention, and you looked good doing it."

Emily nodded. "Yeah, you didn't flash anyone or anything."

Ingrid furrowed her brow as if deep in thought. "It was cool," she said finally.

"But you're still fragile," Keely said loudly. "And that means that we're not letting you out of our sight."

That was the best news I'd heard all day.

CHAPTER 17

*Y*ou said you wanted to borrow the gray dress. And besides, it goes with your eyes," Ingrid said knowledgeably, pulling her knees underneath her oversized striped sweater. We were in Keely's purple-and-pink room, and Keely was yanking clothes from her closet and throwing them toward me, just as she had five years ago, when we'd all hang out in her room before heading to seventh-grade dances. It felt familiar . . . and completely bizarre.

"Sure, gray is fine," I said, barely listening. I'd been dressed, mascaraed, and brought up to date on gossip — both Bainbridge and Hollywood — over the past three days by the three of them. It was nice to not have to think. Within the past seventy-two hours, I felt old barriers break down. My thoughts felt fuzzier, but I wasn't sure if that was due to them or due to the fact that I could barely sleep. Last night, I'd even convinced the three of them to sleep over at my house, just in case. But I hadn't heard a word from my twin. I hadn't heard from Adam, either, but I didn't care about that. I had way more stuff on my mind — like the fact that I had my upcoming date with Matt, and Keely was taking it upon herself to serve as my personal stylist.

And weirdly, I liked the attention. It was a side of me I hadn't known existed — a normal teenage girl getting ready for a date with a crush. But it wasn't just that. It was the fact that finally, people knew I existed. It hadn't taken the Ainsworth nomination or the yearbook editor position or all the debate awards. And having people rush up and ask if I was okay, getting a note from Miss Marsted that said she understood my behavior from yesterday, and being excused from a Calc quiz was kind of nice. It was weird — fainting in a pep rally was the opposite of perfect. And yet people liked me more than ever.

I wanted that to be the lesson my twin had been trying to teach me. And even though I didn't think it was, and I didn't think I'd heard the last of her, for now, I was ignoring it and concentrating on being Normal Hayley. Datable Hayley.

"Um, Hayley, this is kind of important? Gray dress? Yes? No?" Keely asked, shaking the hanger in front of me.

"I guess so?" I hoped that was the right answer.

"Yes," Keely said definitively. "It's sexy." Ingrid nodded in agreement and snapped a picture to text to Emily, who was at the orthodontist but still demanded a play-by-play of the entire outfit-picking experience.

"So, how much do you like him?" Keely pressed.

"Um, I don't know. I guess I'm still figuring that out," I said shyly.

"Where's he taking you?"

"The Firebird," I said tentatively. It hadn't been what I'd expected. It was pretty much the only restaurant in town deemed acceptable by any of the visiting professors, meaning that it served more than pizza and didn't automatically assume Parmesan sprinkled from a can conveyed authentic.

Keely raised an eyebrow. "Wow. That's like . . . clutch."

"Yeah." I didn't tell her I still didn't know what *clutch* meant.

Just then, the doorbell rang, a three-part chime that echoed through the house. Keely and I exchanged a look, and she burst into a peal of nervous, excited laughter.

"That's him!" she said loudly, as if it could possibly be anyone else. She raced down the stairs and I followed behind slowly.

"Everything's going to be fine," I whispered to myself. A fantasy flashed through my mind: Matt and I going to the winter formal, me getting on the train at Thirtieth Street Station in Philadelphia to greet him. He'd catch the train in Concord, and he'd spend weekends curled up in my bed in my UPenn dorm. Maybe it could work.

"Hey!" Matt pulled Keely into an embrace. I noticed how perfectly they fit together. Whenever I hugged someone, it was awkward — my cheek would hit their shoulder, or my lips would graze their lips instead of their cheeks. But Keely and Matt were naturals, as though they'd always done this.

Matt's gaze flicked up. "Hey, Hayley," he said, as if he were seeing me after months away and not only a few hours. He twirled his keys on his finger. I emitted a shaky sigh. *What was I doing?*

"Everything all right?" Matt raised an eyebrow. "Your wipeout the other day was epic. You've got to be hurting. I saw you, like, wincing in the hall the other day."

"I'm perfect." The word sounded off to my ears. I wondered when Matt had spotted me. Had he seen me darting into the cafeteria and sitting, sentry-like, by the entrance, in hopes of seeing my sister? Drinking an extra-large Coffee Hut coffee to make up for the fact that I'd barely slept? Or just looking all-around terrorized, exhausted, and sleep-deprived? And no matter what, if he'd *seen* me so upset, why hadn't he done any-thing about it?

"Well, you crazy kids have fun!" Keely chirped. I tried to shake my weird mood off. I remembered back when Keely used to categorize people by whether they looked like muffins, birds, or horses. *Everyone looks like one of the three!* I'd almost for-gotten that beneath her blown-out hair and perfectly rolled field-hockey skirts she had a goofy streak. I gazed quizzically at Matt. He was a muffin, but in a good way. I liked his half smile, the way his hair flopped over his forehead, like the top of a muffin rising from the pan. Which was an observation that made it even more explicitly apparent that I desperately needed sleep.

"Are you ready?" Matt looked up at me strangely.

I nodded.

"All right." Matt led me toward his car and opened the door. "Sorry it's kind of a mess," he said, pushing a pile of books, including an SAT prep guide, to the floor.

"You're studying?" I asked.

"Yeah. I actually have class for it tomorrow, so I can't get too crazy tonight. My first try kinda sucked. I'm hoping the next time will be better," he said.

"Well, just keep trying!" I said. I was surprised to hear an edge in my voice, but Matt didn't seem to notice. What was my problem? I hadn't seen my sister in days. I was on a date. Everything was *fine*. "I mean, it's not bad to take the SAT more than once, if you want to improve your score."

"Let me guess," Matt said as he backed out of the driveway. "You got a perfect score the first time."

"I did all right." I shrugged. "Um, I like your shirt," I said, changing the subject. It was a plain blue button-down, paired with khakis. A nothing-special, standard-guy uniform.

"Thanks." Matt nodded and reached toward his iPod. As the Grateful Dead filled the car, I allowed myself to relax into the seat. *Everything is fine*, I repeated to myself, careful that I didn't say the words out loud. If Matt called me out, I wasn't sure I could laugh along with him. At least not until I calmed down some.

I glanced back down at the pile of books. Books were something that made sense. I could talk about books. My eye landed on *One Hundred Years of Solitude*.

"So you're a Márquez fan?" I asked, pleasantly surprised.

"No, I mean, not yet. It's actually yours. It fell from your locker the other day."

"Really?" The familiar, clammy, nervous feeling caused my skin to prickle. *Had* the book been in my locker? I didn't remember.

"Yeah. I didn't mean to steal it. I just wanted to look at it. Find out why you like it." He shrugged.

"So, what do you think?"

"The truth?" Matt asked. "I thought it was kind of stupid. Just, like, a waste of time. This family's so trippy. Every character has the same name, and then the same crap keeps happening over and over again. It's like, why don't they just realize that they're in over their heads and move someplace else?" Matt asked.

"Because then it wouldn't be a book," I teased. "You need conflict!"

"Do you? Because I'm usually fine chilling," Matt said.

"Me too," I said as the car crested onto Main Street.

"You never chill, Westin. You're, like, the opposite of chill."

"Hot?" The word slipped out of my mouth before I had a chance to think. My face burned bright red as Matt smiled.

"Yeah. Hot."

Thankfully, before I could embarrass myself further, he turned into the large parking lot in the center of town. He parked, then hurried around the car to open my door.

"I'm really happy we're hanging out," Matt said shyly as we walked toward the restaurant.

"Me too." *Now* everything seemed fine. Better than fine. *This* was what I'd always wanted. Not a perfect SAT score. Not another trophy. I'd spent the last eighteen years running, terrified to ever slow down or stop. And now that I had — and the world hadn't crumbled and I'd still reached the Ainsworth finals — it made me realize how much I'd missed out on in the past. And how much I didn't want to miss in the future.

"You know I had a crush on you in kindergarten?" Matt asked.

"You did?" I was glad that the sun had already set so he wouldn't see me wildly blushing.

"You want to know why?"

"Yes! I mean . . . if you want to tell me." I shivered as we walked down the cobblestoned sidewalk. Matt put his arm around my shoulder and pulled me into him. I could feel his warmth emanating from his jacket, and his scent — detergent, wood smoke, and toothpaste — was a perfect, tingly-inducing blend. I leaned in more closely.

"I liked the way you pronounced *animal*," he said finally. "You said it like —"

"Aminal, I know." My kindergarten teacher, Mrs. Bradley, had made me say the word over and over again in front of the class. *How can you not hear the difference? It's obvious to everyone*, she said. But it wasn't to me. That night, I'd come home, crying, and had stayed up the whole night, hugging Pandemonium, my stuffed panda, as I whispered the word over and over to myself, stopping only when I was one hundred percent sure I was pronouncing it the correct way. The next morning, I'd marched to Mrs. Bradley's desk, told her that her behavior was *animalistic*, and sat down to do a worksheet. I smiled at the memory, then wondered . . . would my twin have done that when she was seven?

"It was cute."

"Maybe it was to you. To me it was pretty much the single worst experience of my childhood. If I need years of therapy in the future, I'm sending the bill to Mrs. Bradley," I joked.

"And what if you became a billionaire? Would you send her some stock options? Because it goes both ways. What if your destiny was a life of crime, until her early humiliating intervention made you realize that you didn't want to break the rules — pronunciation-related or otherwise? Maybe that made you into the driven overachiever you are today. If anything, I think you should be *thanking* her."

"Maybe . . ." Wasn't it the same thing with my twin? I could either blame her or thank her, but one thing was for sure: She'd been impacting my life for the past seventeen years. And the worst part was, I'd never even known.

"Just kidding," Matt said quickly, misunderstanding my silence as disapproval. "Mrs. Bradley was a total jerk."

"You can't call a sixty-five-year-old lady names!" I reached my arm up to good-naturedly punch him on the shoulder, then dropped it to my side. We'd reached the Firebird's red-and-gold awning. I felt a tug of disappointment. Going inside meant that the date was that much closer to ending. And I didn't want it to end.

The interior of the restaurant was cozy and redbrick, with the crackling fireplace, wall sconces, and sprays of delicate flower arrangements on each table proving its position as one of Bainbridge's most expensive spots.

"Hello." The host stepped in front of us.

"What's up, bro?" Matt asked. I smiled, loving how Matt was so comfortable in his own skin that he could simultaneously set up a reservation at a high-end restaurant and call everyone "bro."

"Is this all right?" Matt asked anxiously as we were led to a table.

"It's perfect. No," I said quickly. "I mean, it *is* perfect, but that wasn't what I meant to say. I meant to say it's . . . magic," I decided. I'd had enough of perfect.

"To magic," he said gently, raising his water glass. I raised mine, too, and we clinked, but it was too hard, and a constellation of water spilled on my — Keely's — dress.

I instantly stood up and started to wipe it off but Matt only smiled.

"You know, in some cultures, spilling on yourself means you're going to have good luck."

"Yeah? Where?" I asked.

"What, you don't know?" he teased.

"Contrary to what you seem to think, I definitely don't know everything." I realized that the water was seeping into my tights. "Why don't you use this time to look up what culture thinks spilling on yourself is good luck, and I'll clean up."

It wasn't the smoothest exit, but it wasn't terrible. I hurried to the back of the restaurant, where I was thankful to realize that I was the only one in the bathroom. I hastily began wiping the wet spot on the fabric, but the napkin caused little white lint balls to shed on the gray.

Finally, once I'd done as much damage control as was possible, I left the restroom, ready to head back and talk to Matt about a subject that didn't make me seem super-smart or super-weird. Like hockey. Or Spotify.

But just as I was coming up with a list of Keely-like conversation topics, I stopped in my tracks.

A girl was sitting opposite Matt. Gray dress. Shoulder-skimming brown hair pulled into a low ponytail. The barest hint of lip gloss. It was me.

My heart surged. I wanted to scream, but I couldn't. What was I supposed to do? All I could do was watch as she raised her hand to push her hair back from her forehead. Her blue eyes were wide and her cheekbones stood out from her heart-shaped face. Her bangs — the forever-too-long ones that always seemed to stick to my forehead or hook awkwardly behind my ears — had hints of gold in the strands. The dress hugged her curves in a way that I didn't see when I'd looked in the mirror. She was beautiful.

And it wasn't a word that I was using as some self-compliment. I knew what I looked like, and I knew that I could be cute. But even though she looked like me, the way she moved was far different. I was mesmerized by the way her hand glided over the rough-hewn wooden table and toward Matt's forearm, the way she tilted her head so the shadows of the candle flame flickered across her skin, the way she seemed preternaturally aware that everyone in the room was giving them a second glance. And why shouldn't they have been? They looked like the perfect couple.

A waitress emerged from the kitchen, practically bumping into me. She glared at me, and I watched as she headed to the table where Matt and my twin were sitting.

I opened my mouth to say something, but nothing came out. What could I say? What could I do? She'd planned this, just like she'd planned everything else. Was she going to stay for the entire date? What would she tell Matt? She was wearing a similar dress to mine. Was that a coincidence, or had she been spying at me at Keely's house?

You said you wanted to wear the gray dress. Ingrid's throwaway comment suddenly took on an entirely different meaning. Somehow, when I was looking for her, she'd found *them*. Had she been spying on me the whole time, ready to become me whenever I turned my back? I thought she was finished torturing me, but it was clear: She'd only just begun. *Of course.*

Matt would notice. He knew me. He knew the way I talked to myself and the weird stuff I found funny, the stuff she wouldn't know, no matter how much spying she'd done. Waiters and busboys rushed in and out, but none of them gave me a second glance. It was as if I was invisible. No one noticed that my life was in the process of being stolen from me.

Just then, she scraped her chair back, smiled at Matt, and allowed her hand to linger on his shoulder.

"I'll be back in a second!" I heard her voice over the dining room din. It was lower than mine — the type of voice that would use words like *darling* or *lovely* without irony. Why couldn't he tell? Then, she sauntered away from him as if she had all the time in the world, clutching her phone and smiling at the host, the waiter, and the other patrons as she walked toward the back — toward me.

I took a tentative step forward, ready to confront her, when all of a sudden a busboy crashed through the kitchen doors, his over-laden tray clattering onto the sandstone floor. I jumped to get away from the debris, and as I did, I saw her slip out a rear door.

"Are you all right, miss?" The busboy sat back on his heels and looked up at me. I nodded and numbly headed toward the table.

"Are you okay?" Matt asked, his eyebrows furrowing in concern.

"Do I seem okay?" My voice was sharp.

"Yeah. I mean . . . I guess so."

I nodded tightly. How could he not have noticed that he was talking to a totally different girl?

"Is that the right answer?" Matt asked. "Or did you have another one in mind?" There was an edge to his tone as well.

I shook my head. "No, it's fine. I'm fine." The word got stuck in my throat. I looked away. Before, I'd loved the way Matt's eyes had lit up when he'd seen me in the school parking lot. But now, after seeing them light up for *her*, his gaze felt tainted. The whole night was tainted. I knew that my sister had been sending me a message by showing up, only what was it? That she could steal my life? That she was watching me? That I couldn't try to predict her actions? All of the above?

The silence between us widened as Matt glanced from the table to the bar to the framed landscape painting of rolling Tuscan hills mounted above the fireplace.

Finally, Matt cleared his throat.

"You seem really quiet all of a sudden. Like, shy. What's going on?" he said finally.

"Just tired. I'm glad to be here." I sounded far less convincing than I had earlier, and I knew he knew it.

"Good," Matt said. The same strained silence fell over us again. "So, what sports are you into?"

"None, really. You play hockey, right?" I felt like I was about to cry. Things had spiraled wildly out of control: My twin was out there, she *wasn't* going to go away, and I was trying to act normal on a date. Just then, the waiter arrived and placed a steaming plate of shrimp and mussels atop linguine in front of me.

"The seafood special!" he announced loudly.

Of course. I was allergic to shellfish. Which my twin must have known. My stomach rolled in fresh waves of nausea.

"Fresh pepper?" the waiter asked, holding the grinder aloft like a trophy.

"Sure," I said, watching the flakes rain down on my food. What did it matter? I noticed her abandoned white napkin sitting next to the plate, a blotted raspberry-kiss smirk all too evident. It looked like it was mocking me. I shook the napkin out and smoothed it in my lap, obscuring the mark.

"Great." Matt grabbed his fork and stared down at his plate

of pasta. And I may have imagined it, but I could have sworn I heard laughter in the background.

And then, I noticed something on the floor.

It was a luxurious black leather purse, far more expensive-looking than the canvas satchel I toted everywhere. I leaned under the table and frantically grabbed it, rifling through it and pulling out a wallet.

Matt put his fork down. "Are you leaving?"

I didn't listen. I opened the wallet, feeling my stomach free fall as the girl in the driver's license displayed in the ID window stared back at me.

Jamie Thomson-Thurm. 167 Revere Drive.

Finally, I knew the identity of my sister.

But she had mine.

CHAPTER 18

J pushed myself back from the table. "I need to leave," I said. "Now." She had my wallet. She had my ID. With my ID, she could do whatever she wanted — which must have been her plan. She wanted to mess up my Ainsworth chances, to make me freak out about the future. Or at least, she wanted me to *think* that was what she was doing. *Had she killed Leah?* And if she had, then what else might she do?

"Is everything all right?" Matt rose to his feet.

"No. I'm sorry." I wove between tables, knowing everyone was staring. I felt a hand on my shoulder. I whirled around and shrugged it off.

"Don't touch me!" I yelled in a ragged voice I didn't recognize as my own.

Matt's face fell and two waiters hurried to his side, half restraining him. I knew I needed to say everything was okay, but I was panicking, feeling like a caged animal caught in a trap. Deep down, I knew Matt wasn't the enemy. But I also didn't know how I could possibly explain everything to him. What I needed was to find Jamie. And until then, Matt wouldn't be safe. Better he think I was a psycho and stay away than cross paths with Jamie.

Based on her last name, I could only assume she lived with our father. It made no sense based on what my mother had told me about James running away, but at this point, the lies were starting to bleed into the truth. There was no one left to trust.

My feet thwacked against the pavement as I ran to the Greyhound bus station on the other end of Main Street. I'd never taken the bus, but it seemed like the fastest, easiest way to get out of town. I was done playing detective. I'd fallen into her trap. And I wasn't going to do that anymore.

The bus station was tiny and empty, except for two students with huge camping-type backpacks sleeping on the metal chairs. There wasn't a bus attendant, only a dirty schedule taped to the tiled wall.

I squinted at it. It was barely visible in the dim fluorescent lighting and the numbers swam in front of me.

Just then, a bus pulled up to the curb.

I raced outside and onto the first step of the bus.

"Boston?" I asked.

"Well, we can bring you through Concord, and then you can catch another bus from there." The bus driver glanced dubiously down the stairs at me, surely thinking I was some sort of teen runaway.

"That's fine." I fished a twenty from Jamie's purse, and picked my way through the seats. I wanted to be by myself. But the only seat available was next to a large man holding a cat carrier in his lap.

As soon as the bus lurched out from the station, I dumped out the contents of Jamie's purse on my lap. There was the oxblood-red wallet, containing a driver's license, a few credit cards, and a stack of crisp twenties. I opened the zippered compartment and pulled out a pile of papers.

Receipt from a coffee place. A picture of a brown guinea pig with a white tuft of fur on its head. Was that her pet? It was such an odd thing to carry, but it also made me feel a little less panicky. Murderers don't carry around pictures of cute animals, do they? The picture was faded, and the corner was frayed. It was clear the photo was old. I turned it over. In childlike handwriting were the words *Peanut Butter. I named him after my favorite thing in the world.*

I gently tucked the photo back. More receipts. Then I found it. An index card with my passwords, my Social Security number.

My whole life.

I slumped down in my seat, aware that the man carrying the cat was looking at me strangely. Adrenaline surged through my veins. *167 Revere Drive.* In my mind, I repeated the words over and over, the syllables the only thing I was sure of. Once I met my father, I'd have proof that there had been two babies. I'd have someone on my side. And then — *then* — I could go to the police with proof and confront my mother and make everything go back to the way it should be.

167 Revere Drive, 167 Revere Drive. The words lulled my brain, made me stop thinking of what Jamie would be doing now that she was in Bainbridge.

"Miss?"

A meow, followed by a hiss. The man with the cat carrier was trying to get past me.

"Where are we?" I asked.

"Concord," he announced.

"Concord? I have to go!" I leaped to my feet and raced down the bus steps into another dingy bus station. I headed toward the lone ticket window. The tired-looking clerk raised an eyebrow.

"Boston, please?"

"Bus doesn't leave until seven."

"There's nothing earlier?" I pressed.

The clerk shook her head.

"All right." I shoved a twenty through the metal grille of the window, then settled on a hard plastic chair to wait — while my sister was probably wrecking my life.

When the bus finally rolled up to Boston, my eyes were gritty and dry from being awake so long and my heart was hammering against my chest as though I'd downed two extra-large espressos — even though I hadn't had anything except the water at the restaurant last night.

I blinked as I wavered unsteadily outside the bus terminal. I'd been to Boston a few times before, on school trips, but never often enough to know my way around. All of my fellow passengers seemed to have some sense of where they were going. I just had the Brookline address. I stumbled out to the taxi line, blinking in the weak sun. I flexed and unflexed my toes inside my shoes, then did the same with my calf muscles. It didn't help.

"Taxi?" A driver jerked his thumb toward the black-and-white cab idling on the corner.

I nodded.

"One sixty-seven Revere Drive?" I asked. "In Brookline."

The taxi driver nodded. My breath came in short bursts. James Thomson-Thurm was English. He had two children. He enjoyed parasailing, waterskiing, and opera. He had, at one point, been in love with my mother.

What if he doesn't believe me? The thought crept into my mind. Meanwhile, back in Bainbridge, everyone would believe Jamie was me.

"Right here?" The cab driver pulled up to a four-story Victorian house at the center of a circular drive. Or, *house* wasn't the right word. It was a mansion, straight from an architecture magazine. It wasn't the type of place I'd imagined a professor of medieval history would live. And yet . . .

"Is this one sixty-seven?" I asked, squinting at the address.

"Yes, ma'am. That'll be thirty dollars."

I pulled out Jamie's wallet and peeled two twenties from the front of the stack in the main compartment. A sticky note was affixed to it.

> And you think I don't care about your well-being?
> Enjoy Massachusetts.

The note was signed with a heart.

She'd known. She'd *known* I would come here. The computer history. *Of course.*

"Thirty?" the driver pressed.

I passed the two crisp twenties toward him.

I balled my hands together, my fingers digging into my palms. It was now or never. *My name is Hayley Westin. You knew my mother, Wendy. Almost eighteen years ago, I was born. . . .*

It was the speech of my life — literally. All I needed to do was look him in the eye and tell the truth.

Steeling my courage, I walked up the flagstone path and rang the bell. Almost immediately, as though I'd been watched, the door swung open.

I was standing face-to-face with my father. He looked more weather-beaten than the man in the picture on the back of the book jacket, but the piercing eyes were the same.

I took a deep breath. "First, I'm not Jamie. I'm Hayley. And I . . ."

He laughed, a loud angry bark. "Don't even do this to us. Not now." He grabbed my arm and pulled me inside, through a gleaming hallway and into a large, well-lit kitchen. A beautifully manicured backyard was visible through the glass sliding doors, with trees wrapped in burlap sacks for the winter.

"Wait. Do you know who I am?" I yanked my elbow away from him. He grabbed it back.

"Deborah!" he bellowed. I detected the slightest trace of a British accent. In the very rare times I'd ever pictured us meeting, I thought we'd be introduced at someplace cozy, like the Ugly Mug. I never imagined him speaking to me in a hate-filled voice that made me tremble every time he opened his mouth.

A thin woman made her way into the kitchen. She was wearing a pair of black slacks and a purple cashmere sweater. It was impossible to tell her age — she could have been anywhere between forty and sixty-five — but what struck me were her eyes. Large, blue, and flickering, making it impossible to hold eye contact. She was clearly James's wife, but why did she look so angry with me?

Unless . . .

"You think I'm Jamie," I said slowly.

"We're not playing games anymore. Yes, we think you're Jamie. Yes, we think you're our daughter," the woman said, her voice low, musical, and vaguely threatening.

"I'm not Jamie. I'm *Hayley*. Her twin. Hayley Westin."

Deborah and the man — my *father* — locked eyes, but it was impossible to read what they were trying to tell each other.

"Hayley," Deborah hissed. "How convenient."

Jamie's father shook his head sadly. "Dr. Morrison said this could happen. It's called splitting. It's just another sign that she's a very sick girl. And, of course, knowing she has a twin makes it that much easier to imagine an alternate personality. That's why Wendy and I had agreed to keep it a secret." He shook his head angrily. "Anyway, that place he told us about up in Maine is supposed to be the best, and I think with the right therapy, and maybe some electroshock, she could resume a normal life. . . ." he said, as though I weren't in the room.

"I didn't know about Jamie. Jamie was the one who found *me*, and Jamie's the one trying to take over my life. I came to stop it. And you have to help me. You have to at least believe me!" I locked eyes with James. I knew my voice was getting dangerously shaky, that I was on the verge of sounding like I was having a breakdown. I took a deep breath and went back to what I'd meant to say. "I'm Hayley Kathryn Westin. My mother is Wendy, and eighteen years ago, you and . . ."

James's face crumpled, then hardened. He took a menacing step toward me.

"Stop it!" Deborah shouted. She put her hands on my shoulders. "Jamie. Hayley. Stop it," she said. The scent of her jasmine-and-honey perfume was overpowering. I tried to pull away, but she only tightened her grip. Behind her, a dark-haired boy padded into the kitchen. He was about my age, with shaggy hair that curled over his ears. He had the same blue eyes as his mother, but the half smile looked like my father's on the book jacket. Which meant he had to be my half brother.

I stared at him, trying to get him to understand what was going on. I barely knew myself. "I'm not your sister, am I?" I asked, holding a wide, unblinking gaze and hoping he'd see something — a freckle, a gesture, a scar — that Jamie didn't have.

He turned away, his shoulders stiffening. "I thought she wasn't coming back," he said in a hard voice.

"Aidan, go upstairs. You don't need to see this," James said firmly.

"See what? See Jamie self-destruct . . . again?" Aidan asked, sitting down at the kitchen table, his eyes flicking from Deborah to James, then back again. "Should we just call the police this time? Because I bet she did something she shouldn't have. It was the stolen car last time. What do you think it is this time? Murder? What did you do, Jamie?" he asked.

"I'm sorry," I said finally, breaking the silence. It was another Alice in Wonderland moment. I'd fallen down the rabbit hole and couldn't make sense of the information being presented to me. Was I Jamie? Was I Hayley? Or was I someone else entirely? "If you can just listen to me, I'll explain. . . ."

"We don't need your explanations. And *sorry* doesn't work anymore," the man said in a low voice, as threatening as the sound of a far-off thunderstorm.

"James," Deborah said in a low voice. "Why don't you call Dr. Morrison. We can't talk rationally with her. It'll hurt her, and it'll hurt us. She needs help."

James paused, then nodded once. As he left the room, Deborah and I stared at each other.

"You stole from us. We're your *family*. This is trust. And I don't know if we'll ever get that back," Deborah said slowly.

"I know this sounds crazy. I know you don't believe me. But I'm Hayley. And if I can just call someone, I can prove —"

"Prove that you're manipulative? That you've found more people to pull into your web of lies? No. You won't do that. I know James believes in you, but I don't. I really don't. You turn eighteen in a few months, and then we're done. We can't be responsible for someone who's so willfully irresponsible about everyone and everything in her life. When I think back to you as a child . . . the guinea pig —" She broke off.

"What guinea pig?" I asked, fear climbing up my spine.

"Only my favorite thing in the world," Aidan said. My mind flashed to the picture in the wallet, the childish handwriting.

"Peanut Butter?" I asked reflexively, before I could stop myself.

"Good memory," Aidan said tightly. "Especially for someone who apparently has no idea who Jamie is."

I thought of the picture in the wallet.

Deborah shot a warning look at Aidan, then turned toward me.

"Stop it. For all of our sakes, just stop it." She'd grabbed a napkin from the center of the table and was shredding it into smaller and smaller pieces, which rained down like snow on the table.

Just then, James came into the room. "It's all set. They have emergency protocol for situations like this. They won't be long."

"So what do we do with her until then?" Aidan asked.

"We wait," James said tersely. He folded his arms across his chest.

"Can we talk?" I asked in a small voice. Being in this house, surrounded by Jamie's family, made it hard to think. I felt guilty, as if I were Jamie. Everyone was staring at me. No matter what I said, they wouldn't believe me.

And so I bolted. I ran toward the sliding glass doors and yanked. They wouldn't budge. I turned on my heel to run toward the front and was tackled by Aidan, who was six inches taller than I was. I lost my balance and fell, my head cracking against the floor.

"Ow!" I yelped. I frantically wrestled against his grip, while Deborah and James looked on.

"Let go! You don't want to get hurt!" Deborah called.

Aidan let go, and I took the moment to wipe tears of pain from my eyes.

"I'm sorry," I said helplessly. Everything I'd planned to say had disappeared from my brain. I'd walked into Jamie's trap. And the worst thing was that even though I knew it, I couldn't explain it to these people, who were staring at me with hate in their eyes.

"Sit down," Deborah said tonelessly.

I meekly perched on one of the wooden chairs at the kitchen table, watching the three of them. James kept clenching his jaw, while Deborah stared at the floor. Only Aidan looked at me. I turned away.

Finally, Deborah placed her hand on Aidan's shoulder. "Can you watch her? We'll just be in the next room," Deborah whispered as she and James headed through the archway into the dining room.

Aidan sat down beside me.

"You know you're so busted, don't you?" He asked.

I paused and gazed into his eyes. Could I make him my ally? It was a long shot, but at least he was *looking* at me. I opened my mouth.

"I know this sounds weird. I *know* it does. But I'm really Jamie's twin. I can —" The doorbell rang, cutting me off.

"That's them," James announced to no one in particular, dashing through the room toward the door.

"I hate you," Aidan spat.

"I'm sorry." It was the only phrase I could think of, and even though I kept saying it again and again, I knew it wasn't enough for whatever Jamie had done.

Just then, James came back into the room, two men in white coats behind him.

"She's getting violent," he warned.

That was all they needed to act. One of them lunged toward me, half dragging me from my seated position while the other grabbed my chin and placed two tablets on my tongue. Too surprised to spit them out, I swallowed, tasting their acrid, lawn-fertilizer-like taste.

I coughed to try to spit up the medicine, but it was too late. The pills had dissolved and were already making their way into my bloodstream.

"I'm sorry, Jamie. I hope you know that. And I hope you know we want . . . we want a change. We believe in a change.

But we can't live like this anymore," James said sorrowfully. "You can take her. Thank you."

Fight, a voice in my brain screamed. But I didn't have any fight left in me. I didn't have *anything* left in me. All I wanted to do was curl up into a ball and go to sleep — and never, ever wake up.

"I'm sorry, baby girl. One day, I hope you'll understand," James muttered as the two orderlies dragged me to an unmarked black car.

One of them opened the rear door and shoved me inside. I heard the click of the lock as the two of them climbed into the front, closing a barrier between the front and the back.

The car rolled away from the curb. Even though the windows were closed, I could hear garbage trucks beeping in the distance and the nervous chattering of sparrows in the bare tree branches around us. The world was just waking up, and it was impossible to reconcile the fact that my life as I'd known it was falling apart. And there was nothing I could do about it.

CHAPTER 19

I awoke to commotion around me. The two orderlies were standing above me, unbuckling my seat belt and transferring me to a wheelchair.

"I'm awake!" I said, struggling to consciousness. "I'm fine!"

I wasn't. My brain felt like it was swathed in cotton and my tongue felt far too large for my mouth.

"Steady," one of the orderlies said. He stepped to the side, and I saw a wiry, short man rushing toward me, a stethoscope flopping back and forth on his chest.

"Jamie Thomson-Thurm," he announced. He leaned down toward me. "Jamie, I'm Dr. Taylor, and I'll be taking care of you. Let's get her inside."

The two orderlies half pulled me to my feet. I caught a whiff of salt in the air. We had to be near the ocean. But I knew I wasn't going to get a chance to actually see it. Surrounding me was a series of two-story cottages arranged around a large rough-hewn wooden structure, reminding me more of a summer camp than a mental hospital, which is what it was. It had to be. After all, the property was enclosed by a wrought-iron gate. The very few people I saw wandering around the lawns were either wearing scrubs or had a wristband on their arm. Just like the one on my own arm that must have been placed there while I was unconscious.

Dr. Taylor seemed unfazed by the commotion of the orderlies trying to drag me toward the building.

"I hope you had a good sleep, Jamie," Dr. Taylor said, falling into step beside me. I kept blinking to try to get my contacts to slide back over my pupils and make everything slip back into focus. "Welcome to Serenity Point. I know that you had a couple sleeping pills, so you're probably feeling a bit groggy. That's normal. I've been talking to your doctor back home about your medication, and we might do a few tweaks here and there, depending on your response. It's very important that you keep us abreast of any new feelings or changes that arise as we do, is that clear?" he asked.

"*Yesh* . . . I mean, yes," I said, correcting the lisp that had come out of my mouth. My legs felt like jelly, and I was winded even though we'd only walked a few hundred yards from the entrance to the main building.

"Good. Let's bring her to my office," Dr. Taylor commanded once we stepped inside the lobby immediately past the building entrance. It was empty except for one couch, and a coffee table with pamphlets spread along the surface. *Frequently Asked Questions about Electroshock Treatments*, read one of the brochures. But before I could read the other titles, the two orderlies dragged me down a small corridor. From the outside, I'd assumed the building would look like a hospital, with long, polished linoleum floors and an antiseptic smell. But the walls were covered with terrible paintings of landscapes and the floor had a dingy blue carpet on it. Finally, I was unceremoniously deposited into a small, spare room.

"Sit down," one orderly grunted, nodding toward a couch with a thin, stained cushion.

"Let the nurses' station knows she's here so we can make sure her room is ready," Dr. Taylor said as I tried to get my bearings. The tiny room seemed similar to one of the ones in the guidance suite. But instead of piles of papers, Dr. Taylor's desk contained only a laptop and a single sunflower in a bud vase. The walls were bare and I felt a sudden longing for Miss Keeshan's stupid HANG IN THERE! sloth poster. Anything that would make this place seem more human.

Dr. Taylor perched in the chair behind the desk, steepled his fingers together, and stared at me. "Now, tell me why you're here, Jamie."

I glanced up at the ceiling. A watermark looked like an oddly shaped heart. The sound of the white noise machine whooshed in my ears. *Think*, I urged myself. My brain used to gear into overdrive under pressure. Not anymore. All I could think about were James's eyes. The terrified look Aidan had shot me when he mentioned his guinea pig. The fact that there truly wasn't anywhere to escape to.

"Jamie?" Dr. Taylor prompted.

Trapped. Trapped trapped trapped, my mind screamed. I twisted the hospital ID bracelet around my wrist.

Dr. Taylor leaned his elbows on his knees. "That was an unfair question. I apologize."

I glanced up gratefully into his beady pupils.

"Why don't you start by telling me a little bit about yourself. As you can see, I have some notes, but I'd much rather hear it from you. In your words." He rapped against the stack of manila file folders with his fingers. I leaned forward, trying to see what was inside them, but they were rubber-banded together, making any chance of reading an impossibility.

"I'm not Jamie," I said finally, my voice husky and unfamiliar to my ears. "I'm her twin. I'm *Hayley*. I went to Brookline this morning because I knew that was where my father lived. And I needed to explain what she's been doing for the past few weeks. But that means she's in Bainbridge, and I'm just . . . I need to stop her. And now I'm stuck. And I feel like that's what she wanted."

"You're not Jamie." He glanced at his pad of paper and made a note. "All right. Then why don't you tell me a bit about who you are."

"I'm Hayley," I said again, trying to mask my frustration. "Hayley Westin, from Bainbridge, New Hampshire. I never knew I had a twin. I always thought I was an only child. And then my mom told me that I *did* have a twin, but that she had died. And now . . . well, now I don't know. I mean, my mom lied to me. But I don't know why."

A low, single chime sounded and Dr. Taylor stood up and strode around to the front of the desk. He reached down and held his hand out toward me.

I looked away. I didn't want to speak to him, much less touch him. He dropped his hand to his side.

"Well, Hayley, it's nice to meet you. Unfortunately, we don't have a full session today, but we'll make sure to get the schedule sorted out so you'll have a full forty-five minutes with me tomorrow, and every day following."

"No!" I screamed. "I don't need that. I need you to believe me." The pills had worn off, unleashing my panic. "I need to get *out* of here and call the police. Jamie is impersonating me, she may have killed someone, and if I don't get out of here, then everyone will believe her. Seriously, people are in danger."

Dr. Taylor nodded impassively as he tapped his pen against the folder. "It sounds like you have a lot of anger, Hayley. That's understandable, and we'll discuss it in detail. But the one thing I ask, if that makes sense, is that you bring Jamie to the session tomorrow."

"How can I do that? She's not here. She's in New Hampshire, pretending to be *me*!" I screamed. A hint of a smile crossed Dr. Taylor's face. "I mean," I said, trying to calm down my breathing and my hammering heart, "I think there's been a terrible mistake. What could I do to get you to believe me?"

Dr. Taylor rose to his feet. "We're out of time. I know you're upset. And I feel that after a rest, you'll be better able to talk to me about what's really bothering you."

"I don't need a rest. I'm Hayley. Look me up. You'll find me."

"I'll find *your sister*," Dr. Taylor said tersely, impatience weaving into his voice. "And we will talk tomorrow, Hayley." At this, he pressed a button. A chime sounded, and a bleached-blond nurse wearing a set of hot-pink scrubs walked in. "You have to come to terms with who you are, so you can move beyond it."

"Hi there. I'm Nanci, the nurse assigned to your cottage. Come on, Jamie doll, we'll get you settled," she said, bustling toward me. She had a hint of a Southern accent and her blush was unevenly applied, giving her moon-shaped face a lopsided look.

Dr. Taylor cleared his throat. "The patient mentioned that she'd prefer to be called Hayley for the time being."

"It doesn't matter," I mumbled. If I fought, I'd only be branded crazy. I needed another plan, one that didn't depend on anyone. I just needed to be able to think.

"All right, Hayley, let's hop up to your room. Your roommate's so excited to meet you!" the nurse clucked, as though she were a nursery school teacher trying to convince a child to share the art supplies.

I helplessly trailed behind the nurse, through the long corridors of the facility, then out into the open air. This would be over in a matter of hours, I reminded myself. It had to be. I was too smart to be trapped. It had been a good try on Jamie's part. But I was smarter than her. I was stronger than her.

We trudged along the gravel path, and I wondered wildly if it'd be possible to escape: to sprint from the path, scale the fence, and spring to the nearest town.

Finally, the nurse stopped in front of one of the six cottages that flanked the central building. She walked up the sagging porch steps and unlocked the door.

"You'll be with Sheila." She motioned for me to follow her up a winding staircase toward the second floor. It seemed that the hospital was on the grounds of a former hotel. The main facility was the actual hotel proper, while the buildings flanking it had been family vacation cottages.

The nurse pushed open a door to a room that was bare except for two twin beds. A girl sat cross-legged in one of them, staring into the distance with brilliant aqua eyes. She'd obviously cut her reddish-blond hair herself, and chunks stuck out haphazardly around her pointed, angular face.

"You!" Sheila exclaimed, pointing at me.

"Yes, Sheila. This is your new roommate, Jamie," Nanci said in a singsongy, infant-soothing voice.

"Where's Jenny?" Sheila blurted out.

Nanci pursed her lips as though she'd sucked on a lemon. "Oh, Sheila. Don't you worry about Jenny. She's in a better place right now. How about you focus on getting to know Jamie?"

"What happened to Jenny?" I asked, turning toward Nanci.

Nanci shook her head and gestured to the empty single bed.

"That's where you'll be sleeping. Everyone here wears hospital-issue clothing. That way, there's one fewer thing to think about. Don't you agree, Sheila?" It was only then that I realized Sheila was wearing a pair of shapeless black pants and a gray baggy T-shirt. The nurse squinted at me.

"I think you're a small. I'll get some clothes and some medication, and then you should be right as rain." She turned and left the room. She closed the door, but I realized it didn't matter. The room had a huge picture window looking into the hallway. I noticed a camera in the corner as well, an unflickering red light trained at me. We were being watched all the time.

Sheila coughed and I realized that she, too, was staring at me.

"Hey," I said awkwardly, perching on the edge of my own bed to face her. "So, I'm not here for very long, so . . ."

The radiator hissed and I jumped. Sheila emitted a low, loud cackle that seemed far too loud to have come from her tiny body.

"Everyone says that. Everyone's here forever. Unless they're like Jenny. Jenny escaped. Jenny's not coming back."

"Where did Jenny go?" I asked urgently. But just then, the door reopened and Nanci walked in, balancing a round tray that contained a tiny plastic cup and a large glass of water. Inside the cup were half a dozen multicolored pills. "Here are your meds," she said, holding the tray out toward me. "You'll feel much more comfortable when you take them."

"No," I shook my head. A lie formed in my mind. "I was a wreck when I came in because of the medications. I know Dr. Taylor wants me to get better. The only way I'll get better is if I can talk to him without taking anything."

"You can take it up with him. I'm just doing my job," Nanci said firmly, shaking the cup so the pills rattled together. "Come on, be a good girl. They'll go down easy, and you'll be nice and relaxed." She put the tray on a wooden dresser, picked up one of the cups, and pushed it closer to my mouth.

I panicked, visions of myself becoming an unblinking robot like Sheila coursing through my head.

"I said no!" I swatted her hand away, and the pills — a collection of hexagonal, trapezoidal, and rectangular capsules that reminded me of the blocks I'd once played with as a child — clattered to the floor and rolled under the bed.

"She was bad!" Sheila exclaimed, clapping her hand to her mouth in horror.

"Yes, Sheila, Jamie was very bad," Nanci said through gritted teeth. "All right, we'll try this again." She reached underneath the bureau and pressed a button.

"I'm really fine! I'm sorry!" I chirped, desperate to stop the situation from escalating. "I'll be good!"

"Well, we'll have to hope so, won't we?" Nanci muttered. "But you'll learn soon enough, it's best if you do what you're told. We want the best for you, Hayley."

"I'm *not* Hayley! I mean, I am. But I shouldn't be here. I just really need to figure this out." My voice broke into a half sob.

Nanci's gaze softened. "Everyone's here because they need to figure something out. And you'll learn that you can't do it on your own. Dr. Taylor will help. So will the meds. You just have to trust us."

Just then, another nurse burst into the room.

"What's the problem?" she asked.

"Judy, can you get her some more meds? We had an incident," Nanci said, gesturing to the mess on the floor.

"Of course." The tiny nurse disappeared out of the room. I looked back at Nanci.

"You know, I'm not staying here. This is a horrible mistake that will be fixed, and you'll be sued. You don't want that, do you?" I asked, trying to rationalize.

"Every patient says they'll sue. None of them ever do. Threats are a waste of time, honey." Nanci shook her head. "Now, you can either take your meds like a good girl, or we'll have to resort to other measures."

I gulped. I couldn't imagine what the *other measures* would be.

"Here you go," Judy said as she reentered the room, holding an identical tray filled with the same tiny plastic cup. I glanced at the capsules.

"I'll take them," I said.

"Smart girl," Nanci murmured.

I picked up the tiny cup and tipped it into my mouth, holding the pills under my tongue and hoping I could hold them there long enough to spit them out.

"Good. Now, take a nap like a good girl," Nanci said.

As soon as the door clicked closed, I lay facedown on the bed, knowing the camera wouldn't capture the angle. Then, I spat into my hand and wiped the half-dissolved lump of medication on the sheet under my pillow. Sheila was watching, wide-eyed. I knew either she'd tell the nurses or a housekeeper would discover the multicolored mess, but I'd be long gone by then.

"Can you keep a secret, Sheila?" I asked.

Sheila nodded, unblinking. "I kept Jenny's secret."

"What was it?"

"I can't tell you," Sheila said proudly, rocking back and forth. Sunlight was still spilling through the window, creating large patches of light on the floor. Even though there were no clocks anywhere, it was probably only midday. But the encroaching dread surrounding me made me feel as if darkness was fast approaching.

"Did Jenny . . . die?" I asked finally.

Sheila laughed, the loud cackle that made her sound older and more evil than seemed possible, given her appearance. "No. She only wished she had."

At that, the door clicked open again. Nanci strode in and grabbed Sheila by the shoulder.

"Sheila, I think it's time for a little talk, what do you say?" she asked, glaring at me as she dragged Sheila out the door.

Finally, I was alone.

And I was terrified.

CHAPTER 20

One day. Twelve pills. And even though I'd spit them out whenever a nurse's back was turned, I knew the medication was seeping into my system, and that the craziness surrounding me was seeping into my pores. I felt slow and shaky, with a second or two going by before I realized anyone was talking to me. The Ainsworth final interview was on Monday, less than twenty-four hours away. But all that seemed light-years ago. Now, all my attention was focused on getting through each hour without losing my Hayley-ness. And it was hard.

Even though I'd been there less than twenty-four hours, the routine was clear — and it was clear I'd go crazy if I actually had to follow it for longer than I already had. All meals were at a long, cafeteria-like table, with nurses sitting at each table to ensure every bite was eaten. Nurses monitored each shower door. Group therapy sessions happened in the morning and the afternoon, and there was a mandatory nap when the doors were locked. Sheila continued to stare at me. I'd learned she was sixteen and had been living at Serenity for almost a year. She liked it, she said. I couldn't tell if she was incredibly smart or incredibly out of it, but her wide-eyed stare unnerved me. When I'd fallen asleep the previous night, I'd woken up to her face inches away from mine. I'd screamed, and a night nurse had dragged Sheila back to her side of the room before slowly and methodically strapping her wrists and ankles to the bed with Velcro restraints.

"That'll keep you in one spot," the nurse said.

Sheila bleated a single cry of terror, but then the nurse must have given her medication, because her breathing had slowed into soft, deep snores that had freaked me out even more than seeing her face inches away from mine. Drugs were always used to calm people down, to keep them quiet, to make them obey the draconian rules. I knew it was better for me to stay under the radar and cooperate, but I couldn't help but feel my heart go out to Sheila. Had she gotten better in a year, or far worse? Judging from the way I felt after only one day, I think I knew my answer.

"Jamie?" Dr. Taylor asked, snapping his fingers in front of my face. It was my second therapy session with Dr. Taylor. Sessions occurred every day, with one on weekends and two each weekday, and it was clear that playing along was key to getting anyone to listen to me. "Tell me about Aidan."

"What about him?" I asked. Each session with Dr. Taylor was like playing verbal charades. I'd latch onto a name that sounded familiar and try to pump Dr. Taylor for clues. I figured that until I escaped, the best thing I could do was get as much information about Jamie as possible. I knew my father had adopted her with Deborah, and that Aidan was born only a few months after. I knew she'd been to a few different boarding schools and had a long record of shoplifting. I knew she blamed Aidan for everything.

"They're in the same grade?" I'd asked when Dr. Taylor probed me about the time *I* locked Aidan in the kindergarten coat closet, prompting a full-on panic when everyone assumed he'd been kidnapped. Apparently, the entire town had spent the night searching for him everywhere, while I'd contentedly sat on the couch, watching *Sesame Street* and hugging my stuffed polar bear.

Dr. Taylor had shot me a funny look. "Yes. *You're* in the same grade as your brother. Is that difficult for you?"

The question had given me pause. Because I could *see* how much it would suck. It'd be like having a twin with none of the benefits. Even in my brief time at the Thomson-Thurm house, I'd seen the adoring way James and Deborah had looked at Aidan and the accusatory glances they'd cast at "Jamie." Of course, her behavior warranted it. But what if Aidan had always been the favored child? If I had been her . . . well, maybe if I'd been in a similar situation, I'd have locked him in a closet, too.

That had been the last significant piece of information I'd gleaned about Jamie's family. It was as if Dr. Taylor had sensed that he'd overstepped, that I was eager for any drops of knowledge, and he'd retreated, relying on headshakes and nods.

"Jamie?" Dr. Taylor prodded, snapping me back into the moment.

"I'm not sure what to say about Aidan," I said slowly. The thick file on his desk had the answers.

"Tell me about how he makes you feel," he prodded.

I glanced at the model of the brain on Dr. Taylor's desk. I knew he performed electroshock therapy, and I knew that's where Sheila went when the nurses pulled her out of the room.

"Sad," I suggested.

"All right, anything else?"

"Mad?" I felt like we were playing a game of Mad Libs.

"I wonder if you can go deeper," Dr. Taylor mused, picking up the brain and turning it with his hands. I wondered if his subtext meant that he wondered whether a shock to my brain could make me go deeper.

"I don't know what to say," I said. I took a large sip of my coffee. Coffee wasn't officially allowed, since the nurses were worried about the caffeine interfering with the complicated pill combinations they were giving patients. But Dr. Taylor had made an exception for me, I think as a reward for no longer insisting on calling myself Hayley.

"Well, how are you adjusting here? Your roommate, Sheila . . . how do you like her?"

"I'm worried about her," I said, a brilliant idea forming in my mind. Everyone knew she had hallucinations, and when she did, it was all hands on deck to restrain her. If I could use her to provide a distraction, I could get the file. I could get the phone. And I could get my freedom. I smiled, despite myself, then quickly arranged my expression to a more somber one when I saw a flicker of concern on Dr. Taylor's face.

"Really?" Dr. Taylor leaned forward. "Talk to me about that. Why are you worried about her?"

"I feel like I have to look out for her. I guess it's sort of like the way I felt I was supposed to look out for Aidan. But I couldn't, because I was so wrapped up in my jealousy and anger. Now, I feel like I care about Sheila, and I want to have a good relationship with her. I guess it's a way of transferring my emotions and trying to fix the past," I said, throwing in plenty of therapy-like words that I knew Dr. Taylor would like. I smiled, despite myself. I was pretty proud of my off-the-cuff explanation.

"Yes, that's good!" Dr. Taylor excitedly took a sip of coffee. And then I had an idea.

"I really think I'd be most helped if I could see her now. If I could go back to my room and tell her this," I said. I needed to get Sheila on board, and fast. I was pretty sure I could convince her to help me, but I needed to set it in motion before her electroshock treatment, before I would spend another day longer than I had to here. Then, I'd call Matt. I didn't trust my mother — not when she'd lied to me about Jamie in the first place, not when I didn't even know whether she'd be at home or with Geofferson. But Matt would believe me — he'd been at the restaurant, he *had* to have noticed a difference between Jamie and me — and then, I'd get him to call the police while simultaneously getting me out of here.

"Really? You have another half an hour, and we're really digging up some interesting stuff. I think you might find it valuable to discuss . . ."

I shook my head vehemently. "I need to process stuff . . . please?"

Dr. Taylor paused, his eyes flicking from me to the clock on the wall. It was almost one o'clock, and I was hoping his hunger for lunch would be larger than his hunger for my own psychological breakthrough.

"All right." He pressed the buzzer on the corner of the desk to call for a nurse.

In a second, Nanci came to the door.

"Bye!" I called gleefully to Dr. Taylor, barely able to contain my excitement. This would work. It had to.

As soon as I got into the room, I glanced at Sheila, who was engaged in her usual activity of staring out the window. She turned toward me. She reminded me of a gerbil hyped up on caffeine, manic and jerky and desperate to please.

"I need your help." I glanced behind my shoulder at the always-on camera. I quickly stepped onto the bureau and ripped it from the wall, hoping the nurses were too busy doing rounds to notice it was out of commission.

"You broke it!" Sheila exclaimed, blinking her ultra-large eyes at me accusingly.

"I know. But it's all right. You said you wanted to help me, right?" I asked soothingly.

Sheila nodded vigorously, the tufts of hair surrounding her head bouncing as wildly as flickering candles on a birthday cake.

"Good. Now, do you know what a distraction is?" I asked, amazed that the idea hadn't come to me before. It was so simple. Maybe that had been my problem. I was thinking big-picture, James Bond–style escapes, when I should have realized that my captors were fluorescent-lipstick-loving, graphic-scrubs-wearing sheep who only did what Dr. Taylor told them to.

"I know what a distraction is," Sheila announced importantly.

"Good. So, at lunch, what I want you to do is exactly what you did yesterday. Remember? Just fall to the ground and start yelling. Can you do that?"

"Yes." She nodded, eyes wide.

"Good. But remember, it's just pretend. It's a game. You're pretending you're really, really upset. But you're not."

She smiled, a small, private grin. "That's something Jenny would have done."

"What happened to Jenny?" I was still dying to know. In my mind, Jenny loomed equally as large as Jamie. No matter what

I did at Serenity, I decided, I couldn't become like Jenny. But I needed to know what had happened to her.

Soon, an orderly knocked on the door and we joined the shuffling line of patients to walk to the cafeteria. Some were silent, and some were always chattering loudly into space. We marched down the steps of the cottage and onto the gravel pathway. As was usual, the orderlies were talking among themselves, making jokes about the basketball game on TV the night before, a reminder that there was a whole world beyond the five-acre compound we were locked in.

As we filed up the sagging wooden steps and into the entranceway of the main building, it happened. Sheila fell backward, her head hitting the carpeted floor. A strange, guttural noise emerged from her mouth as she flopped back and forth on the floor.

"They're back! They're attacking me. Help!" she shrieked.

"Who's attacking you?" one of the nurses said, rushing from the front of the line toward Sheila.

"The sloths! They're big!" Sheila was crying and in hysterics, and several other girls had begun crying. I smiled, despite myself. *The sloths?* That was Sheila's sense of humor: twisted, innocent, and not destroyed, despite the past year at Serenity and whatever horrors she'd seen happening to Jenny. As the others pressed into a circle closer toward her and Dr. Taylor was paged, I sprinted toward his office.

The file was still on the desk. I paused. I didn't have much time, but I couldn't resist one look.

On top of the stack of papers was a red sheet of paper with large typed letters in bold black font.

VIOLENT ALERT.

PATIENT HAS OUTBURSTS OF EXTREME VIOLENCE THAT CAN MANIFEST IN HARM TO OTHERS.

Below was a note in Dr. Taylor's handwriting. *Killed brother's g-pig. Explore. Connection btwn that and brother hostility.*

I shut the file, not wanting to see what else was there. Grabbing the receiver of the phone, I huddled under the desk, trying to remember Matt's number. There'd been a 3. And a 5. I felt like I had it. I dialed the string of numbers floating in my mind, my heart hammering against my chest, hoping it was him and not the local pizza place or somewhere equally useless.

"Hello?" a guy asked curiously. I'd done it. Maybe everything would be okay.

"Hey, it's —"

"Hayley," he said warmly. "Where are you calling from? The number says blocked. And I just dropped you off at Keely's."

"Listen, I'm fine, but —"

"Cool. So I told Keely that we'd chill after school tomorrow. Maybe hang out down by the field? Or we can just hang at your place. Still thinking about last night." His voice dropped to a whisper. I wondered what he was thinking about last night. What had Jamie done? A wave of nausea made me pitch forward. I steadied myself against the desk and cleared my throat.

"It was really hot the way you snuck me in past your mom," he said.

My blood turned to ice. "Matt, *wait!*" I interrupted.

"Yeah. You've been awesome. So much fun, no stress . . . what else do you want me to tell you?" he asked teasingly.

To tell you.

Not me. Her.

"What else have I been doing?" I asked. Down the hall, I heard an alarm screech. A door slammed. "What have I been *doing*?" I asked.

Matt chuckled. "What haven't you been doing? I've never seen this side of you. But I'm so, so glad I met it. That shy, book-loving thing was getting old. Even though I did try to read that book you love so much. But honestly, I'm just happy we have other things to do to entertain ourselves."

On the other end of the line, I could hear Matt breathe, his exhalations mixing with a half laugh, a sign that he was surely smiling, waiting for the flirty thing "I" would say, relieved that I was the fun party girl he'd really wanted all along.

"Hayley?" Matt asked. "Did I lose you?"

"Yeah," I agreed. If only he knew how true it was. "Bad connection." I hung up, wiping my clammy hands on my gray Serenity sweatshirt. The screeching of the alarm hadn't stopped and I heard the far-off wail of an ambulance. Sheila was clearly going all out. My heart wrenched, hoping that maybe this could somehow be good for her, that maybe she'd learn that she was a valuable person who wasn't nearly as crazy as she imagined she was.

I picked up the phone again.

Please pick up, I prayed as I dialed Adam's number. I didn't have to dredge it from memory. It was as easy to access as my middle name, as my favorite poems.

Please please please pick up.

"Hello, Adam Scott," Adam said in his baby business-exec voice. I smiled inwardly. Of course Adam would answer his phone that way, as if he were about to get a job offer on his walk from Calc to Physics.

"Adam, it's Hayley."

"I know," Adam said flatly.

"Adam, listen —"

"I don't know why you're calling. We're not friends. Not when you're acting like this. And now you're wandering around the school like some skank, you barely come to class, and you're about to get thrown off Yearbook. Plus, you have the Ainsworth finalist interview, which even Mr. Klish thinks you don't deserve . . . and why are you even calling me? Do you need me to bail you out from jail or something?" he said, laughing harshly.

"Adam, please listen. Please." I clutched the edge of the desk. "I really need to talk."

I heard Adam's sharp intake of breath. In the background, coffee cups clanked, people laughed. Like everything was normal. "Hold on, I'm at the Ugly Mug. I'm heading outside."

"Please don't hang up," I said in a small voice.

"Hayley! I promise I won't. I promise. Okay? I'm outside. Now tell me what's going on."

"I'm in Maine," I said. "The girl who's pretending to be me is my twin. She was the one who made the Facebook page. She was the one in the guidance office that day. It was her. And now I'm in a mental institution, I don't even know what she's doing with Matt, and I don't know what's going on, and no one will believe me!"

A pause.

"Adam?"

"You're in a *mental institution*?"

"Or something. It's called Serenity."

"So the girl I just saw is your *twin*? What?"

Footsteps echoed down the hallway.

"Yes. I'll explain it all. But I have to go. Serenity Point in Maine. Look it up and please, please, please help me. Or stop her. Or just . . ."

The footsteps stopped. The doorknob turned. One black-clad sneaker, then another, stepped in.

"Jamie?" Dr. Taylor asked, sounding genuinely surprised to see me. "What are you doing here?" He was holding a thick file folder, the name *Sheila Neville* written on the front in ominous black letters.

His gaze fell to the phone, the bright display screen making it clear exactly what I'd been doing. He sighed.

"I don't have time to handle this right now. And I don't want you to lie to me. We will discuss this in your next session, but for now, I'm going to escort you to art therapy."

I followed him out the door and down the hall, aware of each nurse glaring at me as I passed by. I knew that disobedience resulted in more medication, more mandatory therapy sessions. At this point, I'd never get out.

"Here you go," Dr. Taylor said gruffly, urging me to step into the brightly colored room. Inexplicably, the walls were covered with orange industrial carpeting while the floor was the same speckled linoleum found in the rest of the hospital. Of course the walls were carpeted. Of course nothing made sense.

Around me, eight patients were stringing dry macaroni onto pieces of yarn.

"Go on." Dr. Taylor practically pushed me onto a chair, then headed over to Molly, the perky red-haired art therapist. I watched as they whispered to each other, catching words like *defiant* and *oppositional*.

When he left, Molly came over to me.

"Are you going to make a necklace?" The question came out more like a threat. I stared down at the table.

"You know, you could make it for your friend Sheila. It might be nice to do something for someone else."

I glanced up. "Is she okay?" I asked.

"I can't talk about other patients," Molly said, a small smile forming on her face. "But I can say that a nice homemade gift might cheer her up while she's recovering."

"Is she getting electroshock? Where did they take her?" My voice rose in panic. If I'd done this to Sheila, I wouldn't forgive myself. She'd thrown herself into the diversion and I didn't even know if it would actually work. Who knew if Adam believed me, or even if he had, if he had enough information to get me. Hot tears formed behind my eyes.

"It's all right to cry," Molly murmured. She put her hand on my shoulder. Even though it was meant to be a protective gesture, her fingers felt clawlike and only reminded me how trapped I was. I would never, ever get out. Adam hadn't believed me. Matt liked Jamie better. The Ainsworth was tomorrow, I had no hope of arriving for the interview, and all I had to look forward to was *maybe*, in the distant future, getting discharged into a family that'd already written me — Jamie — off.

Someone wailed, sounding more like a wounded animal than a human. I looked around to see where the sound was coming from, only to see concern and fear in the faces surrounding me. It had been *me*.

Molly scraped her chair back.

"I think art is too much for you today. Let's call the nurses and get you to sleep."

I didn't protest as two orderlies helped me to my feet and half dragged me to my room, or when the nurse pushed a cup of pills and a glass of water in my hands, or when I finally succumbed to sleep.

I was woken by a bright light in my eyes. It was Dr. Taylor, his fingers flipping up my eyelids. I shook my head and he let go, turning toward the nurse.

"How long has she been asleep?"

"Just two hours. We'd have liked it to have been more." The nurse glared at me as though it were my fault, and not Dr. Taylor's, that I was awake.

"All right. She'll be a little sleepy in the car, but she can nap on the way home. I'll sign the discharge."

"Discharge?" I asked. My voice was creaky.

Dr. Taylor turned toward me and nodded. "Yes. It's not what I would have recommended. I think you could make a lot of progress here if you dug in. But we don't keep patients against their will."

I resisted the urge to question that statement.

"Ready?" the nurse asked, much nicer now that she knew she didn't have to deal with me. She helped me to my feet. I swayed on solid ground. My eyelids felt heavy and I could tell my speech was slurred.

"Will I be better tomorrow?" I asked. If I could get home and get to sleep, I'd be able to make it to the interview tomorrow morning.

"*Better* is a subjective word, Jamie," Dr. Taylor said. "We're here for you anytime you need us."

In the lobby, a burly man with sunglasses stood with his arms crossed over his chest.

"This is Jamie." Dr. Taylor shoved me forward. "I'm faxing her discharge paperwork per her family's request. Jamie, this is the driver who's been arranged by your family to bring you home. Good-bye," he said formally.

I locked eyes with him. As soon as I cleared up everything at home, I'd see what I could do about suing Serenity. But one step at a time. "Thank you."

I climbed into the backseat of the car, far too excited to fall asleep and annoyed at how heavy my eyelids were. I couldn't be foggy. Not now. But as the time it took to open my eyelids after blinking grew longer and longer, I knew I didn't have a choice. I had to rest.

But before I fell into unconsciousness, one word was on my mind: *perfect*.

CHAPTER 21

*M*iss?"

"Yes?" My eyes flew open, taking in the white fences lit by the moonlight, the rolling green pastures, and the gravel driveway leading to the sagging porch.

"You're home," he said. As if I didn't know that.

"Thank you!" The out-of-it feeling was gone, replaced with exhilaration. I was home. I practically sprinted up the driveway, feeling the air in my lungs.

As always, the back door was unlocked. I flung it open. Sadie rushed toward me, jumping and licking and wiggling her tail uncontrollably. *She'd* missed me.

The luminous green numbers on the stove clock read 12:01. The fridge door was the same as always, no phantom pictures. The house smelled like firewood and burning leaves, all the outdoor scents that had wafted through the open windows.

I wasn't sure where to begin. I needed to call Adam. I needed to talk to Mom. I needed to talk to Jamie's family.

But first, I needed to eat.

I opened the fridge, pulled out the jar of peanut butter, and scooped a thick spoonful. Not bothering with bread, I took a bite.

"I see you're making yourself right at home."

I spun around. The spoon clattered to the floor and Sadie ran toward it, unaware that she was in the middle of me and my twin.

"Jamie." I blinked.

"Did I scare you?" She laughed, then sat at the kitchen table. She was wearing one of my mother's yoga tops and a pair of yoga shorts that showed off her toned legs. Dark eyeliner made her eyes seem even bluer. Her hair was loose around her shoulders. As if aware that I was watching, she lifted it up, then dropped it — but not before I got a glance at the hickey on her neck.

"Sit down," she said. It was more of a command than a suggestion. "We have so much to catch up on. Seventeen years is a lot for sisters. I tried reading your journals, but I got a little distracted. Matt is amazing. Why write about it if you can have the real thing?"

I remained standing. I wanted so badly to hate her. She'd almost ruined my life. But I couldn't help but think of the sad-eyed girl from the file, the one who never felt like she belonged in her family. Wasn't that how I'd always felt at school?

"Why did you do this?" I asked. "Why?"

"Does everything need a reason?" she asked cryptically.

"I mean, I know your dad is . . ."

"My dad is what?" In one fluid movement, Jamie burst from the chair and grabbed a butcher knife from the block on the counter. She held it toward me, arching her eyebrow as if to dare me to say something else.

I took an instinctive step back, landing on Sadie's paw. She growled and glanced between us, then bared her teeth and began barking at Jamie.

"Shut up!" Jamie snapped, using her knee to knock Sadie's nose back. Sadie whimpered, tail between her legs, and headed toward my feet. She licked my ankle, and I knew she wanted me to pet her. I didn't. I was frozen, afraid one small move would cause Jamie to violently react.

"Don't look so scared, Hayley," Jamie said, as if she'd read my mind. "I'm not going to kill you yet. It'd be a shame if we lost each other so quickly after reconnecting. Besides, I still need you. Don't worry, you're not Leah Kirkpatrick." She put the knife on the table.

"Did you kill her?" I didn't take my eyes off the knife.

"Did I kill her?" Jamie repeated, as if she were asking herself the same question. "Well, I think that'd be a good debate question. Some people would say I did. Others would say I simply was the catalyst. And then others would say I was just one piece of the plane crash theory puzzle." She smiled as if we shared a secret. "But it turned out well for you. She was going to get your Ainsworth spot."

"And you . . ."

"Fixed things so you would. You can thank me later," she said. Noticing my gaze, she grabbed the knife and placed it back in the block with exaggerated patience. "Seriously, I said I wouldn't kill you. I was joking!"

"I don't get it," I said. "You had everything growing up. You went to the best schools. You had this awesome house and a family and you wanted to give it up?" If Jamie thought her experience had been bad, what would she have done if our situations had been reversed? I imagined Aidan and me playing elaborate games of pretend in their family's lavish, antique-filled home. I imagined family trips to Europe and private lessons and anything in the world I wanted, without *ever* having to worry about cost. But what would Jamie have been like if she'd been raised by my mom?

"You don't have to get it," Jamie said, a hard edge to her voice. "I wouldn't expect you to understand." She sat back down at the table, lost in thought.

I had a million questions: What had really happened to Leah? How had Jamie found out about me in the first place? Why did she want my life? "What was so bad about your life?" I asked quietly. I cautiously sat next to her. Our hands were side by side on the table, the long pointer fingers and prominent knuckles looking like they were a pair. I edged mine closer to hers, surprised when she didn't pull away.

Jamie shrugged. "I didn't like being Jamie. Not the Jamie my dad and his little trophy wife wanted me to be. I felt like there had to be something more out there, something I was missing. And there was."

"Me?" I asked.

"I had to go to one of my brother's stupid debate tournaments last year, and I saw you. You weren't debating him . . . you're better than him, so that made me happy. But it was easy to find your name. At first I just wanted to play around. I mean, I was just kicked out of school and I had a lot of free time, you know? But then, the more I was hanging out here, the easier it was. And I figured, why not try living it?"

I imagined the life we'd have had if we'd grown up together. I imagined us as toddlers in matching bathing suits, staying up late and inventing a secret language, doing whatever twins are supposed to do. No matter what, we'd both been denied that.

"Did you meet my mom?" I asked quietly.

"I did." She shrugged. "She was all right. But I'm not looking for another family. It only makes things more complicated. All I need, *sister*, is you."

"What does that mean?" I asked.

"Well, I'm not going back to Brookline. And, honestly, I don't really feel like staying here any longer than I have to. But I had a good conversation with Mr. Klish today and it seems, in his words, that the Ainsworth is just the ticket for an ambitious young person to reach her dreams. So that's what I need. And I need you to win."

"Okay . . ." I trailed off to allow her to speak.

"So, here's the thing: It's a pretty sweet scholarship. And I don't care about college. But I do need money. So I figure, you win the award, you provide me with an allowance, and I go away. It's easy."

"Where would you go?"

"Costa Rica? Paris? San Francisco? I don't care! Don't you realize, I just don't want to be *here*?"

Her jaw was set, and her nose wrinkled the same way mine did when I was trying not to cry.

"You want me to help you disappear," I said.

Instead of saying something snarky, she nodded.

"I need you to help me. Please. And then, once I'm gone, I'll be well. I'll be able to heal once I get away from *them*. They weren't good parents. There's a reason your mom never talks about James. Please trust me."

I knew that tone. It was pure desperation, the one I'd used with Adam. The one he'd ignored. I couldn't do that to my sister. I noticed a lone eyelash on her cheek, glistening in the shaft of moonlight from the window. I reached toward her and lifted it off with the pad of my finger, holding it toward her. She shrugged, confused.

"It's an eyelash. You make a wish and blow on it." Had she never done this? Keely and I had always done it, the gesture as familiar as brushing a piece of lint off her sweater. But touching Jamie's skin was different. It was like watching myself in the mirror. I couldn't look away.

And I already knew I couldn't turn away.

"You know what my wish is," she said. She puffed out her cheeks and blew.

I thought of the money, halved. It'd still be a lot. I could still make it work. I could get a shift as a barista near campus. I'd make Ingrid share her secrets for how to travel through Europe on less than ten euros a day. Yes, she was sick. But she was my sister. How could I turn on someone so much like myself? My eyes locked with hers. "Okay," I heard myself say.

I felt myself enveloped in my sister's hug, surrounded by a sweet, smoky scent. We hadn't been this close in seventeen years. Maybe this would be worth it.

"Well, you'd better rest up, then!" she said brightly. "And you have to change out of that *outfit*!" I looked down at my Serenity-issued uniform.

Her eyes widened. "I really hope you can forgive me about this. It all got so out of control. I just . . . just got caught up in the idea that I could actually do this. It was the perfect plan."

"I'm happy to do it," I said numbly, allowing my sister to walk me upstairs and tuck me into bed as if I were a child.

CHAPTER 22

I woke up to the smell of coffee.

"I was about to wake you up. How'd you sleep?" a voice cooed. I turned. Jamie was sitting on a chair across from my bed, her knees pulled to her chest. Coffee and toast were sitting on my bedside table, and a heather-gray suit — the one I saved for special occasions — was lying on the window seat.

"I got everything ready for you! All you have to do is take a shower," Jamie said eagerly. Her voice had an edge I hadn't remembered last night. I'd fallen asleep with a sense of relief. But this morning, it was replaced by an uneasy feeling of dread.

"Are you okay? Come on! You don't want to be late!"

"Right. Sorry. I just feel weird. The pills from Serenity —"

"They should be out of your system by now," she barked. "Seriously, just take a shower. And then I'll leave you alone. I promise. I'm as nervous as you are. We are in this together, after all."

"Right." I remembered the flood of warm feelings I'd felt toward Jamie last night. I didn't feel that now. I couldn't stop thinking of the knife blade. The way she laughed when I asked about Leah. The almost-too-easy explanation she had for where Mom was.

"Where's Mom?"

"I told you. She's, like, antiquing with Geofferson. She'll be home tomorrow, and all of this will seem like a bad dream. You've just got to get everything done today. And I know you can do it. You're Hayley Westin."

My heart fluttered in my chest. "And what if I don't?"

"Well, I think that wouldn't turn out very well for either of us, now would it?" She grabbed my wrists. I could feel her fingers pressing into my skin. "We're so alike. Both our parents lied to us. We've always been outsiders. We've never belonged. Now, we have a chance to get what's ours."

"But *I* was the one who was on track for the Ainsworth. That was all me."

Jamie snorted. "You think? Sorry. You're good, but you're not that good. I helped you out. I mean, after I realized that pulling myself up was a lot easier than dragging you down."

"So you did kill Leah," I said flatly.

"Shhhh!" She let go of my wrists and my arms fell slack to my sides. "You're stressed out. It's understandable. Instead of focusing on me, get into the shower, and start thinking of answers for the Ainsworth committee. All right?"

She pushed me into the bathroom and turned on the water. The one window in the room was incredibly narrow. There was no way to escape.

She would kill my mother. Or she'd kill me, or she'd kill us both. It was essential I stop her — but I needed to do it in a way that would make people believe me. I couldn't imagine how I'd explain the story to the Bainbridge Police. There were too many pieces, too many strands, and not enough time. Because the second that she knew I wasn't behaving according to her script, she'd destroy me.

A knock on the door caused me to jump, banging my knee against the faucet. Blood spurted from the cut, the red falling in dark drips on the white tile.

It was only the beginning of the bloodshed. I knew it. If I didn't become a puppet in Jamie's plan, she would kill someone. Even if I did, she could strike. Anything was possible.

"Are you almost done? You don't want to be late!" Jamie yelled.

I turned off the water, wrapped myself in a towel, and stepped out to face my executioner.

Jamie drove me to the U. She didn't speak. Neither did I. I watched as we crested the hill into town, hoping that someone would see our mirror images and . . . stop us? I didn't know. It didn't matter. No one did.

We drove up to the Beland Building, the neo-Gothic admissions office of the U. I'd been there countless times, for school trips and evening lectures. Now, everything looked strange and unfamiliar.

"Good luck," Jamie said. She turned and gave me a tight smile. "You know what to do. I'll be back in two hours."

I staggered out of the car, aware of Jamie's eyes watching my every move as I opened the imposing wooden doors and made my way toward the anteroom of the hall where the interview would be held. I slumped on a velvet-covered bench and held my head in my hands. I knew Jamie wasn't watching me. But I still felt under her control.

A middle-aged suit-clad woman poked her head out from the doorway.

"Hayley Westin?"

"Yes?" I squeaked. I sounded scared and tentative.

She gave me a hard look above her glasses, then cocked her head to the side.

"Are you all right?" she asked.

I swallowed a lump in my throat and nodded.

She smiled. "Good. It's normal to be nervous. In fact, if you weren't, then I'd wonder about your sanity!"

She chuckled and I tried to laugh, only it came out like a bark. She glanced back at me strangely, and I tried to disguise the sound as a cough.

She cleared her throat. "Well then, come along," she said as she led the way up the polished marble staircase to the second floor where the interviews were taking place. "I'm Dr. Dunphy, and I'm so pleased to welcome you to the Ainsworth finals. We just had a young man from Bainbridge. How impressive for the two of you to have made it. I do hope that the competition between you is friendly, though." Her voice held a note of warning as she escorted me into the Searles Room.

"Of course." There was no way I could ever tell her, or anyone, about Jamie. They wouldn't believe me.

"This is supposed to be a conversation." Dr. Dunphy snapped me back to reality as I realized that she'd been talking the whole time. She paused, her hand on the doorknob of the Searles Room. The thick frosted glass on the window made it impossible to see in. "This isn't so much of a test as a chance for you to discuss your goals."

I nodded mutely. It was odd being treated with so much respect after I'd been belittled at Serenity. It was all a matter of perception. In a charcoal suit, pumps, and soft eye makeup, I was promising. Intelligent. A credit to my community. In the shapeless gray sweats at Serenity, I was a mental patient.

"Are you sure you're all right? Take a few minutes and collect yourself. I promise I won't deduct points." Her tone was teasing and maternal, and my heart twisted. I wanted, so badly, for someone to take care of me right now. And there wasn't anyone.

"I'm ready now."

"That's what we like to hear." Dr. Dunphy smiled and opened the door. Inside, two men and one woman were seated in overstuffed green velvet armchairs. An untouched tray of coffee, muffins, and bagels was set on a polished coffee table near their knees. One empty seat — a single, hardbacked chair — faced them.

"Ladies and gentlemen, this is Hayley Westin," Dr. Dunphy announced.

"An honor," one man said, reaching out to enthusiastically pump my hand. His arms seemed too long for his body, reminding me of a scarecrow.

"Thank you, sir," I said.

"Now, the hot seat is all yours!" The other man laughed, not even bothering to make eye contact as he reached forward with his doughy hand and grabbed one of the muffins. Ignoring the napkins, he bit into it, the crumbs scattering down his pants.

"Are you ready?" the woman asked sharply. Or, really, she was a girl, just a few years older than me. Her long dark hair was pulled into a sleek ponytail. A smattering of freckles dusted her heart-shaped face. She wore a black suit and a silver heart necklace that landed at the notch of her collarbone. She was how I used to imagine myself.

I perched on the edge of the chair and half listened as they made introductions. The Scarecrow was Professor Doyle from the psych department at the U. The muffin-loving man was a former dean from Yale. And the girl was Amanda Chang, an Ainsworth winner four years ago and current college senior, double majoring in economics and political science and applying to law school.

But I didn't care about them. I was thinking of Mom. And Miss Marsted. And Adam. I wanted them so badly it hurt my heart. Normally, when I wanted something — like the Ainsworth — I felt the desire creep up my spine and the adrenaline rush my veins. Now, I just felt a dull ache, starting at my temples and entering my heart.

"Tell us a little bit about why you want the Ainsworth," Amanda asked, leaning forward with her elbows on her knees.

"Hayley?" she prompted. I knew that tone. It was the one I'd used at Yearbook. In class. The one that said *I know you aren't prepared.*

Well, she was right. I wasn't.

"I've always cared about learning," I began, *knowing* how cliché it sounded, knowing she was mentally writing me off, because that's what I would have done. I traced through my research interests, how I wanted to connect technology and poetry, how I could see myself making a positive difference in the world, exactly like what they were looking for in a candidate. At this point, I could do it in my sleep. Scarecrow nodded approvingly, so I kept going. But the girl — Future Me — seemed skeptical.

"And what are the challenges facing scholars today?" She asked the question in a way that made it clear she didn't think I was a scholar.

I paused. I knew what I should say: something about how rapid advances in technology made it nearly impossible for anyone to be an expert at anything. I opened my mouth.

"I think it's actually realizing what's really important," I started.

"So, what's important to Hayley Westin?" Future Me asked, barely concealing the sneering tone in her voice.

"If you'd asked me a few weeks ago, I would have said success. And don't get me wrong, it still is. But —" I broke off as a sob formed in my throat. "I need to leave."

I ran out the door and hurtled down the stairs. It hadn't even *occurred* to me to miss the interview. What had I been thinking? I didn't want the Ainsworth. I wanted my life back. All I wanted was Mom and Adam and the Ugly Mug and Sadie sleeping on my bed and conversations with Keely about gunmetal gray versus heather gray.

I clattered down the stairs as the tears rolled down my cheeks and my heart hammered in my chest — and then found myself face-to-face with Dr. Dunphy.

"Are you all right, dear?" Her eyebrows furrowed in concern.

I shook my head. "No. Do you have a phone?" I asked in a small voice. I couldn't do this on my own. But as she fumbled through her bag to find her phone I saw something that made my blood run cold.

It was my car, parked in the visitors' parking lot. Jamie was leaning against it, talking to Adam. Adam clutched a bakery bag in his hands. And then, Jamie turned toward me.

She shook her head slightly, raising an eyebrow.

You were warned.

The words came from my own head, but they might as well have come from hers. She'd given me a chance. She'd known I wasn't following directions.

"You need my phone?" Dr. Dunphy held hers out to me.

"Call the police. Please!" I saw Jamie open the car door, then Adam open the passenger side door. Around me, students were stumbling across campus in their sweats, heading to the dining hall for breakfast, bleary-eyed from a night of partying. No one noticed anything was wrong.

"Stop!" I called. The wind whipped in my face, though, and I knew Adam hadn't heard me. He'd accepted a ride. And once he and Jamie were alone . . . she'd kill him. Of course she would. One fewer Ainsworth contestant, one more way to hurt me.

"The police?" Dr. Dunphy cocked her head in concern.

I didn't have time. I hurtled toward the parking lot just as Adam slid into the passenger seat. A few spaces away, a guy was unlocking his Jeep, a backpack and guitar slung over his shoulder.

Jamie was backing out of the parking lot. I could either try to confront her directly, hoping she didn't run me over or kill Adam, or I could follow her.

I glanced back to the guy with the Jeep.

I needed his car.

I ran toward him.

"I need your car!" I yelled. "Now!"

"Yo, you need a ride? I'm running late, but . . ." he said dubiously, staring me up and down.

I lunged toward him and roughly pushed his shoulders. Since he was already off balance from his backpack and guitar case, the keys clattered to the ground with a thud.

I picked them up, slid into the driver's seat, and pressed on the accelerator. By the time I reached the tree-lined exit of the U, one car was between us.

Jamie turned right, away from Main Street. So did the other car. I followed, heart hammering. At the outskirts of town, the car turned. It was just the two of us.

Jamie glanced in the rearview mirror. A glimmer of surprise crossed her face, only to be replaced by a slight smile.

It confirmed my worst fears. Jamie was determined to kill Adam. It was a fact. I felt it in my bones, in my heart. And I knew I would do anything to save him.

She sped up. So did I. The Jeep was far more powerful than my car, and I knew I could catch up to her. I needed to stop her. No matter what. And if I continued to stay as close as possible to her bumper, at some point, *someone* would see us. *Someone* would stop us. There weren't car chases in Bainbridge.

The car swerved sharply, left, then right. And I realized that Jamie didn't have control of the car anymore. Adam did.

The car took a sharp left, smashing through a fence and causing cows to scatter.

It stopped for a second. I slammed on the brakes, heart thudding, expecting Adam to emerge.

Smoke rose from the hood, making it impossible to see. But then, the car started again, going faster than I'd thought possible, heading toward a pond on the far end of the field. I couldn't tell who was driving anymore, only that it was going in a straight line toward the lake.

Jamie had to be driving. So where was Adam?

I thought of the butcher knife Jamie had held. Could she have used it while he was driving? It was very possible. What did she have to lose? The idea of Adam, bleeding in the car, maybe alive but definitely not okay, was too much.

I needed to stop her. Now.

I closed my eyes and floored the accelerator, focusing only on the car right ahead of me. My goal was just to stop it in any way possible. All I saw in front of me was a brilliant kaleidoscope of blues and greens and browns. So this was how it would end.

I pushed my foot down even harder on the accelerator. One second, two seconds, and then, a thunderlike crash and the feeling of flying.

And then nothing.

If this was death, then it was quiet. At least, that's what I thought at first. And then, my ears began to pick out and separate sounds. The chirping of birds. The lapping of water against the shore. And then a word, so quiet I thought it was in my imagination.

"Hayley?"

I pressed my ear to the ground. I didn't want to move, not yet. I felt like pain surrounded my whole body, but from a distance, as if it hadn't sunk in. If I moved, it would hurt. I felt liquid trickle down my face and knew it was blood.

"Hayley?" The voice was stronger this time. More real. Who was it? Who could want me right now? I knew it was someone important, but everything just seemed a little bit beyond reach. It was as if all I could process were the physical sensations I was slowly regaining.

Slowly, I sat up and wiped my eyes with the back of my hand, unleashing a deluge of blood down my face. That was why I hadn't been able to see. Blinking, I realized my sight wasn't damaged, it had just been obscured by the blood. Right in front of me, smoke was rising from the pile of metal only feet from me that had once been the two cars. Flames sputtered around the wreckage as if it were a macabre bonfire.

And then, everything came flooding back.

"Adam!" I shrieked, scrambling to my feet. My knee buckled, and I fell. And suddenly, the pain was everywhere.

"Hayley!" The voice was real, but I didn't want to open my eyes again. I was too afraid of what I'd see. My face felt wet, and I knew I was crying.

"Hayley, are you okay? It's me. It's me. Adam. Please."

I felt pressure on my shoulders, felt a hand brush away the wetness from my forehead.

"Hayley? Please. Please . . ."

"Adam?" My voice was garbled and unfamiliar; I hadn't said the *d* properly. "Adam." I said again.

"Shhh." I felt him pull me into a hug. For the first time in a long time, I felt safe. But why? And why had I been so scared before? The answers were somewhere close. I knew that, but I didn't want to look. "Shhh," he said again.

And then, a new sound reached my ears: wailing sirens. I opened my mouth and joined their cries, the whole time being rocked by strong arms that kept making me feel safe.

CHAPTER 23

I tossed and turned, falling through space. Although not falling, more like flying, as though I were a puppet on a string, being manipulated by an unseen puppeteer. Everything was dark, and yet I knew my enemy was close by. And I knew her name was Jamie, although I didn't know how I knew it.

"Jamie!" I yelled raggedly, the word echoing again and again and again. Jamie. It was more than a name.

The word was still echoing as a figure emerged from the darkness — shadowy at first, and then more and more solid. Both of us faced each other. Her eyes were large and dark, the pupils practically disappearing into the dark irises. She was my shadow. She was my twin. I knew that now. I'd always known, no matter how much I'd pushed the thought back into my subconscious. We were born together.

We stared at each other. There was no other noise. I held my hand up to her and she did the same, mirror images of each other.

I broke the silence. "We're dead." It was a fitting end. The two of us had entered the world together. Why wouldn't we leave the world together as well?

She shook her head, imperceptibly at first, and then more and more violently. As she did, her body became less and less solid, more and more shadowy. I watched, horrified, entranced. And then I realized that as she was evaporating, I was breathing. I *put my hand against my heart, feeling it beat: strong, steady, singular.*

"She's going to be a little groggy. We've got her on a few pain-killers for her arm and for the knee. And she'll have a headache for a few days. It was a nasty concussion. But other than that, she'll be fine."

I blinked. Circular, white orbs hung above me like stars. I blinked again, attempting to focus, but the orbs above me just swam in and out of my vision.

"Hayley?" a loud voice, inches from my ear, asked. I flinched. I wanted to turn my head away from the source of the noise, but I couldn't. "Hayley," the voice said again.

I breathed in sharply, laughing to myself as I heard it. I was alive. I had a heartbeat and I could breathe.

"See, the painkillers give vivid dreams. Especially coupled with the trauma . . . I'd have someone watch her while she's sleeping for a while."

"Shh, she's coming to. Let me see if she's responsive. She's not sleeping."

I turned, just wanting to be left alone. But the voice was relentless. "Don't move. You're in the hospital. You were in an accident, and you fractured your arm and got a few bumps and bruises, but you're going to be fine. You're safe."

That wasn't correct. I'd never feel safe.

"Hayley, you're in the hospital. Can you hear me?"

"Yeah." I struggled to sit up.

"Take your time." The scrubs wearer swam into focus. Unlike the nurses at Serenity, she had no makeup and a short brown ponytail. She smiled at me. "Good girl," she murmured. I blinked, realizing I had a hospital ID on my wrist, stamped HAYLEY KATHRYN WESTIN in large letters.

"Looks like you're awake," the nurse said fondly. "And we have some people to see you."

I shook my head. I didn't want to see anyone. Not yet. Not like this.

But it was too late.

"Is she okay?" I recognized that voice.

"Mom!" I brushed away the tube from my nose; I didn't want her to see me like this.

"Shh, leave that in. It's just oxygen. It's good for you." The nurse readjusted the tube as Mom ran to the side of the bed.

"Oh, Bunny." Mom's eyes were red and there were dark circles under them. At the foot of the bed was James. I blinked at him. He sighed shakily.

"I don't think I can do this," he said in a thick voice. He turned toward Mom.

"That's all right. She'll talk to you later. When you both feel stronger." Mom's voice was steady and calm. James nodded, relieved, and left the room so it was just the two of us.

"Hayley. Hayley, I am so, so sorry." Mom gently swept my tangled bangs from my forehead.

I winced at the touch, even though it was gentle. My head pounded, and I remembered the last image: me, flying toward the windshield. Adam saving me. The smoke rising from the wreckage of my car as though it were a pyrotechnic display.

"I'm sorry, baby," Mom said, pulling her hand back. Her eyes were wet with tears. "Jamie . . ."

"Is dead." I finished the sentence.

Mom nodded.

"She is. They brought her in, but she didn't make it. I'm sorry. And James came, of course, and his wife is here. I just wish . . ."

I shook my head. "Please don't." I didn't want to hear her explanation. I didn't want anything.

"I shouldn't have lied to you. I shouldn't have lied to myself. I didn't think I wanted any children. James and I had decided we'd put you both up for adoption. We had a couple ready. But then I saw you, and I couldn't give you up. But I couldn't keep you both. So then James decided . . . insisted . . . on keeping Jamie. It was the right thing to do, he said. And we agreed that it would be easier if neither of you knew about each other. We were always fighting, and he was so angry that I'd changed my mind about the adoption. He felt I'd ruined the plan. And I guess I did. After, I wasn't even sure what I'd done. What kind of mother leaves a twin?"

For once, I didn't have the words to make my mother feel better. But she didn't seem to need them. Her lower lip wobbled. She clenched her jaw, then opened her mouth again.

"I was so alone," she said to herself. "And then you both were there, and suddenly, we had one another. But I couldn't keep you both. I wanted you. And James got her. I kept telling myself that she'd died, because it was the only way I could live with myself. It was neater that way. I couldn't see her without seeing him, and . . ." She emitted a long, shaky sigh. "I always hoped she'd have a better life. You were the one who was always working so hard, pushing yourself. I sometimes wished that I'd given both of you to James. But then . . ."

"It's not your fault," I said in a small voice. I sounded very, very young.

"I tried," Mom said, almost to herself. "I love you. I only lied because I love you."

Love. The word jolted in my brain, causing my mind to flash to the accident: Adam, by my side. Adam, always watching out for me, trailing me, sensing that things were falling apart. Matt had never been like that. Matt had fallen for Jamie, the chameleonlike girl who could behave like the perfect girlfriend, absent of her own desires and fears. Matt had been my ideal. But Adam was the guy who knew me and liked me for *me*. I needed him.

"What about Adam?" I asked urgently.

"Adam?" Mom cocked her head. "He's all right. He has a broken leg, but he'll be fine."

"Really?" A tear trickled down my cheek. Was I crying for Adam? Jamie? Myself? I thought of Adam's strong hands on my shoulders, how I trusted him with every fiber of my being.

"Can I see him? I want him here," I told her. I still couldn't look my mother in the face. This was the second time she'd told me about Jamie's death, and this time, I wanted so badly to believe it. I did believe it.

I had to believe it.

Mom's face crumpled, before she quickly composed herself. "Of course you do. I'll get the nurse and see." She rose from the bed. There had definitely been a shift between us, and there was so much to ask: Who else knew about Jamie? Had she talked to James? And how could Mom possibly have confused me with her? But I didn't ask and she didn't say anything.

"Mommy?" I said, just before she reached the threshold. She turned around, tears spilling down her high cheekbones.

"Yes?"

"Actually, can you stay here with me?" I asked.

I knew Mom and I had months — years — of conversations ahead of us, but for right now, I didn't want to talk.

A shadow of a smile crossed her face as she climbed into the bed. I turned toward the window, noticing that the sun was setting. The light refracted from the window against the stainless steel of the IV pole connected to the drip snaking into my arm. I was reminded of the glint of the knife, how Jamie had been determined to kill me. That Mom had, deep down, been right with the story she'd told herself: Only one of us could have survived.

I turned to tell Mom, but her breathing had softened and her face had relaxed. She'd fallen asleep. It wasn't worth waking her up.

After all, Jamie was dead. She couldn't hurt me anymore. And the knowledge that she'd inadvertently put me so close to danger would destroy Mom.

Besides, some things had to stay between sisters.

EPILOGUE
ONE YEAR LATER

*T*he leaves were turning shades of yellow and orange and red as I crossed the UPenn campus on my way to the library. It was good to be away from Bainbridge, and away from my mother, who was still trying to reconcile the eighteen years she'd lived a lie to her life as a newlywed. She was navigating her own uncharted life, and I was happy to give her the space to do that in order to navigate my own.

I glanced down at my watch. It was only four forty-five. I had fifteen minutes before I met with my Psych Stats group.

Quickly, I logged onto Facebook to figure out whether we'd decided to meet in the Commons or at the Starbucks off campus. I scrolled down my newsfeed, clicked on my own profile, and blinked at a status update, written by me.

Hayley Westin: I'm still here.

I took a deep breath. It had to have been some joke written by my roommate before she headed to her Lit class.
My phone buzzed.

Miss you. Give me a call?

I smiled. Adam. He was five hours away, up at Harvard, but we'd been visiting each other every few weeks.

"Hey, baby," I said quietly into the phone, oblivious to the people swarming around me.

"So, how'd you get into Canaday without me?" he asked jovially, naming his Harvard dorm. "I loved the flowers on my desk."

"What?" My blood turned to ice.

"Forget-me-nots. That's cute. Of course, my roommate's a little bummed that I'm getting flowers and all he ever gets from his girlfriend are smiley emoticons, but what can I say, I guess I'm just a lucky guy. It was the perfect present."

"Perfect," I whispered as the phone slid out of my hand and shattered on the pavement.

Anna Davies is a writer and editor whose work has been featured in *The New York Times*, *Cosmo*, *Elle*, *Glamour*, and others. She spends far too much time on Facebook.